Christian Maxwell is resigned when Gabe tells him he's leaving Seattle to protect him, until the truth sinks in, and Chris realizes he may never see Gabe again. Reacting in anger, the two part with cold hostility instead of a warm and loving embrace.

Deciding not to fight Chris's obvious disapproval, Gabe leaves anyway, heading south in his faithful Dodge pickup.

Gabriel Church is a wanted man, and when he landed in Sonora, California, he believed it would be the first stop in his continuing journey. Road blind and far too weary to continue driving, he has no way of knowing he is about to run out of luck.

ASH AND CINDERS

The Gabriel Church Tales, Book Three

Rodd Clark

A NineStar Press Publication

Published by NineStar Press
P.O. Box 91792,
Albuquerque, New Mexico, 87199 USA.
www.ninestarpress.com

Ash and Cinders

Printed in the USA
First Edition
September, 2018

Print ISBN: 978-1-949340-65-5

Also available in eBook, ISBN: 978-1-949340-64-8

Warning: This book contains sexually explicit content, which may only be suitable for mature readers, and depictions of graphic violence, murder; memories of abuse, and memories of potential sexual abuse.

It's just the devil's share. When life evens itself out and every bad guy get what's coming to… It's one of the few balancing things life really offers."

—Gabriel Church

Prologue

ONE WEEK EARLIER

Looking at the man across the room, one would never have imagined how dangerous he actually was. The serial killer was hot and threatening in his own physical way, but there seemed to be a sympathetic kindness scratching below the surface of those mirror-like pupils of his. At times they looked bluish, while other times they appeared to be the color of industrial slate. But, in that instant, they reminded the deputy of humid childhood summers and cool slabs of concrete in the shade beckoning him to rest upon it.

He had been drawn like a magnet after meeting the man he only knew by the name Bobby Johnson. And from the first second they spoke, he found himself wavering under the man's impressive build and mischievous crooked smile. He hadn't known at the time, but the name Bobby Johnson was an alias. Nor did he know that he was meeting a killer who'd claimed a multitude of victims over several years and many miles of this vast country. He only knew there was something unique about his country drawl and those sinful eyes that hinted sexual tension and risk.

Facing Gabriel Church alone in a room without backup would be intimidating to anyone. Even the weight of Deputy Corso's holstered sidearm didn't seem to offer him much security. The killer strangely didn't appear anything but relaxed and surprisingly at peace with himself.

"You know I kinda like the idea of being hunted," the killer said quietly. "It sort of makes my dick hard, as if you couldn't tell."

As he said that, Gabriel readjusted himself in his chair, shifting slightly and opening his legs wider. The deputy could see that, concealed under his faded blue Levi's, there was a sizable bulge indicating he'd been telling the truth. The killer's smile never evaporated once they'd begun talking, and it made the officer think the grin was intended as a challenge or a threat, daring the deputy to make his move.

They were two men sitting alone in a roadside motel room, but the air was thick and muffled every outside noise as if a blanket of heavy cotton down had filled the room's interior.

"You have questions, I'm sure," Gabriel Church said rather flatly. It seemed more a statement than a question. Every bit of the killer's attention danced around the younger deputy sitting across from him in his motel, with his beautifully paralyzed face frozen with anticipation and fear.

Chapter One

"HEAVEN WOULDN'T KNOW what to make of you, anyway."

The words stung him and came as harshly as they'd been intended. But yet he knew they were an accurate assessment of his life thus far. There was no retort that Gabe could've come back with; the unwieldy truth was what it was, and he faced it every day in the mirror. Chris had never resigned himself to the fact that he was leaving just to protect him. Instead of trying to explain himself, he hung his head like a shamed puppy cowering near a piss-stained rug until he said, rather meekly, "You're right, of course; it wouldn't."

"All those fucked-up parallels with a God you've never seen, one you've personally never seen evidence of anyway!"

Gabriel couldn't fight the clearly obvious disapproval thrown in his face. Chris was dead-on correct in his appraisal of him, and he'd been too tired to fight with the man. He'd simply accepted the harsh punishment like the person who knew they'd let someone down whom they adored. And it was one he'd never dreamed he would have. So he'd left anyway, telling himself it was to protect the other man, when really it was to protect himself.

Gabriel Church was a wanted man, in more ways than other fugitives who might be running from the law. He'd landed in Sonora, California, but it was just the first stop in his journey from Washington. He'd been forced to stop there after the copious miles and endless blacktop nearly made him road blind and far too weary to continue driving. However, it was only a brief respite, and it wasn't a place he'd ever call home.

Sonora was a ridiculously small town in comparison to Seattle, but it had a particular quaintness very akin to those upper northwestern states he'd traveled through before. It was a town that had first grown from the glorious days of the California gold rush, originally settled by migrant Mexican miners who went searching for a better life for themselves and their families. Once the glittery veins were all but extracted, the town was forced to turn to the vast tree lines and a fast lumber industry was born. It sprang from the deep woods and left a multitude of sawmills as the skies became smoky dark with new trade and commerce.

But all that remained today was leftover beauty, and since no one could push a fantastic view across the dinner table to feed their family, tourism had become the only thread holding Sonora's tenuous fabric intact. But it was indeed beautifully picturesque. Tourists flocked through the tiny community, flashing photographs from car windows and spending their out-of-town dollars in shops and restaurants, buying postcards and memorabilia before continuing their journey out of the tiny hamlet.

It had charming qualities to boast about, with its tiny red-painted churches mixed alongside homes of every architectural style and size. It sat snuggly nestled into the rolling hillside and the raw, untainted splendor of everything surrounding it. Appearing a city out of sync with the rest of the world, it made one feel everything ran a few ticks slower on the clock and gave the sense of stepping outside of time. For Gabe, it meant a safe place to make a brief rest stop and take a needed breather during his journey to nowhere in particular.

The conversations with Chris, which had been replaying in his mind, were the only distractions from the pull of the highway. But as he drove through town, he, too, became mesmerized with the humble, tiny community called Sonora. It quelled the conversations that had been playing in a continuous loop inside his brain for hours as he drove along Highway 108, commonly known as the Sonora Pass Road. Gabriel passed cars filled to capacity. Each one appeared to be vacationing families finally bound for a week of holiday fun and enjoying the route between the Sierra Nevadas and National Parks. It was an idyllic setting for camping, horseback riding, and hiking in small groups, and was an iconic vacation spot for anyone wanting to escape the dingy streets of East Los Angeles or avoid heading to one of the national parks like Yosemite or Stanislaus. However, Gabe wasn't on vacation; he was driving with no particular fixed point on the horizon line. And he was driving alone.

Gabriel never used to mind being alone in the cab of his Dodge. He was accustomed to the loneliness and being his own company for as many years as he could recall. But that'd been before meeting Christian Maxwell. Now it reminded him of the cold isolation of a prison cell, with him in solitary.

Absentmindedly, his palm rubbed at the bulge in his side pocket where he'd shoved his new mobile phone. It hadn't rung once since he'd left Seattle, and his fingers ached with desire to feel it vibrate through his jeans.

He had told himself he wouldn't use it until he had better news to offer, but he still wanted it to ring. He needed to hear Chris on the other end. His familiar, comforting voice; that beacon in the dark he felt trapped inside; a thing that might break apart the normal repartee that usually played in his head.

He was exhausted with it all, and every conversation the two men had ever shared seemed to drone through his head like a recorder on playback. He tore apart each word and pilfered through its meaning, as if trying to comprehend all that occurred back in Seattle. His normally inquisitive mind was working overtime, and he was edging to the obsessive and compulsive sides of his nature. Try as he might, he couldn't stop the discussions from playing endlessly as he drove in silence.

It was maddening. He felt he needed to pull the truck off the black asphalt road and jump out so that he might be able to scream and yell to the heavens without looking like a fool to those cars passing him on the highway. He wanted to express his rage and pray his shrieking demands would be heard and somehow stop the parade of images in his head. Because they were leaving him broken and scrutinizing every detail and emotion that remained. It was nothing if not draining. Had he not looked up and seen the Sonora exit sign in his path and chosen to take it, he might have found himself doing just that.

He'd been hammered by some heavy blows of late, and losing his lover was only one of many in that series of events plaguing him. He had to question his mission with this second loss of Christian Maxwell in such a short time. Wasn't a heavenly soldier with his conviction intact supposed to be permitted some mercy? A loving God couldn't have created anything as wicked as him on purpose and not promised him a reward for his efforts. It felt as if God were questioning his faith like those stories of Job he'd heard from that pedophilic priest back in Tennessee. He had used the parables of the Book of Job during his sermons many times. He recalled the priest reading from the scriptures: "...and it is written that he will rise again with those whom the Lord raises up."

For the boy of ten who seemed spellbound with the story, his words sounded like music to his ears and were instantly carved deep into his young psyche. They became the words he would carry in his head for years to follow.

Then there was the sex: the sweaty entangling of naked flesh and saliva-traced spots of warmth that Gabriel remembered so well. Those were memories best enjoyed in the tranquility of the predawn hours or the dead of night. The time he spent with Chris was his favorite retreat, his recollections of guttural sounds of unbridled pleasure and the flashes of playful antics as they knotted the sheets and reached to gain purchase over the other's erection like it was a baton handoff in a thirty-meter dash.

Finding partners to play with had never been a challenge. He was far too sexual an animal to live life like some Jesuit priest. But just as that idle thought hit him, another memory came rolling in like a wave crashing on the shore, and he was instantly reminded of another priest, one he met in San Antonio, a man who'd become a gratifying find. He'd been a kind man, all wrapped up in black robes, like an Inuit Eskimo protecting himself from the elements. He recalled Father Kait's shuffling gait when they'd first met and the way he extended his hand in a greeting. How the palsy born from his advanced years became even more apparent in the slightness of that gesture. Gabriel had met few people in his life that he could say had actually surprised or inspired him. But this priest had been such a soul. And Christian had become another.

He'd been an ideal depiction of a grandfatherly type, with his thinning white hair and gently wrinkled smile. Like the grandfather Gabriel had been deprived of knowing because of Bennett's irrational hatred of Sissy's parents and theirs equally of him. A part of the family he'd never have the good fortune to meet or get to know, though he'd secretly always wondered what it would be like to have grandparents that he could spend some time with. For children in his predicament, this became a luxury and an unresolved hurt that Little Gabe learned to never speak about.

He'd seen a purpose and vibrancy still present in the old priest's fading blue eyes. They practically sparkled with his humble, unspoken wisdom and, not unlike a whisper, they hinted at the wealth of every riddle buried there. Gabe saw the man's eyes as some type of calm guarantee he couldn't fully explain. They indicated to him this was a priest who was incapable of judging another harshly, as some in the clergy have been known to do.

Maybe it was due to how much those lovely eyes had witnessed over the years. And those ears of his—surely they'd heard countless intimacies, been privy to all those closely guarded secrets from a multitude of sinners. When someone sat across from Father Kait, they knew their confessions were safe and their confidences wouldn't be broken or shared with another stranger. It became clear if they spent time with Kait and were witness to his gentle smile, and just understood this old man wasn't judging them but, rather, dissecting parts of the whole, and it was their heart and soul he hoped most to expose. With him, they knew from the first encounter it would all be done with the precision of a surgeon's blade and skill. That whatever cancer they carried was about to be excised, without even knowing it existed or how malignant it might've been.

Gabe knew this instinctually. He could tell by the way Father Kait introduced himself. How he spoke so methodically and compassionately and without expressing a need to have one rush into the nearest confessional booth and unburden themselves of their sins as they waited for absolution. Father Kait seemed more interested in the person as an individual rather than the current troubles they were experiencing or the moral wrongdoing they believed they'd committed in their pasts. Though he never had any real inkling of the severity of Gabriel's crimes, or what his confession might've meant to either of them had he been given the whole, unsettling truth.

After leaving San Antonio, Gabe thought about Father Kait more and more, wondering how the old man might be getting on, almost as if they were close friends and not just strangers who'd passed each other along their journeys.

GABE DIDN'T KNOW Father Kait had already slipped his mortal coil and suddenly and unexpectedly died from a stroke. As if those things could ever be considered anything but sudden and unexpected. Mercifully for Father Kait, he made the transition from one life to the next rather quickly, as he was entering the cathedral late one afternoon shortly after Gabe departed the city. One of the last visions he'd had was that of the threadbare red oriental carpet runners that were so iconic to the congregation of St. Joseph's Church of the Acclaimed. One of his last thoughts was of how worn-out the rugs appeared in that second his knees crashed upon the ground. The electricity of a passing neuron sparked somewhere in his brain, telling him he needed to remind himself to have those old rugs replaced soon.

For his part, Gabriel would've been truly saddened to learn the old man had died because he was someone whom he considered his ally. Though in reality, neither man knew the other by any of the degrees that counted most.

Father Kait was everything his priest back at his hometown church of St. Ignatius was not. A man whose name he could barely remember. *Had it been Father Glenn, or possibly something similar to that?* All he could recall from his initial introduction with his former priest had been a feeling he couldn't quite place: a dark and sinister unsettling he was too young to voice. Even as a child, he suspected something awful was hidden behind the black robes. Sometimes a boy simply knew with certainty when they encountered a mocking snake: one with a devilish twinkle in his eyes that always shook the boy to his core and made his stomach ache when no one else was around. He'd felt gratified knowing there was no reason he had to be alone with the priest, and that his mother and father were always close whenever they walked out each Sunday after service.

He was too young at the time to understand what lust was, particularly coming from one he was expected to trust unconditionally, or what lurked behind those imitation smiles. But he learned it, nonetheless, as he grew older and became aware of what people could be capable of doing to one another, given half the chance. He wondered later how many other young parishioners felt the same awkward stirrings in their gut when they were confronted by this supposed man of God. Maybe they never fully understood, like he hadn't exactly, what this man had in mind or the gift he wanted to give them that they'd carry for the remainder of their days. Many years would come and go before he considered how many boys that asshole priest had touched inappropriately, maybe offering them a tight conciliatory grip on their shoulders in comfort right before guiding their small hands to that growing bulge under his black robes. Or how many times he might've whispered a lie in their ears by telling them, "Go ahead and touch it, son. I know God wouldn't mind. Not if it's just this one time."

It was enough to put one off the church for good. But he hadn't turned away, not completely. He was surely twisted by the mix of emotions and confusion he felt as a boy, but he never discussed his feelings with anyone. Not until Chris. Even Sissy had been unaware, never knowing how her son felt going into church every Sunday. But it had been the windows that had transformed him into what he eventually became; those beautiful images that broke through the stained glass and adorned the main hall. The faces of saints shining through the sunlight with the deepest azure blues and the brightest of crimson shades he'd ever seen: a celestial second captured in time, a place where good and evil became irrevocably comingled inside his tiny, undeveloped young brain, where wires became inextricably crossed and reality mired in a fog of his own making. When a boy's first inclinations were born of what it meant to be in service to God, with all that that entails.

Maybe it had been the window with the archangel Michael holding a sword in one fist while, in the other, he held a spear. He was pointing both weapons supposedly toward the earth below, and the figure was haloed in a bright iridescent light that danced around his head. It might have been that precise instant that caused the first break in the manufacture of his young mind. Maybe it was when his mother, Sissy initially confided in him that he'd been named after the archangel Gabriel that fateful Sunday sermon so many years before. He remembered how she'd pointed to one of the windows then gently whispered in his ear, "You know your father and I named you after the angel Gabriel." And, after that moment, everything in his life changed forever. It had given him insight as to who he was and what he was supposed to be. It tied him to some religious prophecy, very undefined in those early days, but one that created a killer when he grew to adulthood.

A man could make himself crazy thinking about the twists and turns of fate. The meticulous route one takes when confronted by that first fork in the road ahead. He knew enough to know when the disease originally became introduced into the body, and knew what it meant to feel the contagion slipping in and yet have no way to expel it. But knowing a thing and preventing it are two very different issues. For "Little Gabe" it may have been the church and the way the light played in the aisle from those gorgeous windows high above his head that bent his will. But it was everything that occurred after that transformed him once again. And most of that would be later proven to be from a would-be author in Seattle and his first introduction to loving anyone completely. Something he hadn't considered even possible because the writer was a man and very different from anyone he'd ever come across.

Chapter Two

AS HE TURNED his tires onto a side street, the aroma from his own sweat-stained pits wafted up to his nostrils. It had been a long drive with very few stops along the way, and a shower was becoming a quick necessity. The engine of the Dodge needed as much of a break as he did, at least by the growling whine it was emitting. His ass was dead numb from long miles of sitting behind the wheel, and his back ached like it had been slowly tortured. It was certainly time to slow his roll and find shelter from the highway.

The city's downtown roads had little to offer in the way of entertainment, which to him was just fine. He didn't have a lot of money anyway, just a handful of cash that Christian had supplied before leaving Seattle. Chris had forced the notes into his hands as his eyes swelled with wetness and threatened to unleash a torrent down his face. But he'd held strong, clearly shoving back his visible sadness. At least until Gabe could no longer see him through the rearview as his truck tore up the road away from him. Chris probably had no idea how difficult it had been for Gabe to drive away or how he'd slumped over the steering wheel or glanced nervously from the right to the left as he sought a fast escape from a difficult moment.

Dredging back those memories wasn't easy, and it made him see how much he wanted to find a rock to crawl under and finally give the highway a rest for the time being. He needed space and distance to consider what he'd done and what he'd left behind. And, more importantly, he knew he needed a cold beer.

His face was wind whipped by his open driver's side window. He'd been trying to conserve fuel by running the air conditioning as little as possible. But the way his hair blew in the breeze and the tiny lines created around his eyes from squinting through the constant sun merely reminded him of how he felt being around Christian Maxwell—freedom incarnate, a sense of unfettered relief that he'd rarely experienced in his life. And still he didn't know why he felt that way when his buddy-companion was close at his side.

Distracted, his fingers went to the truck's stereo knob, wanting to substitute the void created from his recollections with idle white noise of music as it played. If he considered it any longer, he might have to admit that Chris was nothing but bad luck for him. A figure he had placed in the rearview more than once. And one who seemed trapped in that space where he'd always see himself walking away. It wasn't a pleasant thought, and one he had to push out of his skull with tunes from the radio. But just as the background melodies began to soothe him, he remembered the last time the two men showered together, back in that ramshackle motel room before he left to attend to Keen, and he felt his cock come to life in anticipation through the tight confinement of his denim jeans. He wondered if he'd miss that more than anything else, but he realized it wasn't even close to being the real truth.

Chris had become his unholy grail—the thing he'd sought more than any other treasure, yet still a priceless pearl beyond his reach. Nothing he could do seemed to solidify any prospect of them being able to remain together, to live that happily ever after story. Even if he had made a promise to stop his killing in the name of God, it would still only be a salty futility that wet and tempted his lips.

Strange, how his original celestial mission became a backseat passenger whenever a thought of losing Chris forever became his biggest challenge. Their brief relationship had been fiery and sensual, and it had proven to be the greatest oddity in his life. It became the punctuation at the end of every sentence, giving all of his words any of their meaning. Even with that, Gabriel had chosen to drive away twice before. Leaving Chris standing there alone and dumbfounded, with nothing but a vague promise and absent any guarantee the two would ever see each other again, was becoming a pattern he didn't like.

Turning his truck onto a side street as he exited the main thoroughfare in Sonora, Gabe caught a glimpse of a falling star making a distant arc across the night sky. It appeared to him that the heavens were exploding and drifting back to earth. He took it as a sign of confidence. A clear signal meant for his eyes alone, and it brought him a small measure of hope, reminding him he hadn't been completely forgotten during these last furious weeks and months. He wondered if Chris was staring up at the same sky in that same moment. He grinned with a slim degree of faith and possibility, thinking he could be witnessing an event his friend might be able to see, even from those hundreds of miles that separated them. But

Seattle skylines were filled with thousands of lights. Some colored searchlights rocking back and forth across the night sky and acting as a beacon to draw in crowds to their concerts and clubs. He doubted such a faint streak of light could even be seen against the glow of a Seattle skyline, and that was slightly depressing.

He trained his gaze forward, searching for a motel sign. He needed a convenient room within his meager price range and a chance to sleep under clean sheets for a night. Before he could find a motel, a sign caught his eye. It read: Rattlesnake Bar and Grill. He decided a drink was even more enticing than a hot shower and sleep. He had been silent running, as Chris might've said, and he'd been forgetting the taste of bourbon or beer on his lips. A fact he aimed to rectify soon. There was plenty of parking along the frontage, but he circled the block and found inconspicuous parking in a lot behind the strip because some habits were too hard to break.

Unseasonably cool that evening, he could almost catch his breath billowing in wispy clouds as he got out of the pickup and stretched his legs. Standing felt glorious since he hadn't been able to stand upright since the last fuel stop hours earlier. He walked around the block and yanked open large oak doors under the sign that had first drawn him in. Music and commotion met him at the entrance, and his mouth watered with the prospect of a drink. He finally had an opportunity of relaxing without a barrage of old memories occupying his brain.

A band was playing tunes at the rear of the bar, while a bald and bearded dude in his thirties served drinks to a mixed crowd of twentysomethings. The first hint of life he'd experienced since leaving Washington. As he sauntered to the bar, he noticed heads turning to see the stranger who'd just arrived. He felt instantly at home at the Rattlesnake, and, even being older than the general throng of patrons, he knew he was at least dressed accordingly in his denim jeans and tattered sleeveless button-up over a T-shirt. His cap was pulled down to barely reveal his eyes. He could tell the ratio of women to men made for a nice mix of youthful partygoers, any of whom appeared to be seeking company for the evening, and, sadly, in a town with very few prospects.

"What can I get you, buddy?" the bartender asked, his deep manly voice intended to be heard over the din of conversation and background music.

"Bourbon and Coke," Gabe said as he took the first stool available at the corner of the bar.

He surveyed the band and saw they were all males in their early twenties, each tattooed and attired to look more like a grunge band from the upper Northwest. The drummer was sporting a blond Mohawk haircut and banged the drumheads with deft hands and blazing speed. The bar was a trendy place, more sophisticated than he'd expected it would be. After all, Sonora was shithole-sized, but apparently had a specific flavor he hadn't completely gauged. As his glass slid across the mahogany bar, Gabe pulled out a five spot, then tossed it down while scoping everyone he could without appearing obvious.

Gabe jumped, surprised when a young woman came up from behind and touched him on his shoulder, half expecting it to be a police officer or FBI agent who had trailed him across several states, then found him in a dive bar in Sonora. She was clearly under the influence of too much alcohol, and he could see that amorous glazed expression in her pupils, which also informed him she was a girl who rarely went home alone. She reached up and attempted to yank the ball cap from Gabe's head, but he caught her wrists abruptly. Now she showed surprise.

"Hey there, cowboy," she said with a slurry backwoods Southern drawl to her words. "I just wanna see those pretty eyes of yours."

Without releasing his hold, Gabe smiled back coyly, diffusing what might yet turn ugly. "Miss, you never grab a man's hat from his head. It could be considered rude." And then to soften the blow, he grinned more sheepishly before asking, "And what's your name, pretty?"

"Sky," she mumbled drunkenly. To steady herself, she plopped down on a barstool next to Gabe's, rather than risk falling near his feet. She was interested in him; that much was obvious. Just another slutty coed who figured her ample tits and slurred speech would get her free drinks and a romp in the hay with the first sexy man she ran across. A fact which Gabe suspected happened more frequently than not, and one of the first images that entered his head after she'd touched his shoulder.

"Well, Skyler, you seem to be enjoying yourself tonight. Are you alone, or with a girlfriend or simply out with friends?"

"I was with a friend, but she bailed on me already. And I suppose I'm gonna need a ride home later."

The tilt of her head and the emphasis on slurring her words indicated she wasn't nearly as drunk as she would've liked others to believe. Another overused ploy that some women used to set a trap, he figured. And this one seemed too dense to comprehend how much she'd been the only bait that was necessary. Anything else was like hiding the trap in a forest of blind predators and none of them having a sense of smell to guide them. But sometimes Gabe wanted the challenge more than the prize, and Skyler represented little of either. Still, a piece of ass might be just the medicine he needed to stay the voices in his head.

Before he could lean in and offer to buy her a cocktail, a gangly stud appeared out of nowhere and ominously shadowed the two from behind. He was far younger than Gabe and wore a ball cap just like he did. He could have been a paper cutout clone, with his worn-out plaid shirt over his white tee, with nothing but his scraggly beard and his small mannish necklace to illustrate his youth and individuality. Gabe was familiar with the game. The dangerous girl who allowed her crotch sniffed like a bitch dog in heat, yet still playing on the strings of every available male in the room. All because she adored the attention she drew, without showing any concern to the trouble she was instigating. The type of woman who was oblivious to how many drunken or testosterone-induced blows would make contact on bone for no other reason than the seductive scent trails she seemed to leave in her wake.

The stranger didn't say a word when he walked up. But he didn't need to. His presence was clear indication to Gabe of his intention. Fighting a strong urge to stand and face the girl's associate with blood in his eye, he decided to take the high road. Like that unsubtle dance between predators over a downed kill, they were prepping for the inevitable confrontation. It could have easily ended in a far different outcome, but Gabe had no desire to fight for this girl's company. Even if a fast, unattached fuck was the prize she offered to the victor. She wasn't worth it, and in that second appeared strangely oblivious when she put her hand on Gabe's arm, which infuriated her would-be beau further. She giggled seductively and asked, "So what's your name, cowboy? I don't think I've seen you here before."

Without feeling a need to respond, Gabe stood to leave, but not before patting an open palm into the center of the quiet man's chest and saying with a grin, "She's all yours, buddy. Good night and good luck."

He slowly sauntered toward the exit, just as he remembered he'd only had a single drink before choosing to call it a night. There was no question in his mind he couldn't take the lankier dude in a fair fight, or even an unfair one. But he suddenly felt old and tired. And his typical brawl in the back parking lot for pussy seemed anything but ego inflating. Even considering her shoulder-length blonde locks and ample bosom, or the notion she might've given him one satisfying wild ride, at least for a half hour or so. But sleep was becoming the bigger beacon here; at least, sleep without the voices rattling around in his head. And he knew that to acquire that all he needed was to find a nearby liquor store where he could buy a pint of anything strong that could quell the voices and the memories from sounding off in his skull. But before getting drunk, he wanted a shower. A long hot shower to erase the dirty feeling the bar and the experience had given him. Though that was his game plan, in truth, he didn't know how well the rest of his evening was going to go. But first things first: booze, and then off to find a motel for the night.

Within twenty minutes, Gabe had found both destinations. And, after checking into the Queen of the Mines Lodge using one of his usual aliases, he was walking to his room with a black duffel filled with clothes in one hand, and a full bottle of Kentucky Bourbon in his other. The motor lodge was trying painfully hard to appear too much like an old timber mill, crying out too loudly with its façade of rustic splendor and outdoorsy décor. But more important to him, it sat far back from the main road, and Gabe knew it would be a quiet and relaxing breather from the long hours on the interstate. There'd been a small handful of cars out front, so he knew the lodge had few patrons at the moment. He figured most belonged to families on a budget who were traveling through the Sierra Nevada on their way to someplace even grander. Every place one turned their head in Sonora one could see the reflection of timber mills or the echoes of mines where gold was once quarried. The city was holding fast to its roots and springing out of the wilderness like a mirage to every passing tourist heading from point A to point B.

The room was fairly austere, with nothing but bright red curtains, a bed with a matching red comforter, and a single chair and side table as the only motel furnishings. His was a single, and he was certain the larger double-bed rooms were nicer. But those staying at the Queen of the Mines were there because of the view and price, and nothing more. The room was clean and that suited him well. The air was musty and damp from tree mold, but all he wanted was an hour under the hot spray of a shower and the comfort of a bed.

Beside an old rotary phone, Gabe found a printed brochure giving a brief history of Sonora for visitors. Thumbing through the pamphlet, he skimmed each word with some interest. Because after traveling through so many towns in a lifetime, he'd found he was intrigued with history. He particularly liked knowing what made up the origin stories to each of the small or large towns he passed through. Sitting on the edge of the queen-sized bed, he leafed through each paragraph and read up on Sonora as a town. How it could've easily been more Spanish in its style and culture had it not been for the violent uprisings between foreign miners coming in droves to the city and the American miners who pushed them farther to the outskirts and into the likes of Woods Creek, which later became the city of Jamestown, just outside Sonora.

Gabriel always felt he had no real history of his own, which may have been why he seemed fascinated with the stories of other places and other people he met. He had taken a real interest in learning all he could about Christian Maxwell, where he was raised and how well he got along with his parents, every small gadget making up the inner workings of the man. He wasn't going to be the man Chris might take home to the folks, but it was worth knowing the differences in how the two were raised.

Chris still spoke regularly with his parents, though not as much as even Gabe might've guessed. Whereas he hadn't spoken to his folks since that day he drove off their property and never looked back. It had been easier for him than most to walk away from his family because they'd become nothing more than dark shadows slipping like ghosts through those memories of his childhood. They offered no corporeal substance, nor any tangible emotional link that he could bind himself to. He had gotten awfully good at shedding any ties long before leaving Tennessee, and that lesson had come in handy many times in his travels.

"Nobody supports you like your family."

He'd heard it said many times before but had never once believed the lie. Bennett Church had driven him away with his hard-knuckled approach to decency. While his mother, Sissy, a representation of maternal adoration who he once believed he loved, had become even less than a shadow. Until that time she eventually faded into the floral-printed wallpaper and simply disappeared into obscurity. She watched wide-eyed from her kitchen window, amazed with how quickly Bennett could alienate his only son. Even then she knew he was disregarding his daughter like some empty vessel that didn't even warrant his fury or disdain. But while Sissy did nothing to correct the injuries to her daughter's self-image, the damage caused to Gabe was as prominent as it was jarring. It was just as easy to leave his mother behind as to leave that sick fuck Bennett, with one hand held in a perpetual grip around a Budweiser can and a scorned look burned forever into his expression.

At the time, Gabriel hated leaving his younger sister behind. But he had to toss those notions aside quickly for the sake of his own self-preservation. She was relegated to the same pit where he'd tossed all his memories of Sissy and Bennett Church, just a smaller and frailer fraction that he allowed occasionally to emerge. Just one more piece of discarded collateral damage in his life and a thing he knew he had to untether just to maintain his wind speeds.

Together, he and Chris spent countless hours discussing the tortured relationship Gabe had with his family. Obviously, Chris suspected it was the cause of his initial murderous intent. But Gabriel knew it had little effect on the monster he'd become. He knew in his heart it was because God had chosen him for redemption. Just as clearly as he remembered sitting near the aisle and watching the colored glass play out their reflections against the hard-grained floor of St. Ignatius.

Putting it from his mind, he stripped out of his clothing, then tossed his jeans and shirt carelessly on the floor as he moved to the shower. Catching sight of his naked frame in the bathroom mirror, he lingered on the scars he'd gained over time. Life had marred his strong physique by the lines that one only gains after being mercilessly beaten like a stray dog. There'd been many times he felt as if he were some dumb animal tortured by the hands of baleful strangers, those whose only goal was to cause others harm and pain. Still he smiled back at the sight of his own reflection and then turned the water on hot and high. Steam rapidly filled the tiny room, and, using a sturdy washcloth, he scrubbed away the perspiration and road dirt covering his hairy arms and chest. He stood there for nearly a half hour as the water worked to pull every tiny bit of anger and unrelenting emotion from his highway-weary muscles. When he stepped out, he fell quickly atop the red comforter, planting his face into the pillow. He considered making himself a cocktail. But, before he knew it, he was already fast asleep and dreaming of those happier times he'd spent in Seattle with his first friend of any real substance.

Chapter Three

GABE WOKE TANGLED in damp red fabric stained with the night sweats he'd wrestled through. And he'd awoken famished with a belly growling and a mouth that felt stuffed with oversized cotton balls.

Gabe revved the pickup's engine and went searching for a diner with hot coffee. It would hardly be the same experience of sharing those oversized cups at the café down the block from Christian's loft, but he needed a quick jolt of energy that only strong coffee could supply. He found a Homestyle mom and pop diner, aptly called Mothers and Daughters, which was already filling to capacity by the time he circled to find a nearby parking space. When he passed through the doors, the first thing he noticed was the intoxicating aroma of warm biscuits; the second thing was a starched and proper young deputy in full uniform sitting at the counter talking to a busty waitress easily twenty years his senior.

Gabe tried to appear nonchalant as he passed the deputy to reach an open booth. The man was handsome, lantern-jawed, with an affable grin. He appeared to be charming the skirts off the older waitress who was standing with a carafe of coffee in one hand and leaning in to the conversation to the avoidance of all other patrons. The glimmer in her eyes was a cross between the love of an elderly grandmother and the twisted glint that all but implied: *Damn, if I was only twenty years younger...all the things I could do to him might easily have been tallied as one helluva mortal sin.*

The diner was rustic simple, as all places serving breakfast should be. People don't want a great deal of fanfare when it comes to that all-important first meal of the day. They want big buttery biscuits with strong black coffee and fat slabs of salty pork bacon.

Sliding across the red vinyl of his booth, Gabe looked around nervously. He had nothing to fear, but the sight of any uniformed officer always sent a glacier chill running along his spine. It probably always would, he figured, since it came with the job description of serial killer. The diner was noisy that morning—the clatter of ceramic plates being stacked in the kitchen in the back mingled with the multitudes of conversations surrounding him at every table. During their busy morning rush, the waitresses were running on all cylinders as they worked strategic serpentine patterns throughout the restaurant. Every face seemed harried yet still saccharine sweet and friendly as they circled to refill empty cups of coffee or carried food-laden trays to their destination. They were the homespun ladies of Mothers and Daughters cafe.

In no time, a Latina woman in her midforties appeared with a menu and a cordial smile. Gabe requested coffee and a glass of water, then asked for a minute to peruse the menu. In a flash, she slipped away as Gabe studied the wholesomely attractive deputy at the counter. For his life, Gabe never found much interest in people watching, unless he was working a plan that ended with him gaining something of value from a potential mark. Working the pool games and poker marathons for cash became the first of many times he'd utilized those skills. He would often scrutinize those around him, looking for a hidden weakness that he might extort for some benefit. These were simple tools learned early through his drifter existence and necessities whenever a person's survival depended upon them.

Not since he'd become so fascinated with Chris had he noticed himself peering deep into another's identity. Wanting to unmask the mechanisms making the clockwork gears spin and whir to life. His would-be biographer Christian Maxwell had intrigued him from the very beginning, though unexpectedly. Sitting across from him when he asked his questions showed the writer's bravery, or at least his willingness to see it through. It never escaped Gabriel how unique it had been. The man had known he was sitting at a table with a killer, and yet he never ran screaming into the streets or attempted to wave down a passing patrol car. It was almost bravery, and a fearlessness even before that spark turned into a raging inferno in those early days. He remembered every detail of that first meeting and replayed it many times in his mind.

He recalled seeing tiny beads of perspiration erupting on Chris's forehead as he jotted his notes furiously with every answer Gabe gave him. Clearly this was his half-hearted attempt to occupy his hands and keep him from seeing the writer trembling with anxiety, or even notice his dry lips or irises that darted in metronomic fashion. Gabe felt gloriously in control, sitting across from someone who suspected they knew him and understood that he was a murderer, yet trying so hard to remain visibly calm in the face of great danger. It'd set the tone for their relationship from the onset, and Gabe for one had been grateful that it'd occurred exactly as it had.

But the uniformed officer finishing his breakfast was who interested him in that moment. Gabe could tell he was physically fit under his ill-tailored uniform. He was a clean-cut, strapping young man, at least ten years Gabriel's junior. Albeit, rather white-bread and homogenized for his tastes, he was just the type to attract the warm smiles of ladies he might pass along the sidewalk or looking up from a driver's seat as they fumbled with an open purse for a license or their registration.

The deputy pushed his empty plate across the counter, then drained the last remnants of his coffee before standing to leave. He discarded a folded twenty on the counter, easily giving him the preferred treatment of not having to wait in line at the register like most patrons. His sizable tip made the extra effort a worthy addition for those lucky waitresses with the good fortune of serving him. A woman called out as he whisked up a cap from the counter. He didn't wear the traditional deputy hat Gabe was familiar with seeing, wearing a ball cap with a badge emblazed in the center with the words *Tuolumne County* over the top and *Sheriff's Office* beneath the badge.

"Be careful out there, Bleu!" a feminine voice bellowed from unseen parts.

The deputy turned, smiled, then called back, "Will do, Charlene, and you likewise...'cause some of these fellas up in here look a tad rowdy, so, if you need backup, just give me a shout out."

There was an audible titter of laughter from the geezers at a nearby table, and Gabe recognized instantly this deputy was well-known by many Sonora natives. He was surely respected by nearly as many as those who knew him by name. It didn't take long before Gabe's server appeared and slid a warm plate in front of him across the linoleum. It was filled to the edges with many of his favorites; hash browns, scrambled eggs, sides of bacon and peppery sausage links and he immediately dove into it like a ravenous hound with barely enough time to force a smile to his waitress before she slipped away.

BLEU CORSO'S TITLE of Deputy Sheriff wasn't an honorary one, but it wasn't completely accurate either. In truth, he had yet to be named acting sheriff by the Tuolumne County office, although his promotion had been a foregone conclusion after the presiding law enforcement man decided on an unexpected early retirement. But protocol required a paperbound surrender to the rules, and officially the hiring of deputies or even sheriffs was done at predetermined times in a year. Apparently, no one had thought long enough about the guidelines that governed the process, yet everyone felt strangely compelled to follow along blindly.

Deputy Corso had been with the sheriff's office since his graduation from high school. He was loved by most in town, due to his warm nature and serious devotion to maintaining professionalism on every call and traffic stop. Citizens of Sonora learned to respect him despite his youthful face and lack of seasoning. He knew every local by their first name and was always ready to pat a stranger on the back and accompany it with a hearty, countrified chuckle. He made a point to inquire pleasantly on the success of a woman's summer garden or how her grandchildren were doing whenever he pulled a vehicle over for a random broken taillight or rolling through a stop sign. And yet he never shrugged from his duties and gave tickets when they were justified. But it was like accepting solace from a smiling devil because no matter how much one hated to see Deputy Corso trailing them in the rearview and the spark of red and blue, they knew without apology that they'd been speeding. Somehow, the grinning young officer made every offense bearable when he slipped the ticket through an open window for a signature. They knew the flickering green eyes obscured behind his shades, and the sun seemed to ignite his pearly whites when he grinned down at them. It was almost pleasant when he stopped a person's car; after all, who could argue with the boy who had cut their lawns so meticulously a mere fifteen years prior?

An hour after leaving the diner, Bleu was sitting behind the wheel of his cruiser off East Jackson, hidden by the weedy overgrowth and interstate billboard signs. He was clocking tourists with his LiDAR radar and hoping he might fill his quota of monthly citations. One Mississippi...two Mississippi...as each car passed quickly he mouthed the words with his radar gun aimed from his open window. He was smiling and remembering the old joke echoed around the station.

Citizen: Do you have a quota of tickets you have to write?

Officer: No, I can write as many as I want.

Bleu didn't care much for working traffic, but it was an integral part of his police duties, so he shouldered that burden as he'd always done: with a smile and few complaints. After all, there wasn't much crime to speak of in Sonora, and he often felt his presence was more show than any real necessity.

Still, he liked working for the sheriff's office and knew, with his record, his promotion was an imminent conclusion. He liked the jangle of keys in his brown dress slacks, the respect shown in the faces of townies, and the comforting sense of a gun at his hip, even though it almost never left its holster. He took time at the shooting range whenever he could because he wanted to keep his skills honed and at a ready practiced speed. But mostly his job consisted of working traffic stops, making appearances at outdoor festivals, or recording noise and trespassing infractions from those locals he saw far too regularly for his own satisfaction.

Bleu lived his life by simple decrees. The mottos in his head rang as proverbs and country sayings, and each one rang with the soft, dulcet tones of his mother's voice. Her homespun, no-nonsense way of seeing life had successfully carried him through his more difficult days, and every axiom somehow gave his life some meaning and enabled others to see him as the man he was learning to become. He could still recall when he'd perform some idle task for her, like drying dinner dishes, or helping her move a heavy couch to vacuum under, and, being a child who seemed too eager for her approval, he'd always ask, "Is this okay, Momma?" Her responses were simple, uneducated elegance and hit the mark where she deft aimed.

"Well it's certainly better'n a poke in the eye with a sharp stick."

He remembered his mother very fondly, just as he remembered every smile when she offered her sage yet obscure wisdoms. Like little treasures he could pocket and pull out later to examine in detail; even in those rare times when he couldn't quite grasp their strange meanings, like particularly that phrase. Wasn't everything better than some horrible poke in the eye, regardless of the size or sharpness of the protrusion? Yet he could call to mind her twinkling jade-green irises whenever she bequeathed one of her signature, rural colloquialisms. It always produced an ear-to-ear smile on the young deputy's face when her funny sayings came to mind.

Sadly, she was dead now. She'd been taken by cervical cancer when Bleu was sixteen years old; far too early for a proper departure which left a husband and a son feeling the absence with every passing day. Residual scar tissue was the only thing left behind after her painful exodus from this world; that, and a deep, vacuum-like chasm that sucked everything good about his family inside. But Bleu was grateful he could still sense her spirit circling around him as he went through mundane everyday chores. Such as when he changed out of his uniform and into street clothes at the precinct's locker room or in that instant when he was ordering his breakfast at one of the local diners he frequented. She was that warm breath on the nape of his neck, making him feel safe and secure. And he learned early on that he needed to be thankful he could still recall her with such vivid detail. Just as he remembered her comical sayings and idiosyncratic mannerisms or the way she made him feel protected and loved while in her presence.

Her name had been Ruth Tierney when she was young and a bit of a looker, as she would later tell her "lovely little boy Bleu" with an expansive grin plastered on her face. That was until a strapping naval officer just returning from an overseas deployment had unexpectedly caught her attention. At once she fell headlong in love with Edwin Corso after first seeing him at some random social gathering she couldn't quite recall, attired in his pristine white dress uniform. Throughout their brief period of dating, she'd understood instantly that she'd someday marry her attractive soldier. But it was all tragically fleeting. Just as her little boy was obtaining his driver's license, both he and his father lost that delicate connection they'd cherished so dearly, the single matriarchal thread that held their small family intact.

The years between Ruth's death and then had been difficult for him. And though he tried to maintain a good relationship with his father, it never seemed to bounce back to the original days when Ruth was around and running the roost. Ed sank into a dark well of depression for which he was unable to escape. And little Bleu was either too young or inexperienced at the time to have the tools to retrieve him. They became strangers, where Christmas and Thanksgiving holidays were just a quick visit or a wrapped package dropped at the back door with a note promising they'd get together real soon. But they were hollow gestures intended to keep the façade of their family unit unbroken.

The deputy was attractive and young. Most citizens of Sonora respected him, particularly single ladies of a similar age and background. He'd noticed their suggestive gazes. He'd observed their coquettish smiles when they passed him on the street. No amount of feminine modesty could've hidden what Bleu saw in their eyes. He imagined them languishing in their soap-filled tubs as fingers made gentle circles above the mound, daring to explore their own clitoris. With an arch of the spine and a wet tongue dragged across full rosebud lips, they were more like a succubus driven by heat and desire than the women he knew from town. He imagined all this because he'd seen them in their true form, not just women who desired him but those who wanted him completely and wholly to themselves—a man who could offer them more than simply his shared last name.

But secrets are immutable in small towns, and the deputy had his share. As it turned out, Bleu Corso was gay, though deeply entrenched in a closet of deniability. He maintained his best outward appearance of propriety and chose to not act on his more clandestine desires. Bleu had taken out a few random women in town to maintain the ruse of being straight, and he was learning quickly how to master the ability to break off the relationship immediately before any sexual encounter. Thinking himself clever, he'd set the alarm on his cell to ring later in the evening when he was out with a woman, usually occurring at some inopportune moment like when they were eating dinner on their first date or when they headed back to her place, ostensibly for intimacy. He would go through the motions, appearing to have gotten a text or some "official notice" from his station that he was required. He'd then offer up his hasty apology and provide a quick kiss to her lips before leaving her stranded on the steps of her front door. She might smile or wave as he sped away in his cruiser, thinking of her brave policeman racing down the driveway in a cloud of dusty disappointment. But she'd learn later he wasn't returning her calls or text messages. And on some occasions, he'd sit her down and admit that he felt no real connection between the two. He'd ply her with lies and say he thought it best they end it now rather than later. But through all his deception, even he knew he couldn't carry the subterfuge forever. Eventually the women would talk, rumors would spill out and become fodder for the gossip train because if you can't blame yourself, then it's better to shove the knife in someone else's gut and then twist.

Chapter Four

BACK AT THE motor lodge, Gabe felt he was finally standing on terra firma. He'd pulled off the interstate for the time being, had a full belly, was registered at a place he could afford for a few days, and would be sleeping in the luxury of a bed that evening.

The small things please me.

His usual MO would be to troll the city, searching for suckers with fat, overflowing pockets. Typically, he'd scour the city streets for pool halls and hotel bars where women, and occasionally drunk and unsuspecting men, might meet a stranger for sex. He'd become one of those brief, uncommon out-of-town encounters who would roll around sweaty, staining their cotton hotel sheets dark with his perspiration. Church liked the idea of being someone's devilishly unspoken secret. He imagined the mask they wore to hide their shame once they greeted their lovers at the door after a long weekend or out-of-town business meeting. He understood how much he was the cause for those looks that spouses quickly learned to mistrust. Yet no one wanted to ask the questions behind the eyes since they feared hearing a more awful truth revealed.

But he was currently flush with cash, so he didn't need to employ his usual games that night. He plopped down on the queen-sized mattress and clicked the television on. The programs didn't interest him, and, in his boredom, he was constantly yanked backward in time to those last conversations he'd had with Chris. There was a lot he should've said back in Seattle—things he regretted not bringing up in the here and now. His loneliness was taking over, controlling the moment. That much was certain. Loneliness was a sensation he wasn't all that familiar with, and one he'd never have admitted in open company. But he couldn't skirt the depression he felt—his clear and tangible reality, a weighty thing dragging him back to earth like the chains holding fast the ghost of Jacob Marley. And Gabe only knew one way to handle depression: by turning his ghosts into spirits, which meant the overconsumption of alcohol wasn't far away.

"Try to remember, babe, when it comes to life, there's some assembly required," Chris said one night, and it brought a smile back to his face. They'd been making plans to escape Seattle together. Promises and guarantees they both knew weren't in the realm of any possibility. The "what-ifs-and-all" was a game they played together, and though it had made them both feel somehow fused within their combined tragic circumstance, it had still been a mirage. Strange how two such different men could find any common ground to bond over. Theirs being a future they'd never reach, not together. But if he'd been smarter, if things had been different, then maybe he could have found a way.

With all the saccharine sweetness he allowed himself to wallow in, there was still that memory of their first sexual encounter. And, as Gabe recalled that day, the blood began to swell to his dick and fill the veiny shaft. He felt his cock jump with the anticipation before plumping to its typically impressive girth. It reminded him how long it'd been since he'd allowed himself any relief from the building tension, and he suddenly wanted to hear those familiar wet suckling noises, reminiscent of a young calf at its mother's teat.

Gabe recalled the deer-in-the-headlights look on Chris's face, appearing like some intersection between shock and trepidation, like he simply couldn't fathom the possibility the two men were about to fuck. They'd been drinking for hours, back at the Mayflower Park Hotel. And both their heads were reeling from the effect of numerous bourbons and long conversations into the night. Gabe remembered how much it felt like an invasion of privacy. But he'd already agreed to do the interviews, sensing it was too late to turn back. Though he couldn't rightly understand why he felt that way in the moment.

It made him uncomfortable to poke around in the dark, pushing the door in his mind further open with every question Christian tossed in his direction. It allowed an unsettling amount of light to creep in, leaving Gabe feeling exposed and naked. But the booze played its part effectively, and he couldn't stop the answers from falling from his lips. He instantly knew the sensation of being unguarded in the line of questions. Gabe was unaccustomed to this feeling, and even he couldn't believe the level of honesty he offered with every word. The air was thick with sexual tension, and Christian's desire had become a palpable distraction, getting in the way and creating a noticeable wedge between the two.

By Gabe's thinking, the only course correction was to push back against that awkward feeling before it could fully surface and alter the game, as it were. He simply needed to part the man's ass cheeks with his stiff cock and get the deed done. He knew all too well a good defense relied upon a strong offense, and it made perfect sense to put the man under that same heavy cloud which had been suspended over his head that night. He wanted the writer to feel as naked and exposed as he felt. To compel him as much as he was cringing from every stinging question thrust his way. He wanted to share the disease and flip the switch. To make someone else feel as if they were losing the control he was. The good point came from knowing he'd at least get his wick wet in the process, and that seemed all right by him.

He'd known almost instantly that Christian was queer, from the first second they met at the café that fateful afternoon after a long pouring Seattle rain. A man can tell when someone is sizing them up, even with his back turned. And he'd seen that look on many occasions: the hungry wide-eyed caution. Someone waiting with baited breath for the other shoe to fall, and it hadn't surprised him to see that look on the younger stranger's face either. He had his own dirty appetites that needed gratifying, and, if he had to confess, the notion of sex with Chris hadn't been a particularly unpleasant image in his head. He had never fucked a male before Christian Maxwell. But, in the time they spent together, chatting and getting to know each other, the idea had crossed his mind more than once.

What did seem strange to him was it hadn't been a mere flicker, something sparking and then evaporating into nothing as he might've expected it to. Instead it lingered, rattling around in his brain and taking up residence there, until his breathing felt labored and stilted. Gabe had been caught off guard, but, even more, amazed at how much the picture danced around his noggin and refused to depart. He'd found his heart beating fast whenever in the man's presence, with the dichotomy being that it seemed natural and conventional an image, despite his rural upbringing. The movie was always playing somewhere in the background with its raw footage on a perpetual loop. He'd envisioned how he'd take Chris and bend the man to his supreme will. In his own way, he'd suspected from the beginning that they'd end up between the sheets and the nervous and handsome biographer would one day become his bitch.

He'd never considered how his own feelings might transform in the interim.

He blamed it on the shy way Chris was always looking down at his legal pad and the way he tried in vain to avert Gabe's frequent straightforward stares. That was until Gabe forced him to return his gaze, holding him rigid there and preventing him from looking away, just as the apprehension was building around them like some crackling fire ready to consume them both. And in that split second as their eyes were locked across the table, Gabe was all but certain he could read the other man's mind. He could see a wounded soul hidden to most. He unearthed the secrets the writer foolishly thought were too deeply buried to excavate. It became a game Gabe played with him, toying like some curious and sadistic cat batting a smaller creature between its paws. Teasing him with a grin and a sly look simply to watch him fumble with his pen or appear distracted by idle nonsense right beyond his sightline. But the game needed a resolution, and it was time for the tension to be shattered apart. He knew he had to take it further, if only to see where that road carried him. He remembered how he'd dropped his towel from his waist after his shower. How his beguiling pretense became visible. He enjoyed watching Chris gulp in a quick burst of oxygen and how he falsely appeared so unaffected. He remembered how he'd walked into the bedroom, sensing the writer's eyes scanning his ass cheeks as he sauntered off. He remembered how he'd called back over his shoulder, so casual and unassuming, "Are you coming?"

Even now after many months, he could still recall that evening with great clarity. How the pit had formed in his gut. How it then traveled upward into his chest, turning into icy fingers gripping tight around his heart and arteries. How it seemed to freeze there, preventing the organ any damage as it pounded against his ribcage. How it felt like his lungs had been constricted and trapped in a python's embrace. He hadn't experienced this feeling before, or since. And it was why the writer had become so important in the grander scheme of his life.

GABE HAD SUFFERED his sad existence as a boy back in Tennessee. But he'd been forever altered by three things: his misconceptions about God, his disconnected mind telling him that taking a life was not always the sin he thought it to be, and that first contact made with a failed writer back in Seattle. Each event had become a twisted watershed moment intricately tying the whole. Now sufficiently bound together, it was easy to see how one might fail to see that each sliver, every fragment, would someday play a part in the natural resolution that was to come. But fortunately for Gabriel, he was occluded from seeing that future. He was far too busy gazing backward into his recent past.

"You here for the fishing or the mule deer huntin'?"

Gabe looked up from his Johnnie Walker as the bartender leaned over the mahogany to wipe away the residue of ice sweat from his drink. The look of confusion on his face should've told the young man he was buried in his own thoughts, but the little shit was persistent.

"Sorry, I meant you looked like a hunter, and I was asking if you were here for the hunting or the fishing."

"Neither," Gabe said blandly. "I suppose I'm here for the view."

"Well, we got some of the best fishing and hunting in these parts," he continued, undeterred by Gabe's offhanded reply. "Most strangers come here for the hunting, camping, and fishing. At least ones that stick around town, those who aren't making their way through the pass and heading over to the coast anyways." Then with a grin, he added, "You'll have to pardon me, but you don't much look like a man traveling with a carload of his young'uns and a wife distracting you and pointing out all the scenic beauty that we're so proud of."

Taking a swallow of his whiskey, Gabe could see the young man was trying to make idle conversation with someone who'd recently drifted into town. He offered a simple and fresh-faced smile like some small-town welcome wagon greeting him at the city limits with a basket of farm-raised peaches and a brochure showing all their Christian churches to choose from. But Gabe never much cared for small talk about the local color, so he nodded once to illustrate his usual callous dismissal and then hoped the young man would get the point and just walk away.

"Can I get ya a refill?" he asked eagerly. Gabe recognized the man was oblivious to his antisocial gesture, so he acknowledged by pushing his glass across the bar with a half smile. As the server raced back to acquire a clean glass, Gabe surveyed the saloon more fully. It was dead here tonight. Surely it got busier than this? No wonder the kid was so anxious to chat him up. He figured there were only so many buckets of ice one could lug in to fill the beer bins and a limit of limes one could cut into quarters before the need to engage hits you square in the face and you do anything possible to stave off the boredom.

The young man had been right in his assessment of Church as a hunter. He had little interest in stalking deer or elk and couldn't picture himself lounging in a dinghy-sized rowboat with his rod and reel in one hand while he waited for a gentle tug against the nylon. With Gabe's head down and his eyes scrutinizing his cocktail, the young man working behind the bar looked like he was about to say something else but then stopped before turning away. He sauntered off to help another patron, one probably more willing to socialize and save him from another dull evening with very few customers.

Sitting under the blue neon glow of a beer sign, Gabe was reminded of the stained-glass windows back at St. Ignatius and how that particular shade of blue from the saint's vestments appeared to refract and writhe across the hard floors of the cathedral like a snake scrambling away to find shelter. Even then he'd known it was nothing more than a simple trick of the light; the passing of the morning sun as it took new positions in the sky outside. But knowing that didn't make it any less lovely an effect to behold. Suddenly his thoughts were ricocheting backward through time and at breakneck speeds, like witnessing a bullet whirling past his head but somehow seeing it shot in reverse. And just as suddenly, he was back in Tennessee, a boy of ten or so and a part of his church's congregation. He recalled a particular Sunday school class that had been mandatory that he attend, despite his noticeable lack of enthusiasm and dislike of other students in his age group.

By enrolling their son, it meant the family had to arrive extra early in order to make the first available mass. Little Gabe learned quickly how his attendance was both expected and compulsory. He would join in alongside the other sons and daughters of St. Ignatius's devotees and religious elite. They would all be crammed into tiny utilitarian spaces in the farthest reaches of the cathedral maze consisting of austere rooms and overly adorned chapels. Naturally, he would have preferred to have slept later or to have spent time playing with his dogs out in the front yard. But it'd been another typical Bennett Church decree, the kind one knew not to disagree with since the battle was unwinnable when his father set his mind to concrete. He could've stomped around huffing and puffing, but no amount of tears tossed in his mother's direction was ever going to offer him any reprieve. Sissy's will was tailored to her husband's proclamations, whether she agreed with them or not.

Bennett was insistent his boy attended every Sunday bible class. Gabe remembered his father's booming voice one Saturday morning when he was explaining that, rather loudly, to his wife. Sissy had foolishly suggested that Gabe attend a summer camp for something different and fun. She had to have known that the instant she broached the subject she'd regret it because after bringing it up, a row started that lasted for an hour. Bennett trailed behind her with his arms outstretched and his voice raised, and there seemed no place safe in their tiny home to escape. Gabe remembered it clearly because the decorative plates his mother hung in the hallway had rattled from all his stomping around and the pitch in Bennett's excitable words.

"My son is going to have a proper papal teaching, just as I had," he screamed down the hall. And more for Sissy's emphasis, he swore, "I'll be damned adamant about that at least." To the boy it seemed there wasn't much his father wasn't adamant about. Thinking back on it later, Gabriel thought that it odd that Bennett pictured himself as a religious person. He'd once suspected his father hated having to attend mass. He once mused that his father was spineless, and that, had it not been for the starch in his best Sunday shirt, he'd possibly fall face-forward during the ceremony. He sat so rigidly that in Gabe's perception he had to have been glued to the back of those highly polished pews at his beloved St. Ignatius.

The pretty lady who taught the Sunday school class, whom Gabe could no longer remember by name, introduced him to the word "malediction." She said it over and over for the younger pupils, then slowly described how it meant a cursing damnation; the four principal vices of the tongue, as described by Paul in Romans. Looking around, Gabe had seen that many of her young charges wore expressionless stares and glass-eyed confusion, so eventually the young woman said the sermon would be better taught by Pastor Glenn and changed the subject.

But the lesson had slipped out already, and by then it was buzzing around Little Gabe's ears like a mosquito piquing his interest. Now, back in the present, he remembered it once again, an echo from his past. As he drained the last drop of his bourbon and melted ice, sitting atop his barstool all alone at the Firefly Bar and Pool Hall in Sonora California, Gabe knew with a certainty that he'd become his own form of malediction. He was clearly his own curse and another soul's proven damnation.

The original principle expressed in the Bible is there to show how a tongue can shed illumination to a person's character. It's there to remind us, without being literally carved in stone, how we compile our wickedness with every added generation that rejects Christ. It paraphrases Paul's speech in Romans of the sins left behind after harsher words have been spoken. But, more importantly, it teaches us that we have choices with how we operate ourselves through life. That we can do it with deceitful flatteries and infected discourse, and we can utter imprecations against one another with ease. But it was akin to how we are forced to tolerate our own runny streams of diarrhea and shit as they flow forever downhill. It tells us we can choose not to participate, or as Father Glenn might have lauded in one of his sermons: "As written in Matthew 12:34, 'For out of the abundance of the heart the mouth speaks.'"

Chapter Five

CHRISTIAN MAXWELL CRADLED his head in his hands with his own dramatic interpretation of Lady Macbeth. He was practically wringing his palms together and mumbling to himself as if portraying every bit of his remorse and recent regret. It had been four days since Gabriel slipped from the grasp of the authorities and disappeared down that long highway out of Seattle. Chris had been filling the absence created by obsessing over every detail he could find in the local papers, desperate to learn what the police may already know about his dangerously charismatic lover.

He knew Gabriel would wait several days before calling him on the disposable phone Chris covertly tucked in the rear of his nightstand drawer. But he wanted to hear his soothing voice and needed to tell him how much he missed him. What he really wanted more than anything was to taste the familiar hint of whiskey on Gabe's lips. He wanted to curl up with him in his bed and be free of the usual worry that the door to his condo might come crashing down with an explosion of wood slivers and metal deadbolts as agents kicked in his door screaming. He could picture the pandemonium created as his living room became suddenly alive with the onslaught of men in black SWAT gear, with automatic rifles drawn and ready to take down a fugitive. The idea sent cold shivers down his spine and made sleep all but impossible most nights.

Despite the anxiety he felt building and consuming him since this all began, he knew he had to go through the motions of everyday life like Gabe instructed him right before he left. Chris had gone to work as he had every morning before. But more atypically than before, his coworkers found his office door closed and the blinds pulled. Instead of spending his days proofing ad copy and attending administrative meetings, he was scouring the Internet for any news article he thought would be there. But he found nothing unusual in his research. He knew Gabriel visited Detective Keen and his wife the day he disappeared. His reasoning, which had become clear to him, had been solely to protect Chris.

It was another chivalrous surprise. That Church, the sadistic killer, would jump in front of a speeding bullet or throw his body in the path of a coming train. All to protect another person, someone he cared for deeply and hoped to save. He was an enigma to anyone who knew him, but to Chris, he was a man he was learning to trust and understand, though at times even his actions could still astonish him in many ways.

Gabe alone had taken Shea's life, and that had been a selfish act to save his own skin. Christian had no illusions to that tragedy or to every one that followed after that. But he knew Shea's murder had been because of him, and that made him more than complicit in everything Gabriel had done since.

I might as well have killed her myself. If I hadn't visited her that afternoon and told her who Gabriel really was, then she'd still be alive. I'm the murderer here.

In the weeks since his first meeting with the killer, Chris had come to terms with his involvement in Gabriel's crimes. He hadn't gone to the police when Gabriel told him who he was, or when every suspicion he had had been correct. That made him complicit, didn't it? The questions should have torn apart every moral fiber holding his delicate psyche intact. But he'd been too busy watching the magician's hands and seemed to forget all the tricks going on behind his back. He felt the presence of strong emotions the minute he first laid eyes on Gabe. And yet he lied to himself that he'd write his biography of a serial killer and somewhere in the process get the man to turn himself in to the authorities. He always thought he could, and the killer did agree to his interviews, which at the very least showed his willingness to repent.

But, he hadn't gone to the police. And Gabriel hadn't turned himself in. Instead, they fell into a sordid and unexpected relationship. One where a lot of the time they spent together was nothing more than Chris's exploration of why the crimes were committed in the first place. That and trying to get Gabriel to see his own twisted logic as he exposed every nerve with surgical precision and picked at the inner workings of Gabriel's brain. He was trying to get him to see that same awful truth he saw. He wanted to convince him to stop the killings and accept whatever punishment lay ahead. But there was always an absence of clear thinking and rationale when it came to Gabe. Against any of his better judgments, he'd crawled into bed with a murderer and ultimately found some spark of humanity there. A spark he knew that not a single other person would find. Most wouldn't care to ferret out any virtue in the man in the face of such savage atrocities.

He'd discovered a damaged soul inside Gabriel and a goodness plumbed somewhere below the visible surface. He'd seen pain shadowing his killer like some trailing footprint left moist in the sand. But he'd failed to recognize each victim, or the costs of every action the fugitive took for granted. He simply pushed those faceless victims to the dark recesses of his mind, hiding them from plain view as if they were discarded things, recollections intentionally forgotten. Maybe the sex had placated the irrational, or the emotions became so overwhelming that he wasn't right in his head. Now he knew how wrong that had been. Without knowing it at the time, he'd been inhaling that same contagion, breathing in the same sickness, and, as he stood in the cold light of his new reality, he could see that he was equally as guilty of every offense. As guilty as the man who had lain naked under his cool cotton sheets and wrapped a large forearm around his waist to pull him closer as they both dreamed of better days.

Throughout his research Chris fully expected to find a mention of a Detective Keen buried someplace in the newsprint. Anything really that discussed a statewide manhunt or a mysterious killer, but instead he found a glaring absence. It should have comforted him, but it put him more on edge than before because to him that meant the FBI might have taken over the investigation, and he knew they were a tight-lipped bunch. They rarely made any public announcements regarding their investigations, at least not until after they apprehended their suspects. He hoped that wherever Gabe was he was safe and sound and not feeling the same pervasive sense that doors were about to be kicked in with SWAT agents flooding in like waves crashing against rocks. This was the cloud currently hanging over his head, and, like he'd always said, life has a way of biting you in the ass when you are standing oblivious to it.

"You're such a fucking worry-wart."

Chris remembered the conversation with Gabe, walking back from the café at the corner of his block shortly before his lover left Seattle. Both knew it was time to get ahead of the authorities dangerously hot on their trail at the time. Chris was measuring every fear and possibility. His arrest and prosecution, his death or the death of the man he loved, even how he would explain any of those last few weeks to his family or an attorney. Gabriel was simply trying to ease his jangled nerves by giving him another show of his blistering bravado and insane confidence. He had no anxieties, or at least that was how he appeared to Chris at the time.

"Sorry, boss. I personally like to think I'm pragmatic."

When we do crazy things, we can sometimes blame them on a crazy existence, as Gabriel said when they stopped midblock to separate that day. He'd placed one hand around Chris's neck and drawn him in closer. With his other hand, he fingered Chris's jawline in a very uncharacteristically sensitive way, and said, "Don't worry about this shit storm we're facing, boy. The world's headed to the crapper anyways." And then with his twisted grin, he flashed his pearly whites. "It's always running to the medicine cabinet to overdose on whatever it finds...and no matter how many times you wrestle the pills away, it sneaks back for more."

That was his way, Gabriel's disturbed outlook on life. Chris knew it'd been born from his frustration and home life, and it had become his signature view. He always thought eventually everything around him would crumble into dust in the end. As if on cue, Chris could hear the muffled ringing of the disposable cell in his nightstand and his heart froze. "Oh, thank God," he muttered aloud as he yanked the drawer open to answer the call.

"Baby, is that you?" he asked breathlessly. His heart chose not to beat with its regular speed. The proof of that came from those loud thumping sounds, though Chris couldn't determine whether they came from his chest or the rushing blood inside his ears.

"You were expecting someone else?" Gabe asked quietly.

Simply hearing Gabe's melodious, smoky timbre seemed to change everything in an instant for Chris. When a person loved someone and missed them terribly, it didn't take much to feel suddenly safe and orderly by the single sound of their voice. Whatever distance separated them was gone in a flash, and he felt like someone was drawing a warm blanket around his bare shoulders and he sensed that breathy warm feeling on the back of his neck.

"God, it's good to hear that you're okay."

"Like there was ever any doubt," Gabriel said calmly. "I made it to Cali, and I'm taking a few days trying to get my head on straight, but I wanted to make sure you were doing all right."

"Is it safe to talk?" Chris asked with a shaky voice. "Even if it's not, then please lie to me; you can't imagine how much this helps."

In an interval of silence, Chris knew Gabriel was absorbing his confession, like they were allowing that split second to wash them clean. And then Gabriel changed the subject.

"I'm in Sonora," he said flatly. "It's really beautiful here. You should be here to see it."

"You shouldn't be telling me where you are," Chris whispered unable to keep the sadness out of his voice.

"Don't be an idjit, son, it's perfectly safe. It's not like they know who you are anyway. They don't plan on clamping jumper cables to your nips to get you to talk."

Gabe chuckled, obviously amused with himself. And that too shortened the distance between them. With his heart finally beating at regular speed and his breathing controlled, Chris was able to slide up against the pillows and the headboard and pull up his knees to feel more comfortable. Like a fifteen-year-old talking to his first high school love well into the night, he knew no one else could ever begin to understand. Chris understood to steer the conversation away from anything dark or disturbing, so he asked about Sonora, then Gabe's drive out of the city. He listened to that husky voice chatter in the receiver like two bros simply catching up after a long period of not communicating. Though the reality was that it'd been only days since they last saw each other. He found a smile creeping over his face in the warm euphoria that dripped like honey around him.

THAT FEELING OF a camaraderie and completeness was the same for Gabe. Like sitting next to a friend and swinging your feet off a dropped down tailgate, swigging beer from a can, and joking, ribbing the other man mercilessly about everything and nothing at the same time. Gabe could almost hear those echoing words ringing in his head, "I dunno know why, but this dude just gets me." They chatted for long hours into the night. Until both felt they'd run out of anything new to say, yet neither man brought up the events of why they were in separate towns. There was always time for that later.

Gabe's tone became softer and lower, a burly voice raspy with a lifetime of drinking harsh whiskey. Chris loved that more than anything. Gabe trailed his hand along his chest and opened his button-fly jeans as he talked. His fingers gently raking over his dick with every word he uttered to Chris. He was getting hard to the touch, but it was sensuality he knew he wouldn't waste. At least not until their call was over and he could lapse into his dreamier fantasies of the two of them together at last.

"You have such control over me," Chris murmured into the phone.

There was no explanation needed since Gabe knew the effect stirring in his friend's erection. He could tell by the way his words lagged and hung still in the air. How the breathing on the other end of the line became slow and calculated. He knew it because he too felt those same sensations: a driving force that overpowered from the gut, like an ember barely gaining any heat. The only medicine available as a cure was a furiously fast fuck before drifting off to sleep. But they were hundreds of miles apart, and Church didn't like the idea of anyone, including Chris, knowing he occasionally beat off. He was too manly for masturbation. That was something pimple-faced teenagers did because they couldn't get any action. He'd always known that if he needed to get his rocks off a willing partner was never far away. The sexy ones always took for granted the lack of effort they needed to spill out in order to get their sexual gratification fulfilled.

CHRIS STROKED HIS stone-hard flesh but never pulled his cock out or took it further. Instead, they talked; him carefully listening to Gabe's voice while deliberately teasing back with suggestive comments made to entice. Chris's dick was so rigid it was close to causing him pain, and yet he stayed glued to the phone until they both felt the late hour beckoning them to bed.

They said their goodnights, and Gabriel promised to call back in a day or so. A serious conversation was required, but they'd wanted to keep it light and breezy for the time being. It had been several days, which felt more like months since they'd slept together, and both wanted to bask in that state of pleasure before it ultimately had to turn something sour. Gabe's final words cemented their evening as being something damned near perfect because just before he disengaged, he whispered, "Love you then." He lingered for a minute holding the phone in one hand and staring at his ceiling. He knew instinctually that he'd once again forgotten to remain clearheaded and rational when it came to Gabriel Church. But, as he put the disposable phone back into its hiding place in the nightstand, he knew it didn't matter. How could it when all was right with the world, wasn't it?

Chapter Six

ONE OF THE things Bleu hated most about Southern California was the mosquitoes. His flesh crawled at the thought of insects feeding on his blood and feasting on his skin. It was one of the reasons he always wore long-sleeve shirts whenever he stepped outdoors. This made him an unusual picture with other young men his age. He knew he had a good body. He worked out regularly at a local gym, using the discounted rate offered to city police. And in Sonora there wasn't much else to do in the way of entertainment. But, when he ventured out in public, he was dressed more like a mountain man than one of those granola-crunching beach bums so common in the foothills of the Sierras. He was familiar with the type though, their sun-bleached, unkempt hair and Bahama shorts without shirts, dark tans, and reeking of patchouli and pot.

He was considered different in his upbringing for more than his hidden sexuality. Bleu had never expressed an interest in surfing or attending outdoor concerts as a teenager, and he never fully developed an attraction to weed. When it came to other males his same age, he was sure their choices were never going to lead them anyplace good. He suspected his friends had been mainlining the green Kool-Aid their hippy parents were teaching them for far too long. And even as a young man, he felt older, more mature and responsible than his peers. In the back of his mind, he figured someday he'd be in a position of authority, guessing that meant the army or possibly police work. But all his goals and childhood dreams could never have prepared him for becoming a sheriff for Tuolumne County, or such a man deserving of that much respect.

There was a laid-back attitude regarding protocol inside the Sonora City police department. The deputy's cruiser could occasionally be seen parked in front of his residence during his shift, so was not an uncommon sight for his neighbors. Corso could alert the station with a 10-7, which was code for being out of service for a brief stint. Police usually reserved this code for restroom breaks and personal stops, as long as they were within reason, or when they needed to refuel their black-and-whites at the city's designated garage and storage lot.

This was one of those necessary times and not a quick stop to grab lunch before heading back to the streets. As he pulled into his driveway, the deputy radioed in his 10-7 because he felt a desperate need to check his house, half expecting it to be rummaged through with drawers pulled out and possessions stolen. He rented a quaint two bedroom on Daybreak Court, a lovely white-frame construction from the mid-thirties complete with a wraparound porch and shutters at every window. Bleu thought it picturesque when he first noticed it with a tiny rental sign on a post planted in the front yard. Fortunately, it was in his all-too-meager price range, which was not enough for an officer who risked their life on a daily basis, but he never complained. But secret lives are difficult to maintain in small towns, and the night before Bleu had done something he almost never did. He'd picked up a young man for the purpose of sex.

It had gone against his grain to do so, but the urge had been irresistible, and he'd decided to throw all caution to the wind and finally allow himself to live without the usual worry of consequence. He compounded that infraction by allowing the young man to sleep late and remain unsupervised in his home alone. As he dressed to head to the station, he hoped the uniform he wore might give the young man pause should he be considering theft or something worse. But there were times when the weight of his secrets became a burden he could no longer carry, and, if the young man rifled through his things, or absconded with his TV or stereo or the loose change he left in a bowl by the bedroom door...well then so be it. At least he got his rocks off. His name was Jake and he was only nineteen years old, and, oddly, it'd been the younger man who instigated the hookup.

The deputy had been making his final patrol through town the night before. He'd been working an irregular late shift for another officer. A favor for a friend he'd agreed to take on, even though his usual shift ran consistently from eight a.m. to six p.m. He was doing a simple security check, or 10-59, known to officers as a drive-by of a public ground or facility. Corso made it a point to cruise the perimeters of Phoenix Lake whenever he wasn't working traffic. One of his duties was to roust the drunken teenagers who occasionally partied there after school and on most weekend nights. A hot spot for the young people in town, and a place to go and revel in the freedoms of adolescence, to drink their first beers and smoke a little pot while listening to music blasting from stereos through car windows. Bleu knew the place all too well since he and his friends had partied there in the day. And he guessed they'd be partying there long after his retirement from the force.

This was a duty he enjoyed, since it meant taking a relaxing drive through the open air and woody surroundings. He enjoyed that al fresco scent coming off the water and the brisk hint of a season as it passed. Autumn was his favorite time of year. He longed for the solitude, and it was a happy respite from the otherwise hectic days of summer or spring. A time when his mind could stray as he maneuvered his cruiser around beautiful lake homes atop tree-lined grounds. The deputy liked to dream that he'd buy property out there someday, close to the city's largest golf course, and eventually become neighbors with some of Sonora's more affluent residents.

Yet he knew the importance in making his security rounds by the lake, having been reminded of that fact last year, when he was called to work a traffic accident where one young man became their town's latest fatality. Naturally, it was considered the local tragedy, but it was almost an expected outcome, since any constable who worked the area might say, "It was only a matter of time before someone died up there on Phoenix Lake!"

Desolate and dark streets, inebriated teenagers, and dangerous bends taken at higher speeds were lethal combinations. And, being the dutiful officer, Bleu made sure that one of his responsibilities was taking a single pass around the inlets, then shining his spotlight into the gullies and alcoves where kids liked to park and indulge in whatever sins they found comfort in. Unlike some cops, though, he was always polite. Stern but kind, asking they pour out their beer cans and making no point to mention the pervasive odor of weed that billowed from their car windows. He sent each youthful offender safely back home and into the loving arms of their forgiving parents. But that night had been an atypical evening in his usual lake rounds.

He first spotted Jake sitting on the hood of his Camaro, tilting a Budweiser can back as if he hadn't a care in the world. Just shy of ten o'clock, though the music was turned relatively low, Bleu could still hear it creeping around the corner over the crunching sound of his tires against hard gravel. His high beams caught three young men unaware, but, out of the group, only Jake seemed not to have that deer-in-the-headlights expression as he stared calmly back, catching the deputy's eyes.

They were all below the legal drinking age, and he could've taken them in for that offense alone. He could have interrogated them to learn who sold them the beer, and he could've turned it into a drama that might've scared them straight, as it were. But it was already late and that last circle around the lakeshore was to be his final duty before tapping out and heading home for the night. Instead, he parked his cruiser and watched as they were forced to empty their beers on the ground like shamefaced puppies. He gave them the same type of speech that he'd been given when he was their age and found himself trapped in the headlamps of a Sonora black-and-white still gripping a cold Bud in one hand.

Bleu made a pretense of getting their first and last names, as if there was an unspoken retribution soon to follow. Even though he'd never actually written anything down and had all but forgotten their names before the Mustang and driver and a single passenger raced away in a cloud of grateful dust. He could see that Jake was different than his younger companions. He never expressed any guilt and dawdled behind the others in cocky fashion. Bleu had no idea he'd lingered for a reason. There was only ten years difference between the deputy and Jake, who never hid his smug arrogance or disdain for authority as he slowly sauntered back to the Camaro's driver's side door to leave.

"This was okay, officer; the music was shitty and their beers were leaning to the warm side anyway." He opened the Camaro's door to leave.

"Then it wasn't a complete waste that I stopped by," Bleu said confidently. He stared back at the younger man leaning against the door and took him in completely for the first time. He possessed that James Dean swagger, the bravado that was held out almost exclusively for the fresh pretty faces of his world.

"I know it's against the law, deputy, but would it be all right if I took a piss before heading out? It's a long drive back to my place, and the beer's running through me like a sieve."

Without waiting for permission or approval, Jake turned as he slammed shut the driver's side door and sauntered off in the direction of a nearby live oak. Corso was too dumbfounded to stop him, but could almost hear the insanity of the conversation in his head if he'd tried to prevent the kid from urinating in the back woods late at night.

"You graduated from Union High, didn't you?" the boy asked over his shoulder as he began unzipping his Levi's.

"Most did," Bleu stammered out nervously. "You, too, I imagine?"

"You bet, last year," the boy said as if he'd mastered some great accomplishment.

In Corso's unease, he wasn't even questioning how the kid knew where he'd graduated. With four other schools, it would've been a lucky guess to land on the actual one. But his head was beginning to reel, and he seemed mesmerized in watching Jake make a showy pretense of pulling some anaconda-sized prick from his denims.

"I appreciate you letting me drain the lizard, sir." The kid was polite. "I don't think I could've made it all the way home with a full bladder." There was a lilt in his words the deputy couldn't quite track, a secret enthusiasm that appeared out of place. His head was cocked back over his right shoulder to make sure the officer heard every word, yet Bleu suspected he wanted to make sure he was being watched.

And watching he was. As steam billowed off the tree, he heard the splash of urine as it hit, then bounced back off the bark. He couldn't say a word; his mind was fixed on the image at hand, and he wondered how somebody so young could make someone like him feel so uncomfortable. He'd never considered picking up anyone from town. That would've been too dangerous an option to him. But, as he stared at the young man's back muscles moving under the wifebeater tank he was wearing, and his showy one-handed grip on his unseen cock so cavalier, the thought did cross his mind.

When he was done, Jake began wrestling his dick back into his jeans. Even from the back, his charade of stuffing away some snake-sized cock seemed a tad overacted. He made it look as if he were wrestling an oversized, cumbersome garden hose back into a smaller space for storage. As Jake turned around and zipped up his Levi's, his eyes were static lasers sparkling in the moonlight. Even from that yard or so distance and failing light, Bleu could tell he'd left the top button undone on purpose.

"You live with your folks?" Corso asked with a stutter, trying hard to dissolve the tension he felt directed his way.

"Nah, I got my own place," the young man said with a smile.

"Well you should head there, and head there soon," the deputy said. "You okay to drive, not too many beers, huh?"

"I appreciate it, officer, but I only had one beer."

"Well, I shouldn't be letting you drive but—"

Before he could finish Jake moved closer, quick and unexpected, until he was standing a mere foot from Corso. He was too close, clearly trying to invade the deputy's personal space. It startled him and caused him to shift his weight to his heels nervously as he fidgeted with his gun belt and awkwardly turned to grab the door of his cruiser.

"And then again, I could just follow you out," Jake said in a breathy whisper meant to strain the officer's ears and draw him in closer. Corso noticed how the younger man began to finger the loose button of his blue jeans and was caught in a cloud of warm condensation from his breath. Their proximity was alarming, and instantly Bleu felt his dick begin to stiffen as pictures flashed in his head, a full movie with only a split second of time elapsed.

"I could follow you out all the way to your place...or, if you'd prefer, you follow me to mine," Jake said, low and confidently, more animalistic than youthful man.

Every word dripped honey and suggestive inference, and the deputy's heart began racing like a quarter horse nearing the finish line. The noise of chirping crickets and night-foraging animals rustling in the distance were the only sounds he heard. The moment seemed suspended in the air all around them. This was insanity. Corso felt certain he was about to get into his cruiser and drive away, but, before he could, he felt Jake's hand rake across the fly of his dress slacks like a soft breeze. Just a brush against the fabric, but no amount of sheer cotton could've hidden his erection, and he was forced to stand frozen as the kid inched closer and then mouthed wet words into his ear.

"It could be fun, dude. I've never sucked off a cop before. You wanna be my first?"

For a closeted gay man, there are two types of fractured realities. One where one has an out-of-body experience, watching as the spirit rises out of the "unreal self" and hangs in the air above. It witnesses from a distance, perched somewhere above any of the action as one finally accepts the challenge and acquiesces to having sex with another man. It is that shiver of wanton frenzy crawling along skin like spiders, which is the only other thing that can drop a man to his knees. It becomes that firm grip at the back of the head pushing forward as one wrestles a stranger's rigid cock free to wrap lips around it like a hungry nursing pup.

There is also the image of every possibility turned wrong: the arrest or the loss of reputation. That forward step taken so tentatively, which reminds one that once taken it can never be undone. For Bleu Corso, it'd been the former and not the latter.

Maybe it was due to him being in his prime or the overabundance of time spent jacking off in the shower or that tactile need to feel another man's flesh in his hands. Maybe it was his lack of experience or his all-consuming desire, but he didn't pull away as Jake's hand gripped his hard dick through his dress slacks. It was strange for the kid to be the aggressor and not Bleu, but it was pure electricity coursing from man to man, like a spark from a Jacob's ladder as it bounced through the air.

"I got a place," the deputy said with a hoarse stutter, knowing the words escaped on the last remnants of oxygen from his lungs.

"Well then, if you're off duty, let's get there," Jake offered, licking his dry lips with a tongue Bleu wanted suddenly and desperately to taste for himself.

They both turned without words and headed quietly to their respective vehicles. As Bleu got into the cruiser, his mind dashed back to how insane this all was. The boy lived in his town and knew a lot of people. He could destroy him with nothing but an accusation. No more working as a cop and no more respect shining in the eyes of every passerby he met along the way. He would be exposed and shamed, an embarrassment to his family and an unlucky albatross to his friends. But his cock was hard and pushing against the confinement of his underwear, and that made him forget everything else more circumspect or wise at the time. The only relief would be found with him eventually coming, and, even with all his fear and apprehension, he felt his ghost-like insides separate from the man who sat behind the steering wheel. He felt himself float free and could do nothing but watch as the *unreal him* radioed in a 10-7 code to the station, announcing his shift's completion. That voice sounded alien to him as he told Ginda the dispatcher he was finally clocking out for the evening and heading home to get some much-needed rest.

Chapter Seven

SOMEWHERE ACROSS TOWN, Gabe himself was facing his own form of impasse. His room at the Queen of the Mines Lodge was closing in around him and threatening to implode him from all the pressure outside. He'd already done the unthinkable and relieved his mounting desires by yanking his meat furiously until semen shot like a rocket, landing across his chest and stomach. Just as he knew Chris was simultaneously doing, but hundreds of miles away. Now the dingy walls and stale motel air made him feel anxious and trapped behind bars, like he was a tiger pacing back and forth inside a cage, knowing it needed to run and stretch its muscles to finally feel alive and free.

Part of that came from a memory he couldn't let go. Of a time when he and Chris were lounging on the bed back at the Mayflower Park Hotel after a particularly frenzied tryst. The writer was laying snuggly in the crook of Gabe's arm as they were beginning to regain their normal breathing. Amid the pants of exultation, their perspiration was beginning to dry into a sticky residue across their chests and around their necks. Their eyes were fixated stares as both men surveyed every tiny crack in the white-painted ceiling above their heads. Whether lost in thought or that warm afterglow of spent passions, it still felt somehow laced by sadness and regret, as was proven when Gabe finally asked quietly, "Given a different set of conditions, do you believe you could've changed me?"

After a pause that seemed like an eternity, Chris finally said, "I think I already have." Then he began running his palm along the length of the killer's burly chest. The overwhelming scent of manly testosterone hung like cologne in the air and once again the void between the two men lapsed into a much larger chasm.

"Do you think this is how real monsters are supposed to feel?" Gabe finally asked. "'Cause there be monsters here."

CHRIS LAY IN his bed staring at the ceiling, thinking on the complexities of his lover. He never liked when Gabriel became morose after sex. It shattered those grander illusions he'd prefer to wallow in. But he always had his point, he figured. Like when he asked him once about how monsters felt. To him it sounded like a legitimate question. That was if he permitted himself to consider it for any length of time.

No matter how much he wanted it to be different for Gabriel, he knew he'd become destined to feel a lifelong curse of doubt and worry. Not about getting caught or jailed, since he'd already learned that was never a tangible threat that ran through Gabe's head, but rather the confusion and uncertainty that seemed to plague him more and more those days. He knew the man had questions, ones that only surfaced after he and Gabriel met. That balance of good and evil, always teetering precariously by the weight of the lightest of feathers being dropped upon the scales. Questions like those inescapable what-ifs or could've beens; all that was represented by their brief time together and from that first moment their eyes locked at that unforgettable little café so many months before.

It was true that he did feel safe and protected when buried in the man's embrace. And that he found a measure of comfort in every moment he caught one of Gabriel's shit-eating grins or saw that mischievous little boy's face he presented as his greatest guile. But Chris already reasoned his own truth; that as far as Gabe was concerned, he was no more than a parachute in tatters—one that slowed the descent but never prevented the fall. Both men understood one thing about each other, though; this was the first time Gabriel had ever really loved another person, at least this completely and wholly absolute.

"Aren't we all just pieces of crap?" Gabe had said at the time, with a final distracted huff. "Pretending to be something we could never be, fighting to break free of any kinda life we made for ourselves?"

"Who says we can't?" Chris asked as he looked up with a wash of adoration draining around him, staring at the man whose arms now circled him as they lay next to each other. "I mean, break free."

Even in the fading light as he dropped his head and looked down toward his lover, his pale eyes appeared to be glowing. But Chris knew from prior experience it was just another sliver of radiance playing somewhere in the background. Dancing near the base of what seemed simply another of his bottomless glances. Those slate blue-gray orbs had always felt vast and unexplored to Chris, the same eyes that had continually sent ripples of shockwaves racing down his spine. Chris reasoned that whenever most strangers peered into Gabe's eyes, they might've thought the worst: a vampire or an alien perhaps. But only because of the unique colors that were always dancing through those asphalt colored irises of his. They seemed too off-kilter to actually be real, like a man wearing contacts made of mirrored glass.

Even for a failed writer such as himself, who felt very much in love but didn't possess sufficient skill to fully verbalize that particular emotion to others, those damnable eyes were something indescribable. There it was, he thought with a smile. That blank Gabriel expression that begged him to continue or at the very least explain his meaning.

"All I'm saying is that you seemed to have figured out already that we can't change things or break free...but why not? Why not break the mold and do something totally unexpected?" he asked naively. He'd already heard Gabe's view of humanity. That rollercoaster of entropy he figured was the doom of us all. He simply wanted to offer him another way of seeing things, but he wasn't hopeful it'd change for the better. Chris had smiled for his own benefit, remembering what Liz Taylor had said about such things, "Pour yourself a drink and put on some lipstick, then pull yourself together." But you couldn't lighten up a man like Gabriel Church, not while he was waist deep in one of his moods.

"I wouldn't care if it all ended today. I don't think I could ever die any happier than in this moment. What about you?" Chris asked.

He'd hoped his presence reminded Gabe of how sweet life could be once it was solidly sorted out, and the damage placed square in the rearview. He wanted him to feel equally content and relaxed at that moment, lying snug and protected inside the man's arms. It brought back memories of college. Of watching the sophomore boys walk around the quad, still wearing their favorite high school letterman jackets, with tight muscled ass cheeks popping like cherries through their faded jeans. Though he hadn't exactly verbalized his orientation at the time, he remembered an awkward sensation in his gut, almost as clearly as if it were happening all over again. It'd left a lasting impression, one he defined as being something out-of-sorts from the norm.

It was an indescribable feeling, like being in a clique of unfamiliar strangers in a locker room, where every male standing at right or left was bigger, stronger, and more menacing than one could ever hope to be. Fat, pendulous dicks swinging freely as guys headed from the showers to the sinks. Where some laughed and mocked the man next to them by insult and harsh word, where towels were cracked like whips across bare ass cheeks—a place where most men felt camaraderie and bonding of other men despite their nudity and the sense of exposure. Or even possibly because of it. Men different than Christian, who carried sufficient confidence to see their cocks for what they were: an effective tool to get the job done. Or perhaps better, as the weapon some thought they could be.

It wasn't penis envy he felt back then because Christian learned early how he thankfully hadn't been shortchanged in that arena. But it'd been a serious deficiency in his own self-assurance. A masculine energy built from bravado and good-natured boasting. Something that appeared to come quite easily to some, but a thing he felt had been denied him from birth. He tended to blame the absence of that quality on a proper upbringing and the good manners his mother so deftly instilled in him early in life. He'd been taught not to spit on the ground in public or speak too loudly in crowds. He didn't have obnoxious manners and always sat quietly until an adult acknowledged him. Yet he watched other boys his age lacking those assets, and he noticed the unwanted attentions they could draw. He decided from the beginning that it was better to fly under the radar than over it. Nor did he try to highlight another boy's faults or weaknesses, as most boys he witnessed. He saw it as being unmercifully cruel. Even as a child, he knew unwarranted taunting was nothing more than a simple apparatus meant to bolster an already shaky ego. All of that made him unique in the eyes of his peers. And any alienation he felt as a child became that secret he'd never admit to, and that included Gabriel Church.

At the time he had to wonder when his mother would finally give up asking him why he hadn't brought some freshman sweetheart home. One meant to dazzle the family with a conservative summer skirt and blond shoulder-length locks dancing across a white poplin blouse. A girl of proper breeding, who sat begrudging and smiling when she'd been politely asked by a mother with slurred words from being half in the bag already from her afternoon vodka gimlet, "So tell me dear, who are your people? Anyone we might know?"

If she only knew what her son was doing now, he thought. Just as the bemused smirk emerged and stretched a wide smile across his face. His mother at one time had been one of those sorority girls you placed into stereotypes, constructed by legitimacy and with a conservative, moral upbringing. A woman who'd admittedly married well, and only later in life had she realized how much she actually cared for her husband. She was a calculating figure who found the whole idea of love a bit too amusing for words. But she had even higher standards for her son than she did for herself, and Christian was always wedged between the man he was, against desperately wanting her to see him exactly as he truly could be; sweat-drenched and tousled hair after a particularly heated fuck with a man—a man exactly like Gabriel Church.

But in that fateful moment, swathed in their plush surroundings, when Chris asked Gabriel if he could die happy, he wasn't that surprised he didn't get a reply. Instead, he decided not to press the issue and simply enjoy their time together. They came so rarely where Gabriel was concerned.

THERE WAS A moldy odor hanging in the air of his rented room. Gabe stared at the austere surroundings of his three-night stay accommodation at the Lodge. And he couldn't help but compare it to the five-star accommodations he'd shared with Chris back in Seattle. He'd tried to play it off sophisticated when he and Chris first entered their suite weeks earlier. Still, he had to admit it had been the nicest place he'd ever stayed during his lifetime, though it seemed beyond his understanding how anyone would pay so much for a place to crash, simply for a single night's stay.

Maybe the writer with his fancy schooling and rich parents had known that type of life, but he hadn't. He tried to play it off cool and unimpressed, not wanting to appear a rustic bumpkin from the hill country, all gawking and wide-eyed with his first trip to a big city. But he never fully understood how much his simple, unadorned upbringing was a thing Christian admired most about him, or how sometimes the unique differences made for the most remarkable, if unexpected, connections.

He wondered if the mildew scent could be attributed to higher elevation, or by sitting edge-close to the mountains and denser forests, or possibly it was due to the shitty maintenance by an innkeeper who never gave a damn. By the water-stained ceiling tiles he was staring at, he figured it had to be the latter. He was feeling stifled by the confined space, and he knew if he lay there much longer he'd get lost inside recollections of Chris and the sensation of regret being cultivated like a budding flower inside his chest. It was time to take a drive, he figured. The prospect of a meal and a stiff drink seemed the best cure to him then. So he jumped up and headed out of his prison room to the Dodge. If there was one thing he understood, it was how to shove old memories aside. And another tall bourbon under neon lighting had worked amply well before.

SUNLIGHT INVADED THE blinds of Bleu's bedroom, making strange white lines across the hardwood. He'd woken quietly as it crept through his window but wasn't in the mood to jump up and out of bed at that moment. If he did, his companion might notice him stirring and wake up as well. And he wasn't looking forward to those awkward gestures he knew were sitting idle in the pipeline. Instead, the deputy lay there and watched as the lines advanced across the floor until they finally reached the bed. They climbed up his bedframe and atop the mattress as if clamoring to greet him. He listened to the sounds of Jake's breathing and felt the unfamiliar presence of another person in his bed. It was an uneasy and guilty discomfort, and one he couldn't fully comprehend. There was fucking and there was dating; he really didn't know what the hell this was supposed to be.

He'd allowed Jake to spend the night, but that decision hadn't come lightly. As good as the sex was he knew everything he did held its own unique consequence. It'd been late by the time they drifted off to sleep, and one of the last things taking hold of his brain had been an image of him walking Jake to his car in the wee hours of morning, praying no would spot them before they both drove away.

Small town gossip could be deadlier in ways than even the worst day of normal police work. And another man's lips around his dick could be the third-rail charge that sparked an end to his career and stole away his finely honed reputation. But he smiled, remembering every lascivious act done hours earlier.

At that precise moment, his stomach grumbled to life, reminding him how he hadn't taken the time for dinner last night. His need for food simply lost all importance after running into Jake and the prospect of a torrid sexual tryst put everything else on a back burner. The noise in his gut roused the younger man awake, and he rolled over with crust in the corners of his eyes and a licentious grin on his face.

"Hey there, stud," Jake said in a raspy morning voice.

And so it begins, Corso figured, *that inevitably awkward, tongue-tied discussion between strangers after intimacy.* Where men who'd recently fucked hard and passionately and knew few boundaries they hadn't been uncomfortable in crossing suddenly found themselves trapped in a realization of how little each man knew about the other. The deputy smiled over at Jake without speaking but was already calculating how quickly he could get his trick into a shower and then out of his house discretely. Before anyone could witness their departure and draw any unwanted conclusions.

"Want some coffee?" he asked with a grin. One meant to hide his efforts in shattering the possible gracelessness of that instant.

"Sure," Jake said. But before Bleu could jump from the bed, Jake tossed the comforter aside and exposed a rather hefty morning erection.

"Then again, what's the rush?"

If the deputy had concerns, they quickly melted at the sight of a horny young man with a raging hard-on tempting him from the comfort of his bed. He put his better reasoning aside when voices inside his head practically screamed, *Why not? You got the time!*

Within seconds his cock equaled the rigidity of Jake's, and Corso rolled over and whisked the man into his open arms. They kissed fervently as their dicks bounced like combative swords against the other's abdomen. Wrestling like frenzied animals trapped by their excited heat, they grappled for purchase amid the twisting, tangled sheets. Moving in tandem, they shifted their bodies simultaneously as they tried to get their lips around the other man's cock, and then greedily devoured one another with the piety of a monk in devout prayer. Within moments the deputy's stiff member was tapping at Jake's asshole, as if gently knocking on some secret door to gain admittance. It held the promise of a warm inviting place, and both were desperate the deputy gain immediate entry.

With cock-flavored spit as lubricant, Corso finished the act as perspiration beaded across his back. He hadn't taken the precaution of a condom to protect either of them as he typically would've. Afterward both men lay there staring at the ceiling until their labored breathing finally subsided into something normal.

"Now we should jump in the shower and have a quick cup of java before I have to head to work," Bleu said, preoccupied.

There it was again. That self-conscious infused moment where two lovers who didn't really know each other were forced to shed the spell they'd been under and reenter their less interesting realities.

Chapter Eight

OVERCOOKED CHICKEN FRIED steak and cold beer were the only dinner Church could stomach, and, as he ate in silence alone in the rear of the diner, he was doing something he never did: remembering prior kills and replaying them over in his mind. In his lifetime, he'd dug more graves than anyone would ever find. Even Chris couldn't have imagined the number of slain white-lighters he'd made his targets—those people that God had shone a light on for him to send His way. It was like viewing the Friday night game tapes on video, looking for ways to improve strategy and technique. If anyone were watching him curiously, they might've turned to their friend and said, "Now there's a quiet looking dude," but no one plans murders out loud, or changes facial expression when rerunning footage of the hunting and slaughtering of the *so-called* innocents.

He knew there wasn't a word for a man such as himself. He'd grown up with the knowledge of how corrupt his mind was becoming. But then simply knowing a thing and changing were two separate things altogether, at least when it'd been the only life he'd ever known. Like telling an alcoholic to stop drinking or a meth head to put down the pipe, they find reasons for the insanity by sometimes making up the worst of excuses.

But meeting Chris Maxwell had been the signpost he couldn't ignore. The sad look of disappointment in the writer's eyes, and the way he shook his head low and shamefully when Gabe told him it was a futile act to try to change him. That alone became the most important quality that might one day work to transform him. *We've fucked up our water and our air, so what else is left but the dissolution of our self-respect?*

"Can I get you any dessert, good-looking?"

Gabe looked up, surprised, as the young waitress hovered over his table with a salacious grin and an extra pot of coffee in hand. He'd been lost in his own thoughts and suddenly her smile and the sexy twinkle in her eyes reminded him that his original intention after leaving the motel was to get drunk. Or at the very least, get someone to take him back to their place and get laid. The best distractions came from sweaty playtime tangled in the sheets and all the over-heated orgasms that came with that.

"Nothing for me, darlin'," Gabe said with his usual country drawl. He absently bit his lower lip as he glanced up at the waitress with a grin. Her looks were average, slightly below his normal standards, so he paid her little mind. It'd become his way, that mischievous little-boy charm that seemed to work its magic on everyone he encountered. And she was no exception to the rule.

"Well, just the ticket then, handsome?"

He nodded politely, yanking a few crumpled singles and a twenty from his front pocket. He could see she'd been hoping for some kind of spark to occur between them, but her expectations would be shattered on the rocks as Gabriel stood up to pay his check. He was tall with a broad chest, and he possessed that blue-collar ease of a man she didn't need to try to impress. But he whisked the ticket from her hand, then threw a few singles for a tip down before heading to the front register to pay. He could feel her eyes lock onto his ass as he walked away, and it made him happy knowing he hadn't lost his ability to bring women to wet sensual cravings.

The creaking door of the Dodge as he thrust it open reminded him of another time many years before, when he had been less flush with cash than he was currently, thanks to Christian. He'd been sitting in a bar and mentioned to a patron nearby that he was running low on money, and someone across the bar suggested Gabe give plasma for quick cash. Giving blood seemed an appropriate way to earn a few bucks that he hoped to parlay into a bigger sum by playing some pool at the closest bar. He needed the stake to have enough funds to buy the beers he'd need to affect his ruse. If he showed up with no cash but showed an eager eye for a pool game, then the hustle was over before it even began. So he'd shown up at the donation office and filled out the paperwork. But something he thought would take minutes from his day turned into a nightmare lasting nearly an hour and was a ghastly way to gain money.

Gabe wasn't a novice in earning cash, but this was the lowest rung of the ladder, and he knew instantly it wasn't worth the hassle it took to acquire such a measly sum. He completed the paperwork that they'd shoved through the glass-enclosed cubical. Their version of an isolation booth, protecting the staff from getting too close to the dregs of society, he suspected, indigent souls who simply longed for a few bucks to score their crack money or to buy a small pint of 100-proof medicine, just to make it through another sad day.

It was an appalling place that stank from the homeless, unbathed clientele that government-run offices relied on for plasma. Church lied on the application forms they'd given him. Like all the others in that tiny cramped waiting room, their donations were supposed to be clean and untainted from drug use. Yet everyone there seemed complicit in the lie and each person waiting or those behind the glass enclosures knew that it was a pay-to-play scenario that benefited everyone and no one at the same time.

Did the applicant consider themselves alcoholic...checkmark, deny.

Did the applicant give blood or plasma within the last few days... checkmark, deny.

Did the applicant use illegal substances weekly, daily, or often... checkmark to all three, deny.

Gabriel regretted following the advice given him by a man he couldn't rightly remember then and thought long and hard about simply leaving. But then the process piqued his interest enough to see it through. His eyes lingered over those who waited to have their blood drawn. Some were twitching hard from their withdrawal symptoms already, but he knew they wouldn't be turned away by doctors as they should've been.

Church looked up and saw a young man in his early twenties waiting as he had been for his turn behind the curtain. He was wearing a suit, if one could call it that, but it was highly rumpled and threadbare and faded from overwashing. It appeared as if it had once lain in the bottom of a donation box at some church or synagogue and recently had been retrieved as a gift to some lost soul who'd fallen on hard times. The young man was carrying a bible that was as threadbare and old as his clothing. The first thing Gabe noticed was the sardonic grin on the young man's pimply face. It was accompanied by a blank stare from eyes that seemed cold and lifeless. He wondered if the young man was an idiot, but then he saw him open the pages of the bible and watched as he mouthed the words he was reading. He was a devotee, Gabe told himself. A man who'd turned to God when everything around him curdled into shit.

It was unnerving watching him read aloud to himself. It reminded Gabe of those old ventriloquist dolls that mimicked being something they weren't. He sat with his back stiff and his knees crossed but still looked uncomfortable in the ratty, faded suit from yesteryear. The image was creepy to say the least, but it became worse when Gabriel saw a cockroach crawl from the center binding of the bible and then scurry down the man's pant leg. The younger man either didn't notice or pretended not to, but he never moved a muscle, and the notion that roaches lived in abundance inside books wherever this boy hung his coat at night...well it sent a shiver down Gabriel's spine just imagining it. It was an odd picture, his lips moving to the scriptures he read and his whispers barely audible over the serenade of soft lullaby music overhead. The boy flashed a deadpan smile through expressionless eyes giving him a zombie appearance. Gabriel reflected back to the twisted gargoyles carved in white stone that had frightened him once as a child, while even then he couldn't quite pull his eyes from them. They were a fascinating sight to see. It was as if the young man found great comfort in the words he was reading. But to Gabe it was surely a false prophet he was praying to. Who else could offer solace to this twisted man-child and give him the salvation he required? Even to a drifter such as himself, it had to be a tragic existence, and one even he couldn't fully comprehend.

He was about to rise from his chair and then toss the forms and clipboard back to the receptionist when a young woman in a white lab coat called out the alias he'd given earlier as his own name. After the vampires drained him of his plasma, he was given a certificate that he could exchange for cash in a nearby office.

After all that, he still had to wait in line amid the hapless drunks and addicts wanting their minimal rewards. Disgusted, he left the office, but not before dropping his vouchers on the open bible that lay in the lap of the poor religious freak still waiting his turn. He walked out and to his truck and never again felt the urge to exchange his plasma for that paltry a sum. That was truly blood money he figured. Driving the city streets of Sonora, Gabriel took notice of the dive establishments with their mining motifs. Each one sounded more ludicrous to him than the last, such as The Mine Shaft and the Rich Vein Bar and Grill. They flaunted their names, seemingly oblivious to the references to gay clubs merely two more hours' drive farther toward the coast. It was easy to spot the abundance of choppers and hogs parked along the front, which designated them as biker bars, and he could see their popularity here. The highways coming into and navigating through the city were long, open stretches of beautiful roadway. It spoke to the freedom bikers most wanted. But he wondered how many tourists steered clear from any establishment with so many Harleys standing guard out front.

All in all, it was a great little city. But it was very different than the ones where he'd been brought up in. Still, he thought it was the type of town he could embrace if given the chance. Sonora was nothing but a spit in the road, but it sat surrounded by larger sprawling metropolises, everything around it was quickly being consumed by the influx of new residents. Most suspected that in another fifty years or so there wouldn't be any distinctive tiny mill towns dotting the Sierras. But that was years away.

Under a bright azure sky, the city seemed more like a hamlet or village than the growing community that it was. As he meandered through downtown with the windows down and the radio on, all he could think of was how great a place it would be for him and Christian to hole up for a few years. Never far from the coast and buried under a canopy of oak and spruce. It was the type of place he thought he'd like to call home. He wondered how that conversation would go. When his back was firmly at the wall and there were decisions that had to be made and made quickly. He hoped that if he turned his head he'd see Chris in the Dodge next to him as he imagined the strobe of blue lights and sirens at his rear and coming up fast.

"We could always stand and fight." Chris might've said excitedly, the apprehension and urgency making perspiration bead on his forehead. *"Well, if so, I got your back. But if you wanna make a run for it, then I'm gonna call shotgun"*

But it was just a fantasy. A trick of his imagination playing games with his head, and he knew that. But how great it must feel when you have one so eager to take on the calamities of your life sight unseen, as it were, even under the real possibilities of flying bullets and gunfire, arrest, or even the threat of death. Now that had to be true love, he figured; a Bonnie and Clyde romance that would've made a good story. That was if Christian had ever gotten around to writing it.

But fate would never offer him that much of a chance, Gabe figured. He'd been alone for so long that he'd conned himself into believing he'd been happy. He lied many times, telling himself he enjoyed his freedom, and that he didn't even mind the long hours behind the wheel and the endless parade of shitty motels. And that was only when he was flush with cash. There had been many nights when he'd slept in the Dodge or ate from vending machines whenever the money was low. Meeting Chris was like waking up one day and finally noticing how fucked up his life had become.

Chapter Nine

IT WAS A matter of being in the wrong place at the wrong time, he'd told himself, the strike of that disastrous gong still ringing loudly in his ears. The chime of his doorbell startled him with a jolt, sending him leaping from his couch and ready to crawl out of his own skin with worry. He'd tried to steer clear of his condo recently. Arriving home later in the evenings and always remembering to keep the lights off in the living room and the curtains drawn tight. He expected the rap at his door would come soon enough, and, with it, the unwanted visitation by Seattle homicide detectives following up on their earlier interview with him. He'd discussed this with Gabriel the night before. He could tell Gabe had heard the apprehension rising with his tone when they had.

"Don't fret it, babe," he'd offered through a cool country drawl. "You're a clever man, you know how to lie," he said. "Just play dumb. Say you don't remember being anywhere near Shea's apartment. That's the only thing they have; remember, the plates?"

Chris couldn't tell if his lover was saying that to calm his nerves, or if he actually believed detectives had nothing on Chris that might connect him to Shea's murder. But whatever the case, he liked hearing Gabe saying it. He had a way of making everything seem all right. Maybe it was because he was so used to living on the run, a cold calculating killer, that Chris knew he'd normally run away from at breakneck speeds...and never toward the danger as he was now; his arms flung wide and longing as he felt like doing then. He'd already come to grips with the lunacy of his situation and of how he'd fallen head over heels for a serial killer with a God complex and a damned fine chest. The rest was just bad history 101.

He'd been hoping to hear a ring from the disposable prepaid he'd hidden in his nightstand, the one he used to speak with Gabriel. Maybe that was why he jumped so unexpectedly at the sound of the doorbell when it rang. Then his heart stopped abruptly in his chest and refused to beat. He remembered how he no longer had friends visiting him at his place. So it couldn't be an old girlfriend at the door with a bottle of wine and an eagerness to gossip. And he didn't have any family living in Seattle. In fact, he'd lived the lifestyle of a monk ever since first meeting Gabriel, never going out on the town or socializing with coworkers, as he had before.

That realization came as a hard, cold slap across his cheek, reminding him he'd have to examine that change in his personality in some detail, and in the very near future. But not now, not when his nerves were unraveling from the spool so quickly. It had to be the police ringing his doorbell at that time of night. He knew he had to brace himself of all his fear and somehow make it to the door on his shaky legs. Still, the short distance from his sofa to the door appeared more like the trek across some barren wasteland and a journey requiring all his fortitude and skill.

"Coming," he called out, trying to sound carefree. But it squeaked from his throat and ended up sounding queer and frilly.

He expected to see Detective Keen standing there or even the other burly detective he'd brought before. Was it *Gilroy* or *Gillquist*? He wondered. He couldn't recall at that moment. It turned out it was nobody he'd ever met but still clearly some type of investigator. His suit was professionally cut but shabbier and wrinkled more than was normal. This indicated to Chris he was a man who earned a government wage and bowed to a hierarchy of supervisors. In a flash, Christian was assessing the man's character and will, in much the way Gabriel did. Only he wasn't even aware he was doing it. Was this the man who'd eventually run his lover down? Maybe the detective who'd arrest Chris for being an accomplice to murder after the fact? He wasn't certain, and his insides were jelly. But he smiled congenially as he swung the door open and tried to appear nonchalant and unimpressed.

"Yes, can I help you?" he asked calmly.

"I'm Special Agent Richard Jenkins of the Washington CID," the man at the door offered with a nod. "You are Christian Maxwell?" he asked, glancing at the blue folder he was holding. It was apparent to Chris the detective knew exactly who he was introducing himself to. And as a random gesture trying to appear casually indifferent, it failed miserably.

"Yes."

"I understand you had a previous discussion with Detective Keen of the CID regarding a matter that came up during one of his investigations."

The agent took an exaggerated side-glance down the hall to show it was a private matter. He leaned closer and asked, "Excuse me, but do you think we could speak inside?"

Christian muttered something of an apology then stepped aside, allowing the agent to brush past him.

"I know it's late, sir," he began, "but we haven't been able to reach you by phone to schedule a more formal meeting."

"Oh, I'm terribly sorry. I suppose I have been outta pocket recently—work and all," he said with a wave of his hand. "How can I help you now?"

Leading him to the living room, Chris motioned to the sofa. Inside he was a bag of nerves, even though Gabe said he couldn't be implicated in Shea's murder in any way. Outwardly he hoped he projected the demeanor of a man without a care in the world.

Sitting across from him, the detective appeared rather attractive. He was still bouncing somewhere around his mid to late thirties and retained a full head of luxurious blond hair with the hint of gray forming at the temples. His frame suggested that he'd once been quite a school athlete, though his paunchy midsection implied he hadn't stepped foot in a gym in some time. But it was his eyes that made him appear older. They had the glassy knowing suggestion of a man who'd seen a lot of carnage during his career. That he might be a man who'd learned quickly how he needed to hedge judgment of any suspect who might sit across from him at a table. Or how this was a man who needed every fact present before he'd ever fully show his hand. He had a shell-shocked maturity and seasoning about him, the type of man who might represent real danger to Church if their paths were ever to cross. But shoving those apprehensions aside, Chris smiled back congenially, and then waited patiently for the questions to begin.

"Can you tell me about your last conversation with Detective Keen?" Shuffling his folder and clearing his throat, Jenkins went on to say, "From his notes he'd left a message for you and even attempted an interview with you, though his notes weren't clear as to the purpose of his visit."

"So why isn't he here? And why aren't you asking him that question directly?"

Chris heard the stammer in his voice as the pitch rose uncomfortably. It was like a blast of frigid air hitting him square in the face. Something was amiss, something Gabriel hadn't mentioned, and his heartbeat, which earlier had just been racing, now seemed to be locked in stasis. He could see the agent becoming uneasy, and without thinking, he lowered his eyes in something akin to shame and mentally prepared himself for what he knew was coming.

"I suppose you hadn't heard," Jenkins began. "Detective Keen and his wife were murdered in their home recently." His words lingered in the air. "This was about the same time Agent Keen was trying to reach out to you. But of course his murder changed all that, and our office in Olympia was forced to take command of the investigation."

A rush of fear and nervousness hit Christian like a landslide. Though he was trying to appear sincerely concerned but still remotely uninvolved, he was caught in the surprise. Questions were bouncing in his head that he had no time to address in that second, so he maintained the façade as best he could.

"Oh, my heavens no. I hadn't heard." He gazed at the floor in disbelief. "I suppose I haven't been watching the news enough."

Another lie—simply added pretense and more acting than he was accustomed to performing. In truth he had been skimming the headlines, but he'd been searching for word of Gabriel's involvement in Shea's murder. So how the hell had he missed this front-page news story, he wondered?

"Well, I'm sorry to hear that," he said truthfully. "But Detective Keen wasn't alone when he came by the first time. He had another detective with him, so why don't you ask him? I don't quite remember his name, but I think it was Gillquist or Gilroy."

Then his words hit him hard. Suddenly he remembered that he hadn't answered the door the afternoon they stopped by. He was trying to make it appear that he wasn't at home. *So how the fuck was he supposed to know that, or know that detective by name?* His nerves were too jangled, he figured, and he'd now landed himself in a lie by his confession. The heartbeat that once seemed frozen now pounded in his chest loud enough that he suspected Agent Jenkins could surely hear it.

Glancing back inside the blue folder, the agent fortunately seemed to miss the connection. "There's nothing about that in his notes," he said. "But there *is* a Detective Gilroy in our ranks; I'll be sure to ask him about that when we get back to our Seattle division."

And almost as quickly as it began, it appeared to be over. Chris couldn't tell what exactly the purpose of Jenkins's visit was, but, as the tall man stood up, he extended a hand to indicate the interview was ending.

"Apparently I need to check with Detective Gilroy, and maybe he can fill in some of the blanks." And then he leveled his eyes at Christian's and said, "We're investigating the homicide of one of our own, so you can imagine we might have more questions for you later. But for now we have what we need, though I certainly appreciate you taking the time today."

"Yes, of course," Chris stuttered as he rose from the couch. "I am truly sorry to hear about Detective Keen and his wife—such a tragedy. I didn't know him well, but he seemed like a nice, competent investigator."

Jenkins nodded back as they shook hands. *God, I hope he can't tell how clammy my palms are*, Chris worried. But, as he politely ushered him to the door, all he could think of was escape, and then came a flood of questions he knew he was going to have to ask Gabriel—why had he decided to murder Keen?

And his wife! What the hell! What could've driven him to that point? *Was this because of me?* Chris wondered.

Finally alone in his condo, Chris leaned against the door for support. Cold sweat began to bead along his forehead, and it was hard to contain his breathing. As jittery as his nerves were, and even with an absence of words to describe his shock, he still thought he hid it well, masked by truer emotions and not a small amount of confusion. It seemed some qualities from Gabe were rubbing off on him. Then suddenly he felt ridiculously stupid. In his rational brain he had suspected what his lover intended for the detective, but no amount of reasonable scrutiny could have prepared him for the awful truths he learned later, and particularly after he learned of Keen's wife. How tragically it had all turned out, he thought. Hell, even a serial murderer like Gabriel Church had to have some ethical center buried in his core. This was Shea Baltimore all over again.

The room was spinning when he recalled the afternoon Gabe disappeared to "have a chat with the detective." How foolish he was to assume that telephone call Gabe asked him to make, with such strategic timing, was supposed to be a fix for anything. It was just another part in his lover's unknown plan. And one didn't ask for more details when speaking to a tight-lipped, archetypal killer such as Gabe Church. Stupidly, he'd given the killer the benefit of the doubt when he said he'd handle that small task alone. But he never truly suspected it might lead to Keen's death, or that of his wife. At least that was the story he told himself, particularly since hindsight was so damned illuminating. But now he felt trapped, as if he'd been spotted at the scene of a blazing inferno still gripping the matchbook in his grimy gas-covered fingers.

He had questions for sure, but before he would contact his strapping Irish lover, he had to wrap his brain around everything he'd heard from Jenkins. He needed composure first, and a chance to formulate every careful word. He could already hear that gravelly voice saying, "Don't be a stupid little bitch. What the hell did ya think was going to happen at the Keen home, a chat between friends?"

Chris knew he would have a point; after all, the consequences that came with being devoted to a serial killer meant he had to always assume the worst. Hearing the detective was murdered was more than a break in the skin; it was the one murder Gabriel would surely pay for with his life. The others had been significant in number, but this was a homicide detective and one who was on the job. Plus the senseless killing of his wife meant the rusty final nail pounded into the coffin lid. Whatever destiny Gabriel had been on once had now become his own. Clearly, he could no longer hide any guilt like he had with Shea Baltimore. He was intricately tied to murder now, and the plot and origin were his and his alone to deal with. The weight of that knowledge was suddenly unbearable. Chris felt as if strong hands were pushing his shoulders as he slid down the doorframe of his once-secure condo and fought the urge to bawl like a lost babe in the woods.

Chapter Ten

BLEU CORSO HAD lived with secrets all his life. He was raised when the larger world beyond his front porch was still at a distance without the advantage of the social media that blasts news now 24/7. When doors could remain unbolted at night and each of us lived in that blissful state of ignorance; never knowing how cruel and vicious life could sometimes be. But everyone knew the stories, even those as young as Corso. Newspaper articles and television shows that depicted true horror displayed the worst parts mankind had to offer. He was familiar with stories like the Granny Killer, John Glover, and the murders of Gary Ridgeway and Jeffrey Dahmer. But no one in Sonora had made the connection back then. That the darkness brewing in society was suddenly creeping into their safe little town like a sea of plague rats.

Bleu felt an unfamiliar tug in his stomach as he sat in front of the old Zenith and became transfixed by the handsome detectives in TV shows. It was the birth of his curiosity that pushed him to open an application with the police. But it would be years before he made the real connection that it'd been those hunky characters in *Criminal Minds* and surprising rerun shows like *Starsky and Hutch*. But seeing patterns and doing much to disrupt them are two entirely different things. He was attracted to the men in the stories as much as he was the telling of them, and without the conscious understanding of why, he decided to become a policeman early in his life. He was all but certain of his life the day he drove to the police station after graduation and picked up an application on the fly.

Bleu was absently crafting a persona of what he considered to be masculine in becoming a uniformed cop. Even the sight of a strapping, clean-cut officer walking to his car to give him a traffic citation when he was seventeen had been enough to get his motor revving and his dick dancing excitedly in his jeans. It had become a foregone conclusion that Bleu Corso would someday be a deputy somewhere.

His good ole boy manner and the way he interacted with Sonora citizens was enough to advance his career goals with lightning speed. Yet he always lived with a shadow hanging ominously over his right shoulder—that his orientation would become public knowledge and he'd be expected to resign from the force. But a hungry libido can take dangerous chances, and his trysts, though necessary at the time, were continually making their own hazardous choices.

Picking up Jake for a romp in the sheets hadn't been smart, but he knew if he didn't exercise some demons they'd linger and make life difficult later. What if the young man talked? He wondered. What if someone witnessed his recent trick leaving his house? They were all good concerns he understood, but at least he wasn't plagued by constant erotic images, having for the moment assuaged some of his desire, at least for the time being. He could finally concentrate on real life and the job at hand.

Corso recognized Sally's voice from dispatch. She was requesting an 11-97 from his car. This was a typical security and location check, which usually told the officer his car had been radio silent for too long.

"Linoberg and advancing on South Washington here, Sal," Bleu replied into the mic sternly and waited for the next directive he knew would follow.

"Perfect. Deputy, there's an 11-10 request at the high school, and you're the closest car," she stated efficiently, even though it seemed laced with some subtle indecency. "There's another vandalism report. See off-duty officer Jacob Wilkes at the scene." Then despite her professionalism, she added, "Thanks, handsome," as Bleu clicked his response of "10-4" with a grin on his face.

He was already traveling toward South Washington, so she was right: he wasn't far away. As he turned onto the street and headed to Sonora High, he was wondering about Sally. He knew she had the hots for him because she never hid her attraction well. Little did she realize he had no interest in a single mother of two, five years older than him, with her looks fading faster than she would've cared to admit. His dick had recently found a more preferable warm spot to burrow.

The rest of the deputy's day was much like that. Spent running around town taking reports with the occasional traffic violation stops in-between. It was boring enough to make one question their reasons for being so hell-bent on becoming a cop. Yet Bleu did admire the respect he garnered in his freshly starched uniform. And the occasional free cups of coffee or lunches didn't hurt either.

As good as it was, there'd been time to remind him just how tangled his life was becoming. Tall and twisted like the roadside kudzu growing near his dad's place. You never knew where the road was gonna take you when it bent, but all his careful planning was getting sidetracked by his choices of partners for the bedroom. He was still a simple farm boy with bigger aspirations and far from the realization of what choice was, or what was preordained from birth.

His father would never understand him liking guys, but, had his mother lived long enough, he'd always hoped she would have. Through his cruiser window, he could smell the hint of October wafting in on the open breeze. It reminded him that no matter how much he wanted the status quo to remain, he knew eventually things were going to change, and maybe not for the better.

Growing up in Sonora usually meant young people took for granted the city's beauty and rustic charm. The way streets were lined with quaint shops and businesses designed to appear as if they'd been crafted over a hundred years earlier made you feel as if you'd stepped backward in time. You could almost feel the gold rush energy present in the air and you knew with certainty that you were standing in a mining town, trapped somewhere in the late 1800s. The architecture, unpaved sidewalks, and even the paint schemes on every shop along Washington Street, became a premeditated creation. Every building seemed more high school play set design than actual storefront. Tourists took notice, which was the intent. They stood in small clusters with their cameras flashing and took pictures of others standing by streetlamps, as if they were more prop than anything with function.

Most kids had seen their share of Sonora and wanted nothing more than to graduate and race away from their parents, to head to the big cities with their beachside communities more favorable to their lifestyle. How could they even begin to appreciate the native fauna and the changing colors of gold and red as the leaves turned with every season? How could they enjoy a town that had so little traffic and quiet neighbors with nothing of importance to report in the local papers? There wasn't anything fun to do there. They only had a couple of movie theatres, and cruising through town with the windows down and music playing was nothing but a bust.

Bleu, being different than most, did appreciate the gifts Sonora offered. And even with his dreams of escaping to metropolitan cities like San Francisco and San Diego, he never relished the idea of leaving Sonora for good, not completely. His job as a deputy sheriff was constraining with its button-down reputation and high profile visibility, whereas the big cities had a sea of faces. And many belonged to hot young guys he had yet to meet. How could he not dream of diving in and wallowing in every wave with abandon?

I need patience. I'll get better hours assigned, and then, when I have a free weekend, I'll travel into San Francisco and spend the weekend screwing any and every one I can. He wouldn't have to explain his actions to his father, or the mayor, or the presiding Sherriff. He could just go nuts, so to speak.

Sally was still calling out duties from her isolation booth of a dispatch desk, and Corso took random calls while letting other deputies catch others. There wasn't any hurry in his day, and as he turned his cruiser off Stockton and hit Washington Street, he noticed a weathered Dodge pickup parked at the pumps in a 7-Eleven. What caught his eye wasn't the unfamiliar truck but the driver standing with a nozzle in hand.

He was a big man in faded denim jeans tucked over what appeared to be old brown work boots that had seen better days. The deputy observed how striking he appeared as he turned his cruiser into the lot and shifted into park. The big guy wore some form of tank top under an unbuttoned flannel shirt that had sleeves rolled up to the wrist in a carefree fashion. He was clearly muscular by the strain of the fabric surrounding his guns. And, even from that distance, Corso could see the five-day growth of beard and presumed the man to be in his mid to late thirties. There was something sexy in the image of him leaning next to the pickup with one foot propped up in his open door, like a rebel outlaw stance. It gave Corso pause enough to scope him further in his rearview, and even though Bleu traditionally liked his men younger and with more of a street thug appeal, he found himself staring, nonetheless. Usually, seeing a nineteen-year-old with his scratch prison tats and unkempt hair would make his dick hard under his dress slacks, but, whether he was his typical type or not, Bleu had to admit the dude was hot from a distance. He looked like sex on a stick, he mused, and a man worthy of a second glance no matter whom you were.

Being in law enforcement, Corso knew the cars of most of the locals. This man was obviously another tourist. If any officer tells you they don't run the tags of drivers they find alluring, they'd be lying. Partly by instinct, and partly because he liked the handsome face, Bleu typed in the numbers of the Dodge's front plate while trying to appear inconspicuous as he did. Before the report hit his cruiser's tiny monitor, the stranger was replacing the pump's nozzle and getting in to leave. Bleu heard the squeak of a rusty hinge as the big man hoisted his body behind the wheel and heard the engine roar to life.

As the pickup turned onto Washington and disappeared, the DL data hit the screen. *Bobby Johnson—38, resident of Portland, Oregon.* There were no traffic violations or outstanding warrants. The data pulled in no red flags and was by all accounts innocuous. It did not reveal information as to the subject, Bobby Johnson, having been robbed a few days earlier. There was nothing about how Johnson had been fleeced by a well-practiced serial killer who had taken the license plates of a Dodge of similar age to his own and pocketed the wallet left casually on the back seat while Bobby was presumably humping his secretary in a rundown Motel 6. When signals fly through the atmosphere, when they are pulled by detectives and bureaus across the continent, the output is only as good as the information loaded. And so far, Bobby Johnson's misfortune did not come up on the radar of a deputy sheriff based out of Sonora, California.

Had Bleu requested the same information at the precinct he might've gotten a different intelligence returned, but a simple dashboard relay in a black-and-white cruiser had its limitation. Without a reason to require a random traffic stop of the vehicle, the deputy should have gone on about his business. He should have stepped into the convenience store and purchased a soda as he normally did around that time of day. He should have taken the time for a casual wave to the staff, all of whom he knew by name. He should have strolled past the counter to use the bathroom as was his custom. But instead, Bleu shifted into reverse, deciding to trail the pickup a little farther down the street. Maybe it was lust, or maybe it was a policeman's intuition. But whatever the reason, he pulled out onto Washington and weaved through the lines of traffic to reach the Dodge with its burly, intriguing driver.

Chapter Eleven

HUNDREDS OF MILES away at that exact moment, Chris was arriving home from work. The hours at his office should've been enough to lose that morning-after headache he'd been suffering throughout the day. But it was nothing if not persistent. His head felt as if it could split open at any minute, despite the three ibuprofens he'd popped around noon. He hadn't been able to concentrate on any of his normal duties because he couldn't push aside the news about those last few hours Gabe had spent in town.

After a quick shower and a change into street clothes, he was beginning to feel better, with the pounding in his skull finally beginning to subside. Still, he remembered he had an unopened bottle of Scotch on the kitchen counter and decided its medicinal effects would definitively crush his headache into memory once and for all. With a drink in hand and comfortable attire, he could sit in the privacy of his condo and wait for a call from Gabe on his disposable. He knew he'd phone tonight because he'd learned how much of a shared static-like connection they possessed, which united them. If he could say one good thing about Gabe, it had to be how both had a communal and unspoken understanding, even across the vast miles that separated them. And as unpredictable as he already knew the man could be, there were still certain things Chris knew he could depend on. Like the fact that Gabe would call tonight and they'd surely talk for at least an hour or so. They'd catch up with other, maybe talk enough dirty sex that both would be jacking off later that evening, or they'd sit quietly and listen to the masculine breathing on the line across all those invisible airwaves.

He needed to hear Gabriel's voice, but, even more importantly, he wanted to ask him about the detective and his poor dead wife. He had to be careful though; saying the wrong thing would mean he'd no doubt hang up. And like a drugged-out junkie in need of a fix, he really just wanted to feel close to Gabe and listen to his words while fantasizing about lying next to him naked and listening to the sound of his irregular beating heart.

Several hours and three large Scotches later, the expected ring of the track phone startled Chris and began a metronome-paced pounding inside his chest. It had gotten dark by then, and the city skyline had burst into a sea of twinkling lights far into the distance as urban nightlife spilled onto the sidewalks. The evening sky had turned the color of a dark bruise, all framed by a shadow of blue edges with hints of fading crimson hiding beneath the surface. Chris was visibly nervous when he answered the call.

"Evening, lover," he said in a hoarse whisper.

There was a slight pause before Gabe's gravelly voice broke the silence. "So how's my baby doing tonight?" he asked, equally quiet.

"Been better, I have to admit, but missing holding your body, that's for sure."

"There'll be time for that later," he said with a degree of finality, even though Chris could picture the corners of his lips turning up with a smile.

Security instantly washed over his frame like drizzle from a warm summer rain. But unexpectedly, an explosion of random images appeared, crazy imagery sending icy, raw shivers through his veins. Pictures of him in a black suit and tie and gripping the handle of a black mahogany coffin as he was ushered down the steps of a church he didn't recognize. He knew all too suddenly that the weird phantasm couldn't be real—as certainly as he knew it had to be Gabriel lying inside the box. He shuddered involuntarily with a sense that no man should ever have to feel the weight of a good friend in their hand as they carry them to their graveside. Then, as quickly as it had come, it was gone. And the ice inside his veins began to dissipate.

"So where are you now?" he asked, shaking that awful myriad of images from his brain.

"Same place as before, but best you don't really know exactly where... remember?"

This was Gabe's way; his secretive methodology in his efforts to shield Christian as much as possible. But as comforting a notion as that should've been, it was also constructing a very unique form of prison in itself, where too much uncertainty can often kill a relationship.

"Well, I hope you're safe wherever you are. And I can't even imagine how you'd be spending your days. So, what's the end game here?" he asked as his voice began to rise with irritation. "Are we supposed to connect up soon? Find that place where we can both hole up and be together, or is this your way of pushing me into a corner, and making me think you have real feelings for me that you don't? Are you hoping I'll fade like smoke from your back tires as you drive away?"

"Well someone's a little grumpy tonight," Gabe said flatly. "And a tad overly dramatic I'd say."

"Sorry. I'm just frustrated. And I got some bad news recently, something we need to talk about, I think."

He was already breaking that promise he'd made earlier, that he wouldn't broach the subject of the detective's murder, or that of his innocent wife. Not until they'd at least shared some time together not discussing the evils of Gabriel's past. But he couldn't help himself. Chris was frustrated, horny, and he was depressed, and there were big things coming between them that he hadn't expected. Walls were being built brick by brick, and he hoped if Gabriel were there with him, or if he could be wherever Gabe was in that moment, that it may have made more sense than it actually did. That he could simply fall into his arms and find that comfort and security he'd always found before. Or that his lover would say all the right words he desperately needed to hear; that they'd at last make some sense, and he could finally leave some of what he'd heard on the road behind him.

He needed to see a future that didn't include the horrors that now made up his life. That both men could erase their bad histories and have fun for a change, like they did early on when they walked the busy sidewalks of Seattle and were unafraid of being spotted or recognized...before the totality of death crept into his life with Shea Baltimore's murder. And *now* there was the detective and the man's wife to consider. A man he knew by name, which made it even more personal. It had been hard to imagine the faces of Gabe's prior victims once. But it was becoming tactile and real now in ways he knew he couldn't hide from anymore.

"Goddamn it, Gabe, I just want to see you. I want to feel you close for a change. And even more importantly, I want all this shit behind us once and for all!"

"Patience there, boy," Gabriel said, his Kentucky drawl becoming even more pronounced. "Just because I need to lay low for a while doesn't mean I can't see you. I was actually thinking on a plan I had in the works, one where you rent a car, then drive to meet me somewhere in the middle. We could spend a couple of days drinking and fucking. Ruttin' around like pigs on the floor of one of them fancy hotels you seem to like so much."

Then as suddenly as they hit, all those feelings of anxiety and fear he was feeling slipped off his back as effortlessly as one of those complimentary hotel robes falling to the plush Berber rugs of some high-rise downtown suite. That image brought new life to his privates, and his cock jittered with excitement at the thought of it, just as it had back at the Mayflower.

The few nights they'd stayed at the luxurious Mayflower Park had been brief in retrospect, but they were some of the greatest moments in Christian's life he could remember. The thought of reliving those romantic hours made him forget all about the news he'd wanted to discuss with Gabe. He simply melted deeper into the fluffy, faux leather cushions of his sofa and allowed himself the chance to consider Gabriel's proposal.

"Then it's settled, tell me where and when," he said in a defiant, hopeful tone.

"I'll let you know tomorrow; we'll say by this weekend then. That way you don't have to miss work or draw any attention to yourself."

The prospect of seeing Gabe changed everything, and the remainder of their time spent on the phone came like a rambling hike without any direction. *It would have been pointless anyway. Gabe wasn't one to give anything more than a vague answer, and he would never have revealed his exact location on the phone.* There were short periods of silence between them as well, as Chris absentmindedly ran his fingers along his chest, tracing wide circles and sporting a Cheshire cat's grin. They discussed everything and nothing at the same time, just as lovers were inclined to do. They talked about the weather and all the picturesque places Gabe had recently driven through. And again, Chris noticed how the man omitted any of the city names and highway references from his words. But that didn't matter, he knew that because he'd finally get another chance to see his lover again. In the hour or so of their conversation they were clearly wallowing in fat, contented happiness. They shared a few jokes and laughed. They even jabbed a few insults at each other, like a stabbing thrust to the gut with a jagged blade of testosterone. Had anyone been listening to their conversation, or had they intercepted the call and tapped the line with no regard to their privacy, it might have sounded more like two frat brothers talking about getting together, but it was significantly more than any wickedly sordid bromance or man crush.

WITH HIS SHIFT over, Bleu was eager to call it a day. He hadn't gotten much sleep the night before, but considering how he'd spent that time, he wasn't about to complain. He pulled into his driveway just as his city was getting ready for primetime television and dinner plates were being rinsed off in sinks all across town. He didn't have anyone to come home to, but for the moment he was all right with that. It didn't hurt that his tryst with Jake the prior evening would leave him spent and sated for another twenty-four stretch or so. The kid had been flawless in the sack. He'd swallowed Bleu's rock-hard member like a high-priced hooker or an eager crack whore with attributed skills.

He'd wondered, in the moments he was fucking Jake, how many times the kid had taken a dick up the ass. He'd bucked and writhed like it had been his first ride on the receiving end, but the signs were there it hadn't been his first rodeo. When he'd been the same age as Jake, he hadn't had the confidence to pick up a stranger for anonymous sex. He rather admired the kid's brazen acceptance of his come on and thought maybe that was what sex was all about: the self-assurance that you were desirable, that others wanted your good bits as much as you wanted to share them.

After unlocking his front door, he entered to find every corner of the room was dark. He'd forgotten to leave a light on in the living room when he left that morning. But he'd been busy trying to get out before his neighbors roused and caught a glimpse of him and his overnight guest leaving. He hadn't even had time for a leisurely cup of coffee because there was that awkward morning-after tension. He worried a great deal about his reputation around town. And since the electricity in his nerves had drained from his body with the semen, he no longer cared to make idle nice with his young sex partner, he wanted him gone.

He worried that Jake would brag to his friends about his *date*. He worried a phone call might be overheard by a parent and that long build of gossip would eventually turn an ugly shade of hate and retribution. But what could he have done? He'd been horny, and the young man looked very enticing standing there in the pale moonlight and in the privacy of a dark country road where few cars traveled. It was a reminder that sometimes his prick took the chances his head would never have allowed.

Tossing his deputy's jacket on the chair by the door, he clicked on the lights and headed toward the fridge. There was a musky odor in the air, reminding him how little time he'd spent at home recently. The tables and shelves showed signs of untended layers of dust, and the icebox wasn't much better. It held only old takeout boxes and the refuse of dinners he hadn't finished. He hadn't spent enough time cleaning or shopping lately, and for a change he wondered if he didn't really need a companion in his life after all. Frustrated, he closed the fridge and headed upstairs for bed.

He remembered the Dodge pickup he had followed earlier and the hunky driver behind the wheel who hadn't struck him as the typical Sonora tourist. He'd trailed the vehicle for a few blocks and was considering pulling him over when he received a call from dispatch and had to relinquish the chase. But he hadn't forgotten about it. He told himself if he saw the driver and truck again in town he'd definitely pull it over. He'd have to make up some pretense for the stop, as the law was pretty specific about such things.

After a quick shower, Bleu crawled into bed naked and yanked the covers up around his chest. The bedding was still a rumpled mess from last night's sex act. But he was far too tired to hassle with pulling fresh sheets from the cupboard and making up the bed. Besides there was the faint scent of Jake's presence still lingering in the cotton fabric, and he rather liked that. It was a perfumed reminder of everything that happened the prior evening: every grunt, every thrust, and every wet and impassioned kiss on a stranger's face. Bleu found himself burrowing deeper into the sheets like a caterpillar craving his cocoon. He allowed the fragrant scent of testosterone and sweat to pull him in deeper as his mind drifted aimlessly. And just before he nodded off, he suddenly remembered he hadn't gotten Jake's telephone number, maybe due to him not wishing to offer his own number for privacy. Whatever the reason, as he lay under the cool sheets and the moon began making its patterns on the bedroom floor, he thought what a shame that was. He would've liked to have added Jake to his phone's contact list because one never knew when one's dick would demand another encore performance. And with salacious images of the younger man's bare chest and peach-fuzz covered ass cheeks dancing playfully in his head, he finally acquiesced. He allowed himself to coast free until he felt finally safe and warm all buried under a heavy blanket of black.

Chapter Twelve

GABE LAY AWAKE on his bed and scanned his surroundings. He chuckled when he thought how ridiculous it was that they called this a *lodge*. It wasn't nearly grand enough to carry that distinction. It was an austere room, by all accounts, and seemed to have a musky odor hanging in the air like a permanent guest. Still, it was off the beaten track, which had been the only saving grace to him.

It had been instinct. Whenever he chose a motel or boarding house as a respite from the highway, he always chose places off the interstate. That was when he had the funds to acquire a place for a short time. He looked for places with multiple egress points and a certain amount of anonymity. It was his ritual to drive around each establishment until he was satisfied with the accommodations and safety, long before he decided it was secure to check in. It was a reflex arc thing to him, a calculated action without being aware he was even performing it. He knew that he would never have survived being one step ahead of those who might be tracking him had he not been keenly adept at making wise choices. He was grateful Chris had pushed money on him. Just as he was grateful he'd given him his first disposable cell to use, which was a luxury for him and something that everyone around him simply took for granted.

But he wasn't stupid. Even with newfound flushness, he still knew better than to take unwise chances. He wasn't always conscious when he did it. His life had become a series of decisions made by rote. Such as where he stayed, how long he lingered, and whom he encountered, fucked, or robbed for food and fuel money.

After making his dutiful call that night, he felt better. He could hear the tension in the writer's voice from the beginning, but by the time they both said goodnight and hung up, he could tell the man was at least calmer in the end. He recognized a lilting excitement in every word whenever he spoke, thinking how he couldn't even remember the last time he'd heard Christian so happy.

This whole thing was as difficult on him, but sometimes he could forget that in the face of his own survival.

He lay naked atop the scratchy motel comforter. He'd slipped off his shirt and jeans during their conversation, but only after his cock danced enthusiastically under the denim. It appeared that it had become equally excited after hearing his would-be lover's voice on the other end of the line. It reminded him how he hadn't fucked anyone since driving out of Seattle, and he wondered if he could even hold off until the weekend and Chris's trip to a spot partway in the middle. He knew what Chris would say if he were asked, *"Don't do it, and baby...keep it tucked inside till I can make it up to you."*

He knew Christian Maxwell was probably the only one standing that didn't think he was a misanthrope, just another fucked up individual wanting nothing more than the total destruction of humanity. Then again, he knew he'd never allowed anyone else in, certainly not long enough to make clear judgments about him or his life. Certainly no one other than Chris knew anything about the white light surrounding the victims and a whisper of how many murders he'd done over the years. Even that investigator that had been tracking him hadn't guessed. He hadn't known a thing about his reasoning. But he'd had to die anyway because, if he'd been left on the board as a player, he'd have pursued him with the usual tenacity of a seasoned homicide detective. And more importantly, he was the only person who'd ever made a connection from him to Chris. That was as far as he knew at the time.

The first time he realized how much he'd screwed Chris's life came with Shea Baltimore's murder. If only he'd done the right thing, simply disappeared before it ever became an issue, or when he made a friend a subject in an ongoing police investigation. Hours after leaving the city, the only thing occupying his mind was the wind whistling through the crack in the driver's side window and the hum of his engine. Then he recalled an old memory he'd long since thought forgotten. A quote he remembered from their priest back at St. Ignatius. He hadn't been more than nine or ten at the time, and the sermon he recalled had been on John the Apostle. He remembered something about there being *"many rooms in my father's house, and I leave for there to prepare a place for you."* What struck a chord in him had been the second part of that verse; *"where it was written that I would come back for you, so that you may be where I am and because you know the place I am going."*

The words had rung in his head as the truck's tires pounded steadily against the asphalt. He'd driven for hours throughout the night. As he did, he'd thought about that particular verse and wondered if he'd ever really make it back to Chris one day and questioned whether they'd ever be able to stay together after the road that he'd put them on. He knew the rules had changed considerably once he killed a homicide detective and his wife. But one thing he knew with certainty was that the writer was the only person who really knew him well, and the only man other than himself who possibly understood where they were both headed.

THE NEXT MORNING was business as usual for Deputy Corso, a quick shower and fast cup of coffee as he slipped into his uniform before pressing his cruiser to the station for his shift. Every officer had to meet with the captain prior to their regular shift, which ran in three separate duty increments for a small city the size of Sonora. Bleu was typically one of five other officers in whichever shift he'd been assigned. They ran in early, evening, and midnight swings, and one of the first things you learned was a need for consistency in your work shifts. Getting used to sleeping during the day hours then being upended by night duty could play hell on your internal clock. But maintaining an unvaried shift wasn't as easy as all that and depended as much on your personal relationship with the captain as much as anything else.

Bleu Corso was an up-and-coming golden boy. There was a foregone conclusion that he would advance further in rank as long as he didn't fuck up his career by anything—such as write-ups for excessive force used or being affiliated in any way in an internal affairs investigation. Still, his relationship with Captain Kowalski was tenuous at best. Kowalski was old school law enforcement, a dinosaur from another era who few actually took seriously as either threat or mentoring supervisor. He was out of sync in the new world order. Officers were expected to show zero racial bias, unlike Kowalski who was accustomed to the occasional slur regarding a suspect's heritage or ethnicity. His locker room jokes about *Wops, Pols, Beaners*, or *Paki's* were familiar to everyone at the station, but he seemed oblivious when they hung their heads in embarrassment or simply smiled out of politeness with the faintest of chortles as they abruptly ducked away to escape his gravity.

Kowalski strutted around the precinct barking out commands like a drill sergeant. His uniform shirt barely contained his barrel chest and sagging belly, and every button down the length of his dress blue seemed strained to the point that others feared they'd pop off unexpectedly and then shoot across the station like bullet spray. Portly would've been a charitable description of him, and his 1950's ideology was regarded by most as disconcerting. And not just the tangy seasoning of a veteran cop who'd put in plenty of hours behind the wheel of a black-and-white cruiser.

Maybe it had been envy on Kowalski's part, seeing an upstart officer on another zenith rise when he was so close to forced retirement. Or maybe it came out of Corso's fear of getting tagged as queer before the bars on his shoulders might protect him. But there was noticeable distance between them, and it was a distance neither man seemed willing, or able, to close or negotiate anymore.

It wasn't as if Bleu hadn't tried. He secretly hated himself every time he noticed he'd been laughing too heartily and appeared too enthusiastic after hearing another of Kowalski's harsh and demeaning assessments about the suspects currently held in the gen pop of their Tuolumne County jails. But he told himself he was simply biding his time; that whenever the old dude was finally put out to pasture, he'd see changes were made inside the precinct and those newly hired officers would be expected to be tolerant and accepting of their suspects in as much as they were other cops.

He'd also see the chicken scratch drawings presently adorning the men's room stalls were painted over, every crudely depicted illustration of an oversized, engorged penis with the telephone number of the city's only gay bar scrawled beneath it like some sordid invitation. The dicks were vulgar, unrealistic representations, appearing more as if they'd been done by a simple child. Or in the very least an artist who had seen too few penises in their lifetime, save their own. Every dick drawing was rudimentarily cast with precum oozing from the head and clearly etched with a convenient house key in lieu of any paintbrush. The words promised readers that their satisfaction was guaranteed, as long as the recipient could stomach the sight of a faggot on a bended knee and worshipping from his phallic altar.

Corso didn't know who did the majority of the artwork, but he presumed it had to be Silas Jennings, a fat rookie about his age who walked around with a blanket stare that was best described as being unadulterated confusion. He had never been the type of cop Corso would've spent his off hours socializing with, and, fortunately because of his higher rank, he didn't have to.

Minutes speedily passed. The regular metronomic clicking of the second hand from the clock in the station's single conference room prompted Corso to check his wristwatch more than once. It must also have reminded Kowalski how rubber needed to hit the pavement because he quickly handed out all his assignments and printed alerts for the officers to review later and then disappeared into his office, barking casually back over his shoulder, "Stay safe out there, fellas," as the door closed behind his fat frame. Deputies scattered like ants from the mound as they headed toward their cruisers parked in the lot out back, thankful for the opportunity of escaping the rigid atmosphere of the precinct and their captain's sizable orbit.

Black-and-white cars fanned out in all directions, one after another with military precision. Each one to their designated sections of the city to patrol those streets assigned to their individual cars and answer dispatches without a partner. "Unis," as they were known in police circles, never carried more than a single driver. At least that was the case in Tuolumne County where backup was a simple radio call away. It was the best way to permeate the town with as many uniformed officers as the city could afford, without placing any staffer in serious jeopardy.

It was nothing but a gift of chance that an hour into his patrol the deputy rounded a corner and stumbled onto the same two-tone Dodge he'd seen the day before. He easily recalled the husky driver behind the wheel, as he did the tan-over-white coloring with its rusty dented sidewalls and heavy black smoke pouring from its exhaust.

He decided this time he wasn't going to lose his quarry in traffic and made a sudden jerk of the wheel, sending his cruiser barreling into a nearby parking lot of a local drive-thru called Sonny's Place. He remembered the name of the driver from yesterday. Bobby Johnson, a man without any standing state warrants. But, for reasons he couldn't fathom, he felt a tiny spark inside his belly, one that was strangely turning into a full-fledged tingle. Because somehow he didn't think this guy looked much like any Bobby he'd ever known. Something didn't feel right, and the face didn't match the name. And sometimes that was all it took for a cop with experience to initiate a traffic stop.

WITH BLUE LIGHTS flashing behind him, Gabe exhaled deeply with exasperation. He knew something as ordinary as a police stop could be frustrating to any driver, but for him it could mean something else entirely.

Naturally he'd spotted the Dodge Charger police sedan earlier and he knew he was carrying the license of a dead man. But he also knew from personal experience that didn't always present a threat. He pulled safely to the side of the road to wait but didn't turn off his engine.

He watched as a strapping young deputy emerged and sauntered slowly up to this driver's side window but didn't immediately reach for his wallet. He knew it was better to wait until he was asked for any documentation rather than make abrupt motions that might startle a fresh-faced officer such as this one.

"Afternoon, officer," he said politely. "Did I make an illegal turn or something? I know I wasn't speeding." He flashed his pearly grin and raised a hand to shield his eyes from the morning sun blasting his face.

"No, sir," the officer said, "but might I see your driver's license, registration, and insurance please?" He was very professional.

With a nod, Gabe reached for his wallet and pulled out the dead fucker's ID. And when he handed it out his window he caught the young man's green eyes. He's quite a handsome dude, he thought. He noticed the man's square jaw with its slight suggestion of razor stubble visible to him even in that blazing sunlight. His first thoughts had been how people no doubt trusted this officer. That he appeared clean-cut and forthright. This could play to his advantage since he had a fake ID, but no registration and a barely passable counterfeit insurance card. It wouldn't hold up to a radio check, he was sure, but he carried it as a last-ditch effort because police rarely stopped him. He knew his only chance of escaping the deputy's further scrutiny would be if he utilized every charm he had.

"As you can see I'm just a tourist, I was headed down the coast to visit a few friends when I thought I'd check out the sights here. It's really a lovely city you boys have here," he said with a broad smile utilizing every ounce of his sex appeal. "Did I fuck up a turn back there or something?" he asked, still shielding his eyes.

"No sir, we're checking for a stolen vehicle we got a call on that seemed to match your Dodge."

"*We,*" Gabe asked with an expressive face? "Do you have a partner in the back of your Charger I can't see from here?"

The deputy smiled back engagingly. "Well, you know how it is."

"I know cops and judges always refer to themselves in the plural, sure. But it always made me think they were talking about the mouse in their pocket." Leaning closer, Gabe asked, "So, do you have a little mouse in your slacks there, officer?"

It worked as effectively as he'd planned because the deputy smiled sheepishly and hung his head before he handed the license back through the window with his nerves rattled. He'd obviously forgotten about the insurance card and registration in the face of Gabe's advances, and he decided to make sure it was ignored completely.

"Say, fella, you're obviously local. Can you tell a tourist where he can find a really good steakhouse around here? I've been hankering for a raw slab of beef meat and I was hoping for a good meal 'fore I had to head outta town."

"You can try Dotty's off I-120. They have nice steaks and plenty of fixings."

Resting an arm on the roof of the Dodge, Gabe could tell the deputy was relaxing a bit, and the idea of the two men getting it on wasn't exactly a repugnant notion. He watched as the officer took an anxious glance down the street in both directions. Almost as if he was scanning a crowd to see if anyone was close enough to hear his conversation clearly.

"How long you in town for, Mr. Johnson?"

"It's Bobby…and only till tomorrow, I think." Gabe put his license back inside his wallet. "Besides the great steaks, what's the nightlife like in Sonora?"

"On life support," the deputy said with a chuckle.

"Surely there are places a guy can go for fun without running into tribes of sightseers, I'd imagine."

"Well, when you find a spot let me know."

"So you *would* consider meeting me for a drink somewhere?"

The rising lilt in his words came off playfully, and he was exploiting all the powers of persuasion at his command. Yes, Gabe thought, the cop was attractive. But he was more concerned with getting away undetected, and he knew his best hope was in utilizing all the charms he'd once plied on Chris. He didn't even know why he suspected the officer could be had, but there was something lurking behind those green pupils telling him this deputy had secrets. Maybe it was the confident way he bobbed his head as he approached the window, the nearly imperceptible nod that, had it been a greeting, Gabe figured it would have been a cocky, *Was sup, dude?*

The trappings of overcompensation were all the invitation he needed, a dance between strangers Gabriel knew all too well. When your only armaments are your wits and an ability to adapt, you learn rather quickly how to survive in the real world. And not unlike a trained psychiatrist,

Church had developed his skill in gauging others with a pinpoint accuracy of a sniper from SEAL Team Six.

The deputy's confidence stammered like his voice. He stared down at his boots embarrassed, as if they might be able to sprout tiny wings from each heel, anything that might carry him from this awkward situation. "I...umm, I don't know, Bobby," he blurted out. "That's probably not appropriate."

"Well, I figure you're the kind of man who doesn't need to flash a badge to get noticed. And hell, I'm only talking about having a drink with a new friend," Gabe countered.

"Well, I could meet you for a beer after work, I suppose," the deputy muttered under his breath, as the corners of his mouth tipped the balance in Gabe's favor. "But I don't get off 'til late."

"You pick the bar, and I'll be there. Maybe you'll have a chance to tell me about the lovely city and everything it has to offer."

"Sure, whatever," the deputy mumbled back. "You staying with friends or renting a room during your stay in Sonora? I mean, if I need to call and cancel or something."

His voice cracked with the question, and suddenly Church realized he was digging himself in too deep. His plan had been simple distraction, which worked beautifully. But now the cop was being a cop, and he didn't like where that was headed.

"Sure." he said evasively. "But you name the bar, and I'll do my best to find it. And, even if you can't make it, I can still have a beer all by my lonesome, on your recommendation anyway." He then flashed his bright enamel and allowed the sunlight to hit square in his eyes and create a twinkling he was certain the officer noticed. "I don't mind my own company, but I do hope you can swing by for a quick drink at least. It could be fun."

His last words positively dripped with innuendo. And to further drive the inference, he raked his open palm along the length of his denim-covered thigh. It could have been an innocuous gesture, like drying his hand of perspiration. Realizing he hadn't properly introduced himself, Gabe peered closer at the nameplate pinned to his chest.

"Well, Deputy Corso," he drawled. "Is that what I should call you if you do show up?"

"It's Bleu actually."

"Cool, like the color then."

With a chuckle the younger man said, "Its Bleu, spelled *a tad back-ass-ward,*" he said, "With the E first, before the U. It's about as unusual as I am, I suppose, but it's a family thing." He said as his voice trailed off almost apologetically.

"Well that's great, officer. I was named after my uncle Robert," Gabe said in yet another confident lie.

"There is a little place about ten minutes off 108, on Campo Seco Road," Bleu said. "It's called The Iron Mine. Pool, tall drafts, and bikers mostly, not the place where vacationing families go, but you might like it. It's simple...unpretentious."

"See you know my speed already," Gabriel whispered. "And you didn't even have to pull out your radar gun to get there."

His slow glance seemingly took in every inch of the studly officer. His sardonic grin was both suggestive and innocent at the same time. Then a fast October gust blew strong in that moment and ruffled the deputy's wispy brown locks on his forehead. It reminded Gabe of Christian and how pure and unsullied he'd appeared when they first met. The space separating them was heavy with static electricity, then the sounds of passing cars and horns off in the distance yanked them back.

"So, when you getting off?" he asked. Gabriel let the double entendre hang seductively in the air between them. His shit-eating grin never dissolved from his face, almost as if he'd just whispered something wet and sexual.

Bleu's earlobes turned pink. "Well, I'll get free of the precinct around seven," the deputy advised, "but I can't make it to the Iron Mine until around eight, if that's cool?"

"That'd be perfect. See you there, I hope, Deputy Corso." Then he looked up imploringly, like a child searching a parent's face and asked the questions, "So are we done here? Is it all good?"

Gabe hadn't set out to entice a date from a good-looking stud like Corso. Particularly considering the man was a Sonora law enforcement officer. But it was true that he'd been a little starved for attention. Yesterday he'd been thinking he needed a little more adult fun of the bouncy castle type. And since Chris was far away at the moment, he needed to have it subbed by a player yet unnamed. But this whole meeting had been nothing but a magician's hands moving faster than his audience. He didn't want to take the risk by flashing an insurance card or vehicle registration, since neither showed the name of Bobby Johnson, which would likely make for more questions and follow-up. Actually, if it hadn't been for a driving need for identity theft, he would have already forgotten the name of that paunchy electrician from Queen Anne he'd murdered a few months earlier.

Faces didn't stick in Gabe's head for long, not when they were white-lighters he met along the way, and not when their destinies seemed so tragically pre-ordained once he'd spotted them. They were merely one face out of the many. At least this Bobby guy was special in the fact that, even dead, Gabriel had found some use for him.

Chapter Thirteen

FEELING BETTER THAN he had in a long while, Chris woke with a start the moment the sun blasted through his bedroom windows. As he got ready for work that morning, he felt a gnawing pit inside his belly, knowing it was due to being able to see Gabe soon. He felt a mixture of excitement in that and his anxiety of being escorted to the wall, like an accused convict heading to his execution.

Blindfold or cigarette, they might ask. Well he didn't smoke—he knew that shit could kill ya. And he fully expected to see every bullet as they flew through the air, knowing with steadfast conviction that the words *Gabriel Church* had already been etched into the casing prior to ever being discharged from those offending rifles.

As he poured a cup of coffee and gathered his wardrobe in his typically meticulous fashion, he thought about making reservations for a car and a hotel later today. A heady prospect, he couldn't wait to be alone again with Gabriel. His life had become something he could never have envisioned before meeting Gabe, and it felt like a veil had lifted or the scales had been yanked from his eyes.

You walk around oblivious. You interact with plastic fabrications of people and drift through your surrounding like they are nothing but mere set designs with painted flats and hastily positioned decorations. But they are only mirages, meant to look authentic and not the simple props they really are.

Meeting Gabe had changed all that. He'd learned the lessons of what he really wanted in a lover and what made his dick hard during all his late-night passions. It felt as if he'd been reborn. That everything he knew before was now suddenly false. And surprisingly, that hadn't occurred to him before. He wondered what he'd say whenever he finally outed himself to his parents and wondered if they already suspected, even though he hadn't allowed himself to believe it could be true.

"Mother, I wanted to let you know I'm gay, something I very recently realized. I have fallen in love with another man. Oh, and by the way, he's

a serial killer and currently running from the police. So can I freshen up your vodka for you because we have some time?"

Yes, that would go over splendidly.

If the tenuousness of the situation had taught him anything, it was how much he could adapt. He would simply become something different than he'd been before: for his friends, coworkers, and for his family. He wasn't the man he thought he'd successfully crafted so long ago, but that was made clear by the images flashing through his brain constantly after his first meeting with Gabriel…grainy photographs of him being escorted by police at either side, with cuffs restraining his wrists and with chains between his ankles preventing him from walking above a shuffle. He saw his own face with a dazed look of confusion plastered like a deer caught in the headlights and perpetually frozen in time for anyone to see, captured in the still of a random reporter's photo and headlines that sent chills racing down his spine.

Even with everything unraveling around him, Chris was still eager to make the drive out of town. He was enthusiastic for a vacation out of the city, away from any spirits floating around the condo or downtown streets of Seattle and an opportunity to have some much-needed sexual tensions released. And with someone he truly cared for, since it had been far too long since he'd gotten off. At least while there was someone else in the room.

WITH THE SAME mounting tensions others shared, Bleu spent the remainder of his afternoon worrying about an upcoming meeting for drinks with a stranger. Someone he'd pulled over in traffic but knew next to nothing about. And by the way his cock had danced under his dress slacks, he knew there was a chance it could turn out to be something more than friendly local hospitality. He couldn't forget the suggestive and calculated deliberation of the man's hand running up and down his thighs. Even such a small signal wasn't lost on the deputy, who was busy noticing how big the driver's mitts were. He had to presume the dude had a girthy appendage hidden in his jeans.

After some deep reflection, he was genuinely surprised that he was about to experience something that felt anything but natural to him. Something he'd never had to face before today: a practically blind date with a stranger, one who happened to be male. Granted he was one hot fucking male, but the situation felt strange enough that he didn't need the added pressure brought on by the dude's handsome features or those intimidating guns of his.

With his grin never evaporating, the brutish man behind the wheel had spoken volumes without uttering a single word of intent. For the deputy, it had been unnerving and titillating at the same time. Never before had someone been so blatant or suggestive toward him during a routine stop. He'd had women cry and occasionally lean into the wheel so that he might be able to glance down their cleavage, but never before had a man attempted it. It left him slightly unfocused, wondering how this dude could tell he was gay. Did his sexuality ooze off or surround him like an aura?

He'd already run the man's name through the database, but, being a good detective, he knew he had to reach out to the places investigators went to when learning about a suspect, so he typed into Facebook.

When he didn't find anything for a Bobby Johnson from Washington, which had been the state he claimed to be his residence, he began a search using other social media sites. He expected to find something of a digital footprint for the man, but found he was a tad anxious after thinking that he might actually run across one. In his mind, he worried he'd run across a profile and find a picture of Bobby sporting a grin taken from a random social gathering outdoors. One where he might be holding a can of beer in one hand and BBQ tongs in the other. Or one more important to him, where he'd been standing arm in arm with a lovely unrecognized woman, obviously his wife.

Maybe he'd skim across postings about his children, as well, or see photos taken at little league games or school recitals. And he wondered what his reaction would be once he did. He was a newbie himself, and he didn't fuck around all that much. There were limits to the short list of anonymous sexual conquests that he'd had over time, but, to his knowledge, he'd never been with anyone straight and married.

The questions idling through his mind then became whether he'd go through with a fast, furious screwing if the option was laid out for him to choose. He also wondered about expectation. He could tell this dude was a top, which was a position he typically preferred for himself. But when he'd agreed to drinks, he knew he may have placed himself in a situation where it'd be him biting the pillowcase and taking the brunt of what this guy had to offer.

He suspected this guy had the right equipment and that it might take two full hands to grip his erect cock. And as that picture played in his mind, he found himself grinning sheepishly as he imagined Bobby whispering, *"Well, I do have a few inches of circumference to work with...you wanna see it? You either have it or you don't."* He was suddenly flush with embarrassment and scanned the station, hoping no one had witnessed him smiling at his desk alone like an imbecile. He'd taken a break from his patrol, and, in lieu of lunch, he raced back to the station to search the shared computer in the bullpen. But it was getting time to hit the streets again, and he didn't want others to see his search parameters, so he cleared any cache and put the monitor to sleep even though he hadn't learned anything new about his upcoming *date* he didn't know already.

In the hours after stopping Bobby's Dodge truck, the deputy was pulled into his own drama after dispatch received a call of a confession to murder. His unit, along with others, sped to the address given, which was off Redbud Drive. Everyone was understandably on high alert. Homicide rates in Tuolumne County were so much lower than the national average that most considered them nonexistent. But, on the rare occasions when they occurred, everyone knew it would be big news and a topic of idle conversation at diners and bars for weeks to come.

Corso knew Kowalski would be called to the scene, and because Sonora was the county seat of Tuolumne, he knew their County Sheriff would be there as well. He'd met Sheriff Jacoby several times, and he hadn't been any more impressed with him than he was with Captain Kowalski. Jacoby was an oddity. A fat, uneducated man who'd worked his way through the ranks with a career that spanned decades. But his success couldn't have been attributed to his effective police work as much as him simply outlasting any competitors for the title. Both Kowalski and Jacoby would typically be called when the offense was of the highest order. And in a town of less than five thousand, with statistical crime rates bordering on the enviable, he knew he could expect them to show.

The last time he remembered seeing his captain at a scene was over a year earlier. There'd been a five-car pileup on the interstate and it prompted heavier news coverage because of two tragic fatalities in the crash. Kowalski's face had been the only image captured on film that day, with all that carnage and twisted smoking metal as his dramatic background. More publicity or community assurance than anything, Bleu suspected. If Kowalski knew that he'd be retiring the following year, he might not have made the effort to drive to the scene just to appear on camera.

Corso radioed back to Sally to request new information about the caller and any circumstances while racing his unit to the address on Redbud with sirens blasting. He was surprised by the lack of urgency in her tone when Sally explained the caller identified herself as Maude Hannity, and that she'd dialed 911 to let someone know she'd effectively poisoned her husband of nearly twenty years. Bleu heard a slight chortle in Sally's voice when she described the situation. Apparently, Mrs. Hannity had gotten "sick and tired of Ponder's constant bitching and his unhappiness with his life." Sally further explained that Maude only called the Sheriff's office to have them stop by and "haul this piece of shit off her kitchen floor." She had done all she could do to contain the laughter she knew would be caught on the recording. The deputy left his sirens on but gingerly reduced his speed.

The call became routine after that. Maude Hannity offered herself freely to the officers arriving on the scene. She didn't fight or claim innocence as a palm shielded the back of her head while she was assisted into the back of a nearby cruiser. Seeing a middle-aged and somewhat frumpy woman such as her being led away was a tad surreal for Corso. He thought he'd seen it all. But this setting seemed off-kilter, and the cast of suspect characters were anything but predictable.

Requests went out for the use of Mariposa County's SID van. Tuolumne had long shared the Scientific Investigation Division's equipment of Mariposa because cost outweighed any need. Crime tape was stretched across the entryway as protocol, but all knew this was surely a residence that had never had anything but Christmas lights strung where the tape now extended. Of the few officers who stayed, most entered and exited quickly. They surveyed the body of Ponder Hannity lying dead on the cold rustic country tile of the Hannity's kitchen. Onlookers littered the cul-de-sac, full of curiosity, and even from a distance they could see the officers exiting the home while shaking their heads in disbelief. Most people, those not in law enforcement, didn't realize that seeing this type of crime was just as shocking to officers as it was the neighbors who craned their necks and peered across the driveway like timid field mice scanning the horizon for foxes or birds of prey.

Regardless of the tragedy, it was a waiting game after that. Cops milled around the lawn while waiting for the SID van to arrive. They gossiped in small groups, chatted with onlookers and made notes to fill the time. And as dull and routine as it became, it was still the biggest thing to happen in Corso's day for quite some time. In all his duties, and seeing other cops and officials he rarely encountered, he nearly forgot about his date for a drink with Bobby. When he remembered it, he thought this would at least provide a modicum of conversation should they come up with nothing in common to discuss.

Kowalski hadn't shown up to the scene, and Bleu suspected he knew why. The captain had probably been en route when Sal informed him about the circumstances of the call. The same as she did with him. He probably figured it was small potatoes and turned his unit around to head back to the precinct. Everyone knew he no longer needed to kiss the ass of Jacoby anymore because in a few short weeks he'd be outta there, and it would be someone else's problem. In his head, Bleu knew that it would be his problem soon enough, the hassles, the bureaucracy, the kissing of those fat cheeks on Jacoby. And that didn't offer him as much comfort as he thought it would.

After closing up the Hannity homicide, Corso headed back to the station to log out. He wanted to get home for a quick shower and a change of clothing. He didn't think it appropriate to wear his uniform out on a date. That was if this was truly a date after all. Bleu suspected he risked those threats plenty in his life: the whispers, gossip, and innuendo of why he wasn't married yet, and who was that unfamiliar fella he'd been seen talking to the other day? He knew he didn't need to add any more oxygen to that steadily growing fire. Part of him was still unsure as to whether he'd show or not, but as he went through the motions of his daily routine, he never stopping working toward that goal. No matter where his head seemed in any particular moment, no matter how much he vacillated over showing up to the Iron Mine, inside, he still knew he had no real intentions of backing out. Not at the last minute, and not after reflecting back about those piercing cobalt eyes that Bobby apparently liked to flash his way.

Chapter Fourteen

DARKNESS HAD DESCENDED when Gabe pulled into the parking lot. Without a laptop and without knowing every nook and cranny of Sonora, he had to stop at a gas station and ask for directions from the man behind the counter. He was going to be early. That was if the handsome deputy even showed. As he circled around the block, he thought about what Chris would say if he knew what he was planning. *Yes, I did what I had to just to get out of a difficult situation.* Besides, the officer was attractive enough, in his clean-cut strapping way, and he was clearly interested in seeing where this meeting would take them. He reminded himself how long it had been since he had sex, or how long it would be before he hooked up with Chris. And that was how each lie he told himself began: an awareness to adapt, or one more action for his survival, and not his lust working yet another angle.

Gabriel wasn't someone you said *no* to—even Chris knew that. If he ran across a door marked DO NOT ENTER, it would be an invitation for him, since killers rarely followed society's rules of convention. Chris might've understood why he felt it necessary to flirt his way out of a potentially bad scenario. But both men knew it would better if you didn't ask him to like it. As he pulled the truck into an empty space, he thought about that, and decided this was something he wouldn't share with Chris when they met next.

He entered via the street-facing façade and noticed large paned windows with neon advertising. The red lights from the neon turned the sidewalks out front a bright, friendly hue. A martini glass made from neon tubes hung behind the glass. Slightly tilted, the green neon framed a single olive. He doubted there were many of the Mine's regular clientele who ever ordered martinis, since it had a distinctly happy-hour vibe he'd noticed even before opening the door.

Cigarette smoke billowed into the street as he entered, which seemed strange. This was California, so he was surprised to find any bar where patrons could still smoke indoors. California was filled with vegans and bohemians and those who only shopped at Whole Foods Markets and were not afraid to approach a stranger they saw smoking in public to inform them of all the known dangers of cigarette smoke. They were like Ninja assassins here. Everyone had a cause and everyone seemed fearless in their attempts to enforce their values on others. Gabe had given up smoking long ago. It was a habit he'd inadvertently picked up after leaving home at seventeen. But when you're a drifter and money is tight, you have to decide to give it up, or decide to do things you'd rather not, just to maintain the habit.

During that slow period between post-work revelers and before the later crowds filtered in, there were plenty of vacant tables to choose from. The deputy had been correct, since there were two pool tables sitting idle in the back, right next to a line of old video games that stood like the Queen's Guard soldiers. Though he doubted they ever saw much attention.

Music filled the space but wasn't overpowering. A nice place where people met after their shifts, he suspected, and a place to chat quietly about their coworkers. A tragically stereotypical young man in his mid-twenties was tending bar. His appearance all but screamed "junkie," like a replica of someone pulled from the pages of a dark graphic novel. He wore a black cotton shirt with long sleeves that hung loosely over his dirty acid-wash jeans. His head was shaved except for the Mohawk he proudly sported in the center. It made Gabe think he'd crawled not simply from the pages of a dime novel, but from another period altogether. Once he spotted him, he instantly pictured him slamming needles of crack cocaine into his arms in his van out back, a van from the same bygone era where his haircut originated. He had an aura of a kid who got high frequently and wasn't simply a chemical-friendly lad who only smoked weed. He looked far too hardcore, and far too close to gone. Gabe had seen his type many times before, and, by the way his pupils darted back and forth, it should've been a dead giveaway to almost everyone. Stepping up to the end of the long bar, Gabe seized on the notion this kid had chosen his shirt deliberately, possibly to hide the pockmark injection scars dotting the insides of those skinny arms of his.

"What'll be, mister?" the kid asked as he rushed up, the wet bar rag still gripped in his hand.

"A draft, tallest you got, but I'm meeting a friend, so bring it to my table."

With that Church threw down one of his many stolen credit cards to indicate he wanted a tab run. Then he turned abruptly and sauntered off to find a quiet table for him and the deputy should their meeting go as planned. Out-of-the-way dive bars, such as this one, were the only places Gabe knew to use a stolen card he'd lifted from some fool's wallet. They rarely had surveillance cameras, and, if the card came back declined, he could still resort to cash. In these types of establishments, no one ever asked many questions, and he'd grown to utilize those lessons he'd learned early.

The kid looked at him suspiciously when he slid the beer in front of him, but Church wasn't worried. It was a cautious look, which suggested he knew the kid was holding a stash somewhere on his person, more than enough to have him turn on his heels and race away in fear. Watching the young man scurry back to the safety of his spot behind the bar, Gabe recalled another time when he'd once ended a white-lighter who looked a lot like this kid. He was about the same age and same build, anyway. He couldn't remember the details clearly, he never did. But seeing his ruddy complexion and scruffy youthful attempt at facial hair brought back an image like a firecracker exploding in his head.

He remembered gutting the boy with a hunting knife, and though he couldn't see every particular, he remembered that he'd dumped his remains into a black unfathomable body of water and also remembered seeing the corpse floating slowly downstream.

That was how it was usually. The specifics escaped him later, as if they were enveloped in a fog, which was why it'd been so difficult during those initial so-called interviews with Christian. It wasn't remorse, just his forgetfulness.

Gabe watched as drinkers came in then left the bar. He got up for no other reason than to hit the head or walk over to the bar to reorder. The bartender wasn't keen on checking back at his table, that much was apparent. Maybe he thought he was too good to perform the job of cocktail waitress, but whoever hired the kid had failed to recognize the aroma of spoon-cooked heroin reeking off his body like scent trails. Gabe didn't wear a watch, so he was guessing at the time. He'd never consider asking the fruit fly schlepping drinks and chatting up his regulars. But before he could decide whether to leave or hang longer, he saw moonlight burst in from the open door and saw the deputy enter.

He wasn't in his uniform, thankfully, and he'd replaced his pressed slacks for denim. In lieu of the starched blue shirt with a badge, he was wearing a red Wrangler shirt that gave him a more masculine appeal. When he'd been leaning over his driver's side window, Gabe had noticed how the Sonora police didn't have tin badges, and instead they had a fabric emblem stitched on their front lapels. It simply read Sonora at the top and Police at the bottom. He remembered it because it appeared odd that its design showed a pickax crossing a shovel with a sun behind that. He already knew the local heritage from the motel brochures he'd skimmed through, but it was unusual that was the design law enforcement had chosen. He presumed it had to be some kind of city seal, and something duplicated on the flags and local government offices.

He was walking back to his table with his third beer in his hand when Bleu entered. Gabe waved an arm and smiled lightly in a gesture that said, "Welcome, join me."

"Well, you look more comfortable than when I last saw you," Gabe bellowed over the music. The deputy grinned sheepishly and weaved through empty tables to reach the spot Gabe had picked. "I didn't want to come in uniform," he said, "It wouldn't help the Mine's business to have cops drinking here." He chuckled. Taking a seat, he looked around to see who was working, but before he could rise and head to the bar, the kid was standing breathless behind him. "How 'do, officer, can I get you something cold to drink?"

"How 'bout a pitcher of draft and an empty," he said off-handedly. And without waiting for a response, the young man turned on his heels and disappeared behind the bar to fill the order.

"I take it the young man knows you," Gabe whispered as he sat down. "So are you a regular here?"

"Not exactly, but we have run across one another. I can't discuss it though; it's a police thing, not a social one." The deputy murmured back, discreetly sidestepping the whole unspoken truth.

"So what's the boy's deal?" Gabe asked "'Cause I read addict off him. Did you have to arrest him in the line of duty?"

Bleu considered briefly, then said, "That's the problem being a cop; it's never proper gossiping about a resident's past histories with the law."

"Sure, I understand," Church said apologetically. He liked this man. He seemed devout in his ethical stance, which was refreshing given who and what he was.

"So have you seen much of Sonora during your visit?"

"Not enough," the killer said as his eyes twinkled against the bar lights.

"You said you're headed out soon, meeting friends on the coast, was it?" The deputy asked, quickly changing subjects.

"I did," Gabriel said leaning back in his chair. "But how was your day today? I mean, if there's anything you can talk about, but in general terms."

They were complete strangers with only a hint of suggestion between them, so Bleu recounted his story about a homicide, saying he was leaving out the names to show the victim some respect. It was just the connection required, and they talked in an engaging way about the oddity of a woman poisoning her husband of many years and how unusual that crime was in a town like Sonora. They continued talking when the subject turned to tourism and local history, and as innocuous as it was, it seemed to do the trick. By the time the deputy was downing his second draft, they found they were chatting like old friends. The only difference being Corso's stories were truthful, while Gabe spun lie upon lie with an easy comfort.

When the second pitcher arrived from a visibly anxious and eager-to-please server, the mood began to change. Using his fabricated persona of Bobby, Gabe asked Bleu about his decision to join the force, whether or not he enjoyed it, and what future plans he had for his career. It was simple idle conversation but it came from a genuine interest. It gave the deputy a chance to talk about his life more. And with every fragment he revealed, Gabe was busy calculating his chances for bedding the handsome officer, and whether or not this straight-laced fella would agree to go bitch and give up the goods.

The beer was taking its toll, and every time the officer spoke, he flashed a perfect set of pristine white enamel. He carried the same southern drawl to his words Gabe did, which forced him to ask about where the deputy had grown up and how long he'd lived in Sonora. He was surprised when Bleu confided he'd been born and raised locally, which made him wonder again about the inflection of his speech. He wrote it off as a boy who'd watched far too many westerns growing up. But he never knew how closely he'd touched on the truth.

BLEU BECAME UNEASY after Bobby made a somewhat suggestive double entendre his way. It was hard for him to discern whether they were directed at him or whether this was chatter with his newfound acquaintance. Suddenly, Bleu felt unmatched and inexperienced, and stuttered back with casual indifference. He watched as Bobby relaxed his posture and then ran a palm across his chin with its three-day growth of beard in a sensual gesture. His calculated glare somehow defied his pleasant, apathetic smile.

It felt akin to a party taking place behind closed doors, something fun one knew was happening just out of sight. Bleu couldn't separate the man's words from the flickering light occurring in those steel-gray eyes of his. It sent a cold shiver racing down his spine. One that strangely got hotter along its path as it closed in on his groin area.

This was like no experience he'd had before. Certainly not the same sense of young Jake and his toned stringy body. He was in the company of someone greater. A real man's man—someone he felt was only toying with him in that moment, like a cat with a mouse.

"I appreciate you telling me 'bout this place, officer, though I didn't get the steak I was hankering for. But your town has to have some more fun to offer to its more adventurous tourists?"

Bobby's crooked grin and the way he leveled his gaze back at Bleu was unquestionably a come-on. But their conversation hadn't relaxed him near as much as it had Bobby, he suspected. Bleu was beginning to really see where this was heading, and like a little boy lost in a mall crying for his mama, he felt nervous and alone.

"Suppose that depends what kind a fun you're looking for, Bobby," he stammered out with a feigned grin. "Now the kid behind the bar might have his own ideas of what fun is, but that's not mine. So, if I'm to play Julie, your cruise director, then you gotta define your guidelines."

Finally the alcohol was taking effect. He was able to lean back in his chair and feel the power creeping in. He felt more confident and it showed. He was batting the ball back onto Bobby's court and becoming just as sure that he knew how this evening would turn out after all.

Bobby looked down at his glass then stared back into Corso's green eyes with a devilish grin on his face. Every motion made seemed slower, as if he were moving through an encased block of ice. The long pause was methodic and measured—an unfamiliar signal to Bleu, one he hadn't seen before then. After what seemed like a minute dragged through mud, he finally said, "Dunno. I got a room at the Queen of the Mines Lodge. "We could grab a bottle and head there for a spell...maybe see where we might want to go from there?"

With the draft beer sufficiently melting his inhibitions, Bleu stood up quickly, causing his chair to rock against the wood floor. "Why not," he said. "I don't have any plans." Which was true, and that proclamation allowed him to suddenly realize how boring his life had become—work and then home and back again. And the only distraction came from those rare incidents when he allowed his freak flag to fly, as he had with Jake.

"I know where your motel is, so why don't you go ahead. I'll stop to get a bottle from the liquor store, and I'll meet ya there in a few," he said, a burp from the beer stifling his words. "Do you have a preference...scotch, bourbon, or something else?"

"Whiskey, please. I'll leave it to you for the origin and state." A true aficionado knew there were tons of blends, but also knew very few whiskeys could be considered authentic bourbon. Generally, it meant the whiskey had to come from Kentucky, but the law merely defined bourbon as having 51 percent of corn grain in the mash. There were also requirements to the distillation, but a true whiskey lover knew it was the required aging in charred, white-oak barrels that made the flavor so signature. "Maybe a black label brand," Bobby offered as he lumbered up, then headed toward the door. "Let me settle up for the drinks," Corso said, turning toward the bar.

"I'll get the drinks here," Bobby interjected. "That is, since you're getting the stiff stuff." He oozed indecency, Bleu thought. Every sentence dripped his own suggestive meaning, and he wondered how much of that was on purpose and how much came from his libido.

"You need anything else?" he asked over his shoulder. But before Bobby could answer, Bleu leaned in close and quietly asked, "By the way, what room you in, bro?"

He fought to hide his self-conscious blushing and hoped the beer they'd consumed helped to hide any embarrassment he felt.

"I'll be parked right in front," Bobby said, snickering. "Look for the Dodge; remember, the one you didn't mind pulling over without cause." Both laughed a tad too loudly at that, and then the deputy was gone.

GABE HEADED TO the bar to pay out his drink tab with *Drug Boy*. But he only left a minimal tip. Although it wasn't his money to spend, the kid had unnerved him and seemed rude. In his eyes, everyone gets what's coming to them, but he was slightly inebriated and didn't grasp the meaning of that random thought.

Chapter Fifteen

GABRIEL ARRIVED BACK at the lodge first, as he expected he would. He wanted to hide the 9mm in a place where the deputy wouldn't find it. He'd brought the Glock in earlier because he liked having it near him when he slept. But instead of stowing it back into the Dodge, he decided to put it out of sight yet still within his reach should the evening not go as planned.

By the time Bleu arrived, he found Bobby's door ajar. Warm light from his room was leaching into the parking lot like an immoral invitation for something he wanted to do but didn't want to have to confess to later. Seeing movement inside, he grabbed up the high-priced whiskey bottle and the six-pack of Coke he'd bought for the occasion. He'd also thought to buy a bag of ice, but it was in the trunk. No doubt making a watery mess all over his carpet lining as it melted. His heart was racing with excitement, and seeing Bobby step into the doorframe, he noticed that he'd removed his shirt and boots. Standing in a halo of bad motel lighting, he looked quite content in his white socks and jeans,

He had a magnificent physique for one slightly older than Bleu. He seemed to swallow up the space between the doorjambs. His muscular chest and abs were peppered with close-cropped hair that frothed over his bare nipples, making trails and patches to parts unseen. Stepping out of his vehicle, the deputy called out to him, being careful not to speak loud enough that other guests might hear.

"I see you made yourself comfortable already."

He didn't know why he said that; it sounded ridiculous to his ear the second the words came out. But he was nervous and didn't have any witty quip in his arsenal. Bobby simply nodded back without words, and then retreated inside like a spider tempting a fly into his parlor.

GABE MADE THEM both drinks after placing the ice in a bucket and leaving the remainder of the bag to drain inside the bathtub. Music was playing from an ancient desk radio the motel provided, and Gabriel had chosen country music to offset any vacuum of silence he suspected might lapse between them. He could tell Corso wasn't exactly out and proud, and he understood why. He knew better than most what it was to be raised in the shaming confines of a rural home. Not to mention he had a reputation to uphold since he doubted the denizens of Sonora would take kindly to a queer deputy patrolling their city.

Thinking about Corso growing up brought back memories of his old childhood, and, although he hadn't been gay back then, he certainly knew how Daddy Bennett would've taken the news had he known. He felt a twinge of pity when he thought how hard it must be hiding who and what you were when you were a peace officer living in a small town. Gabe didn't know how many times this young man had an occasion to draw his pistol, but he suspected it was near to never. He surely was more proficient with a firearm than Corso. But bravery comes with many faces, and one could reason he was fearless by simply being who he was and not jumping out of his chair and racing from this motel room still clutching the pearls to his chest.

They talked for almost an hour, with topics ranging from the weather to girls they dated in high school and reasons why neither man had any desire for a monogamous lifestyle. It was all *bullshit*, but it greased the proverbial wheels and gave the whiskey its best chance to work. Gabe spun his lies with precision, as if he knew the differences that separated him from others more than the similarities he might've shared. He was well-versed in fabricating a life to compare with normalcy, regardless that it went against every grain he understood.

Gabe crafted stories of his high school football career and how he'd wanted to go collegiate had it not been for his injury. All manufactured from his head with a paintbrush, and where almost nothing he offered could've been truthful. He had, in fact, never played high school ball, as he never even officially graduated. The accounts he shared as his reality were probably more telling than the words spoken, and had Christian been sitting there, he surely would have said that. He would have leaned over and indicated to Gabriel in a quiet voice that he did have dreams and aspirations of growing up in a normal house. That whenever he drew facets from his forgery, he was showing everything he'd really wanted from his life in ways he couldn't even comprehend.

Fortunately, he wasn't sitting with Chris but a deputy who knew nothing about his real life or even his actual name. They joked back and forth while sipping their drinks until Gabe was beginning to tire from the game. Bleu's handsome features and his unscarred face were enhanced by his quick mind and jovial personality, causing Gabe to finally ask, "So Deputy, you're a smart, good-looking man, and, as we both know, there's no pale ring line circling your finger. Despite the obvious answer, I'm keen to ask you, did you ever want to marry?"

Bleu obviously hadn't expected the question and leaned back in his chair exhaling deeply. He looked as if he were soaking in a bath and reticent about stepping out into the cold air yet. He set his whiskey and cola on the table beside him then placed his palms together, making a steeple of his fingers. To Gabriel, it appeared he was formulating his words carefully, about to unleash some earth-shattering bit of news.

"Well, I figured there's always time for that later, and I suppose no one has gotten my pot percolating."

You're a bad liar, Gabe wanted to say. His proclivities clearly were a shade darker than he cared to admit, and that got him wondering if the deputy was simply a bad fuck or someone with a few unpleasant habits he wasn't willing to address.

"I get your meaning, buddy. I came close to marriage a couple of times but..." Gabe's lie trailed off like wisp of smoke before he added, "Ya know what I'm talking about, deputy, right?"

It felt as artificial as two strangers staring up at a titty dancer in a smoke-filled strip bar; sharing lies about wives or work while they drank themselves into stupors, knowing they'd have to head home soon and fuck the missus before the kids were up and raising all kinds of hell. As they commiserated about all those poor shits who'd been dragged unwilling down the aisle, they laughed and poured themselves another drink.

Bleu appeared relaxed enough that Gabe felt he could take it a step further. He purposely spilled a few drops of whiskey on his chest as if by accident, then chuckled in his baritone way. Each droplet turned his chest hair dark as he palmed the spillage in a gesture of absently drying himself. A calculated move meant to titillate, as he raked his bare chest, he noticed a twinkle of discomfort in the deputy's eyes.

Hypocrite...isn't this the reason why you're here?

There was ritual in every action, though clearly nothing either man had ever shared during their time together. Like a hand grazing across loose fabric, becoming tighter with every stroke, or a single pause between sentences that feels as if it's expanding, threatening to envelop the room.

From a distance one would've heard their voices getting lower, the silence becoming contributory, like a separate accomplishment to the same crime. Even though the stories kept coming, and they chatted normally, eventually there were slow measured breaks where very little was said. Ultimately Gabriel decided to fragment the growing awkwardness the best way he knew how: by reaching down with his free hand and unsnapping the top button of his jeans while Bleu watched with great intensity.

WITH THE SIGHT of Bobby hunkered back in his chair, so relaxed, a raised glass in one hand, while the other tempted without words, Bleu's reaction to him was hard to control.

He was hearing Bobby recount a story about some gambling and hunting trip he'd taken recently, but it was likely another lie to amuse. As if in complete indifference to his tale, those blueish-gray pupils of his were busy constructing a different narrative.

Bleu couldn't discern whether it was the lighting or the cocktail, but those depthless orbs seemed magnetic. They flashed like high beams on a dark country road and all but whispered to the things they wanted to do intimately with him, making him uncomfortable.

GABE COULD SEE the effect he was having on the deputy. It felt like bedding a virgin to him, the way this sexy man shifted nervously in his chair but said nothing about the way he'd loosened his jeans snap, like some monstrous snake needing to uncoil.

If the deputy had seen the bulge in Gabe's Levi's from across the room, he'd covered it well. Blood was filling his member fast, and he felt a little trapped inside his own passions. Gabe could distinguish there were things he could do that might make it easier on the younger man, but he stopped short of making it so tranquil as to allow his trepidation to dissipate completely.

Setting down his drink, he reached up in a slow motion and clicked off the reading lamp overhead. It was only a 60-watt bulb, so didn't extinguish much light, but it had meaning, and he was sure Corso was picking up on that. He didn't care for sex with married men and wasn't the type to seduce straight men into bed for the sheer thrill of it. He never spent any time in video booths at bookstores or loitered in the dusky parks at night. And he doubted if Corso did either.

For Gabriel Church, it was the challenge of the hunt as much as the physical act itself. He was a narcissist, someone who enjoyed the adoration and worship of his naked form and saw it as nourishment. Seeing a glimmer of hope in another person's eyes, whether they were female or male was a satisfying resolution for a near perfect encounter. He could sense the other person's mouth going dry, could feel the tittering of a heartbeat from across the room.

It was power, and it spoke to his divinity. He'd learned that lesson as a teenager, and it had rippling effects running through his adulthood. His initial intention had been to flirt his way out of further scrutiny from a local lawman. But it had twisted into something more decadent after seeing Bleu squirming in his chair. He'd tested the waters, and the man hadn't run. That was a promising start. He stood up and advanced on Corso without speaking. He smiled when the deputy's reaction was a wide-eyed stare of quivering confusion.

Placing one big hand on the back of Bleu's neck he maneuvered his head until he felt those warm breaths across his bare navel, adding more fuel to an already unyielding erection. Recognizing it could easily go either way, he patiently waited for a sign from the deputy to show he was successfully melting under Gabriel's touch. He knew he risked another awkward miscalculation, and that the young officer could still bolt like a rabbit as he tried to escape the veil of his small-town shames. But this hadn't been one of his first rodeos. Gabriel had spent a lifetime analyzing other people's desires, and then manipulating his approach to best suit his victory in the sack. The evidence of his experience came quickly, after the young man leaned in closer and began raking his wet lips across the manly hair of Church's bush with absolute subjection.

In a matter of seconds that later felt inconsequential, they were standing completely unclothed inside the motel room and facing one another like naked combatants preparing to wrestle. It reminded Gabe of those bare-assed Roman soldiers who tested themselves in hand-to-hand before jumping into the baths and playfully splashing around the fountains and sprays like juveniles. There'd been a particular indelicacy of movement whenever Bleu attempted to wrangle out of his clothes, but for Gabe it came like fluid silk, and his command of the moment never lessened.

Raised in the Catholic Church, Gabriel had seen the ironclad control possessed by the ecclesiastical whenever it came to a good man's cock. From a young age, he knew it was one of his greatest features, and wielding it on another unsuspecting partner could be intoxicating to him. He found the deputy's shaft was no shrinking violet either; nothing in comparison to him, but then again few were.

The radio was playing a bad country tune in the background, and the air was thick with testosterone and promise. He allowed Bleu an opportunity of examining his body and watched his awestruck face as he explored every hairy crevasse and dimple of the massive frame standing before him. Corso was toned but hairless for the most part, reminding Gabe that he'd be seeing Christian this weekend. They were a lot alike. Both were intelligent, both were clean-cut, square-jawed boys from proper homes. If they had their scars and blemishes, they were better hidden on the inside than anything he displayed.

Without needing a request, the deputy fell to his knees and gingerly accepted Gabe's shaft in his tentative grip. But getting blown while standing wasn't exactly ideal to Gabe, so he crab-walked backward to reach his chair while holding Corso's jaw in his tight, oversized palms. Dropping into his chair like a king assuming the throne, he sat with hairy legs splayed apart while the deputy went to town on his manhood like a dog with a gristly bone.

Of all the masks the killer had assumed over the years, he'd never lost touch with his real desires, and he liked the wet sounds emanating around his midsection, and he enjoyed knowing that others prized him like a god. His head went back and his mouth opened with pleasure in that carnal moment, and never once did he consider whether Chris would've been heartbroken with any of his lustful deeds.

BEFORE THEY EVENTUALLY moved to the bed, there were flashes in Corso's mind, each one consisting of him interacting with citizens and wearing his uniform. The picture of him in that moment as he suckled on a stranger's cock was scandalous by comparison. He'd always been proud of the reputation he maintained in the community. But in this second, he felt it was weak and insignificant, as if he'd been living a hallucination. *It's strange; the kinds of things that can enter your brain at the worst possible moments.*

Bleu did things that evening that should have made him feel uneasy. Unfamiliar and untried acts, such as when he allowed himself to get fucked when it was a position he normally took with lovers, particularly when his partner brandished such a sizable sword that it made him feel as if he were being impaled near the point of death. Yes, there were a lot of new experiences that night. There were lies spilled on the floor like semen on those dingy sheets. He was acquiescing every traditional thing for want of something else, and he did it all without ever knowing Bobby wasn't Bobby but someone else.

Throughout two separate rounds of sweaty, engaging sex, Bobby never placed Bleu's dick between his lips. He did kiss him—though even that felt passionless and parched of any real sense of connection. Like a tide of the moon, it was meant to drive the waves toward the shore and nothing more. Every time the big man's mouth was cradled in the nape of his neck it felt somehow contrived. Though for his part, the warm breathing and sounds of fevered lovemaking had successfully worked their magic and managed to allow him to drift those naiad waters all the way to an explosive climax. The second time Bobby entered him, he ejaculated almost instantly. His hands had barely grazed his own cock—he was surprised to learn it wasn't even necessary—and he was a little shamefaced when he shot bullet sprays of semen across Bobby's comforter.

At some point, one of them got up and turned off the lights, and, after ripping off the covers, they curled front to back and lay naked together in a noncommittal embrace. The sounds coming from Bobby's side of the bed were relaxing and peaceful and reminded Bleu of an article he read once that stated they'd taken a survey to find the most restful sounds people liked to hear whenever they were sleeping. The winner, as it turned out, was the sound of croaking toads in a Malaysian pond at dusk, or at least according to their rather ridiculous online survey.

Besides the heavy masculine breathing softly wetting his ear, Bleu heard a heartbeat that seemed slightly strange to him. Even before he drifted off, he found himself counting every beat and concentrating on the pauses that came in-between. It seemed to him to sound like a muffled effort, like a stubborn artery valve that didn't really want to fully close. He thought about asking Bobby, but noticed his breaths were at least coming regularly, and he presumed he'd fallen asleep.

Hours passed by comfortably until the lawman decided to extricate himself from a situation that might feel more awkward in the cold light of dawn. Quietly slipping from under the sheets, he rummaged around in the dark for his pants and shirt, careful not to wake his host. Although he suspected Bobby was simply feigning unconsciousness because he too would understand what Bleu was doing. That the morning would bring its stale reminder of their night of passion, and that straight dudes didn't want to see the men they'd recently plowed under any other guise than too much alcohol in their bloodstream and recognition of how hard their cocks had been only hours earlier. Bobby murmured and rolled over as he pulled a sheet to his chest.

Taking a look over his shoulder, Bleu stood at the doorway and stared at the figure lying there. This view of Bobby was like seeing some alabaster statue, a marble reproduction of a Greek god without a name, sleeping like a baby, and his first inclination was to leave his telephone number scratched in a pad on the nightstand. Thinking better of it, he smiled, a congratulatory pat on his back for learning new things in a short period of time.

Getting into his car, he noticed the first rays of daylight peaking over the skyline and decided he had to haul ass if he wanted to take a shower, grab some breakfast, and get into his uniform before his shift. As he drove away, he felt more relaxed; believing no one of any consequence had witnessed him with Bobby. Or those guests of the motel hadn't awoken to watch him skulking to his car like a guilty married man in his walk of morning-after shame. In truth, he felt a little pleased with what he'd done. Like a wild-eyed cat with the mouse tail still peeking out its whiskered lips. But with every new and fresh experience, he still had that gnawing in his belly about the man he'd woken up next to. Pulling out into the main road, he decided that he had, in fact, not spent enough time researching the man. There were still tons of unanswered questions rattling the cages. No matter how forthright Bobby had been the night before, he couldn't seem to lose that unfamiliar twinge that told him something wasn't right there. He wouldn't feel better until he decided to accept his instincts as a gift, and he reckoned he'd do a deeper look into Bobby's background as soon as he had time between patrols.

Chapter Sixteen

"YOU GOTTA TAKE your pleasures seriously." Gabe had said those words to him once. It had been right after they made love that first time, while lying in bed at the Mayflower wrapped in high thread-count cotton sheets. It seemed to be a philosophy of Gabriel's, and one he was particularly proud of. Chris had looked at him red-faced while nuzzling in the crook of his arm, feeling slightly debased since he was still sticky in several hidden spots from their lovemaking. He was quietly breathing waves across Gabe's chest and recalled how his chest hair bent and swayed with every breath. It reminded him at the time of stalks of grain billowing and bowing as if pushed by a strong wind across the plains.

Chris was still trying to rationalize his feelings back then. All his feelings of deep attraction to such a disturbing figure and he was only midway through his justifications by the time they made it to the bedroom that night. He'd gone through all the lies in his head back then, the ones where he told himself it started innocently enough. But by the time he sat across from the killer with the intent of interviewing a sociopath, he was already hooked and being pulled, fighting, into the boat.

He was so excited at his prospect of seeing Gabe again that it was too difficult to focus back on those early days, where guilt was an alien intruder and he was beginning to comprehend that he was falling in love with a *monster*. By the time he allowed himself to be seduced by Gabriel, it was already too late to turn back. But he knew he was as culpable as the killer because he hadn't walked away and hadn't informed the FBI of Gabe's whereabouts. It was a shared sickness now, a disease that had spread from a serial murderer to him by his sheer complacency.

Too late to bathe in the river now, no preacher in white could hold his head below water to wash him of any sin. He was in this for the long haul, and, like it or not, he knew Gabriel would be his undoing and his salvation at the same time. Probably, he suspected, as he ran down some deserted road on foot while many cruisers flashing red-and-blue lights raced to intercept him.

But for now, he was preoccupied with his plans of seeing Gabe and all that entailed. They had chosen Central Point, Oregon, as their midway safety spot. Or, more aptly, Gabe had chosen it since it was the halfway mark, he claimed, though he hadn't divulged the name of the city he was holed up in. Chris spent a great deal of time choosing a place to stay and, after googling every hotel Central Point offered, he was getting discouraged until he stumbled onto The Bent Willows, which was a B&B with some promise. He thought staying anywhere more traditional might be too dangerous and figured an out-of-the-way bed-and-breakfast was a sound choice. The pictures online showed a large, white country inn that could've easily doubled as an individual home for someone of means. Built in the Tidewater architecture style, with stark clapboard walls and a sun porch wrapping the first floor, it seemed to Chris to be a perfect romantic getaway. In their photographs, he saw the landscape dotted by juniper and maple trees, but no willows that he could see. It boasted of a pool and a quiet courtyard in back, but Chris knew they'd rarely get to see the outside of their room. That was if he had his way.

Pictures of the interior accommodations were what finally sold him. Each room displayed a queen-sized bed with a dark mahogany headboard. The beds were covered by luxurious floral pattern comforters with matching pillows in shams. It never dawned on him when he wrote down the reservation number what the owners of The Bent Willows might say of two men sharing such a room.

Traveling along I-5 was the easiest route, and it seemed the most innocuous place he could've chosen. He hoped Gabe would be pleased with his choice as he called to see if he could reserve a suite for the weekend.

BY EARLY AFTERNOON his sexcapades with the deputy were no more than a blur, a faint edging over the horizon. And all because Gabriel didn't do guilt and had given up regret a long time ago. It hadn't crossed his mind whether this incident would become a topic of discussion for when he connected up with Christian or not. And inside he didn't care. He had his feelings for his would-be biographer; that was apparent. But this was sex, and sometimes the two didn't always intersect.

His room was beginning to have an odor of stale perspiration and sticky sex, so, after making himself a cup of coffee from the pot provided by the lodge management, he pulled on jeans and opened the door to air it out.

It was still rather cool, considering the lateness of the day. As he stood there nearly naked, sipping the bitter beverage, he stared out at the foothills of the Sonora Pass Mountains. A stunning scene and a place very much suited to his personality. Maybe it could be an ideal spot for Chris and him to set up camp, a fresh start away from the bustle of Seattle and as far away as possible from those bluegrass pasturelands of Tennessee.

He stood in the doorframe wearing only the tattered jeans and sipping a crappy cup of coffee, noticing the majesty in the emerald thicket of trees and the frost-tipped mountain ranges huddled in the distance. And, in that moment, it dawned on him that he hadn't thought about the next possible white-lighter since leaving Seattle. He wondered if that had something to do with Chris, or possibly him being blinded to the obvious while his head had been down and he concentrated hard on other things...things that seemed more important than they would've only a year ago.

He remembered a conversation he once had with Chris, when they were lying naked on the floor of the Mayflower Park Hotel. They'd just finished a round of remarkably good sex and were feeling the effects of their exhaustion. They were leaning against the sofa, all exposed atop the fine white Berber carpeting and sharing a bottle of bourbon that they passed back and forth. Chris had asked him how it felt to grow up and know you were different than your peers. Through his quiet and slightly slurred questions, he asked Gabe whether he even knew at the time that his thoughts had been skewed or somehow separate from the other children's. At the time, Gabriel thought it Chris's way of learning something new about his lover, asking him questions to determine whether he reasoned, even from that young age, just how hardwired his brain had become due to his unconventional relationship with Bennett and Sissy Church. But later, when he thought about it, he figured that had been Chris's way of asking for himself, as much as for Gabe. Like he was tracing an imaginary line of his own sexuality to find its origin point or see how it had taken him to that particular place in time, even without the obvious signposts there directing him.

"How does it feel," Chris asked, truly interested, "I mean, to see things through your eyes?"

Thinking hard on that, Gabe answered as best he could.

"It's like looking out a window to the outside world but seeing everything through a haze, like a window covered in ice and snow."

When he saw Chris's wide-eyed curiosity, he continued, "But before you can totally take in the whole image, the glass suddenly shatters, like someone threw a brick into your home in anger." He grabbed the bottle from Chris's lap. "It's like I can see myself standing there as the shards get dangerously close to my face, and in every fragmented sliver I can still see parts of the complete image frozen inside the shattered sections that are still flying toward me."

He'd seen Christian nodding out of the corner of his sightline and couldn't decide whether he was getting drunk off the bourbon, or whether he was struggling to understand everything he'd heard. Remembering that one conversation as he stood in the doorway of his room at the Queen of the Mines made him suddenly appreciate how much he had changed since meeting Chris. How he felt himself transforming and evolving simply because he knew there was someone else in the universe that identified with him, or at least someone who was currently wrestling to comprehend the dark places of his soul. He was learning a great deal more about his character.

DURING ONE OF their late-night conversations, Chris finally mentioned his visit from Special Agent Jenkins of the CID. It had been the beginning of a difficult conversation that lasted for over an hour, and it had been one he was dreading having to make. They argued bitterly that night, and accusations and reprisals flew across the air signals until both were left emotionally drained and beyond the point of weariness. But, as unpleasant as the call had been, when Chris failed to mention the detective's name or his actual title, the trouble began. Had he told Gabe that it hadn't simply been a visit from another Seattle homicide detective on a follow-up, but rather an investigator from the Washington Criminal Investigative Division, he might've heard more worry in Gabe's voice.

"I don't want to discuss my motives tonight, not here, not now, so fucking relax, you asshole!"

At least those hadn't been the words he presumed Gabriel would screech in his ear. Not about how stupid he'd been for not seeing the obvious, and that he should've known what was actually going to occur at the Keen residence. It was Shea Baltimore all over again, and another incident of his inability to see the cold-sliced reality whenever it came to Gabriel and his reasoning. Gabe was more concerned about the lie of omission than he should've been, and not about the murders of a law enforcement officer or that of his innocent wife, randomly caught inside the fray.

THEIR HEATED DISCUSSION masked certain facts that Gabe might've noticed earlier had he been informed of each facet. He might have suspected the next steps such an investigator would've taken—like when the murder of a prominent homicide detective in a city the size of Seattle could begin an investigation that might prove fateful to his survival or destiny. Sometimes it was simply too hard to fully concentrate with Chris panicking in his ears. Or when he was left to assuage any of Chris's new concerns and griefs he spewed regarding that detective and his once-pretty wife.

Chapter Seventeen

THE WASHINGTON CID truly possessed a lot of pull. Special Agent Jenkins ensured that every case that Detective Keen had ever been a part of was reopened and scrutinized without budget restriction, and with specific acumen to do the job effectively. He was tenacious when it came to losing one of their own.

He started with Keen's most recent homicide case, that of Shea Baltimore. He dissected it through clear eyes and discussed it meticulously with long-seasoned investigators. His job was made easier by laws recently changed so dramatically on the heels of Snowden, 911, the NSA, and Homeland Security. An organization with the prestigious history of the WCID easily obtained phone records for potential suspects in the murder of a homicide detective. CID didn't need a prior warrant to ping cell towers for any suspect or involved party whenever it came to a cop killing.

Judges are at their individual discretion when it comes to issuing subpoenas and search warrants for phone records, at least as far as triangulation data gleaned from the examination of cell tower locations. Maybe the ACLU would have been appalled, but when Jenkins made his verbal request via a brief conversation with Judge Leon Little, he was informed that a probable cause warrant wouldn't be necessary for his requested circumstances. Since there was no wiretapping or any phone recordings to be played in a courtroom, any expectation of privacy a person thought they held was not an issue his court felt obliged to fight. In his words, "A respected agent of the CID was requesting a simple triangulation data for a possible suspect, and/or potential witness in a homicide case." He didn't even need to utter the words, yet both men understood with clarity that it'd been the murder of a law enforcement officer, one currently on the job during the moment of his murder. If there was any apprehension in the judge's words, Jenkins hadn't heard it. And even if there were any questions or misgivings lingering there, they were suddenly lost in the mire of that one simple, unassailable fact.

When a state bureau of a criminal investigative unit requests latitude/longitude triangulation data in the homicide investigation of a detective's murder, any previously coveted common sense flies fast out the window. And thanks to the Electronic Communications Privacy Act of 1989, technically one only needed to show the data contained "specific and articulable facts" relating to an investigation. And the special agent had that in spades.

He may not have been able to pull the private phone records for calls and conversations of any of the suspects and possible witnesses listed in Keen's case file, but he could at least find out where each person, noted by name, was during the time of his murder or shortly thereafter, which was more than an adequate beginning.

During their careers, Detective Scott Keen and Agent Richard Jenkins had never crossed paths. But one can learn a great deal about an investigator by their notes. He reviewed Keen's final case file many times. Enough to see clearly each scent trail the detective seemed to be following. Each case file was actually a banker's box, and this included the Baltimore homicide. The banker's box had stacks of spreadsheets Keen had requested, each page a vehicle tag and name, and, by studying the sheets, Jenkins could actually observe Keen's investigative process as well as the simple deductions he made along the way. The chicken-scratch penmanship he scribbled was often barely legible, but he noted his thoughts inside the margins whenever he crossed off a tag or name, or highlighted another to indicate it needed to be further investigated.

Keen had produced a legal pad with a list of potential names via that spreadsheet. He crossed off the improbable suspects as he trekked through his inquiry, in much the same process as Jenkins would have done. He thought he might've actually liked this man had their paths crossed in better context, such as a shared investigation or even a social function for police. His own newly originated case file naturally held information pertaining to each victim, and a photo of Keen alongside his wife had been retrieved from the box. And like any good investigator worth his salt, Jenkins had put that picture on his assigned desk to act as his inspiration. Seeing a victim's face staring back at him every day had its way of pushing him to find some resolution, a practice Keen shared in his work as well.

While assigned to work directly from Keen's precinct during the probe, he had occasion to meet many officers and detectives who knew the man professionally. Most said better things out loud than they would've to

Keen's face directly because no one likes to speak ill of the recently deceased. But when another detective from vice walked by and noticed the photo of Keen and Carol on the special agent's temporary desk, he stopped and noted how Keen did the same thing during his investigations. How he also placed victim photos on a whiteboard, in much the same way as Jenkins. It was an idle comment, speaking to Keen's propensity and manner. But somewhere inside Jenkins a connection was fused, and the man became more driven in finding the murderer of one with nearly equal skill to his own.

With proper police work and due diligence aside, the information Jenkins uncovered seemed more disheartening than probable cause. None of the names listed in Keen's case file showed them anywhere near the detective's residence during the hours closest to the coroner's TOD. It appeared it had all been a monumental waste of his time.

But, after scrutinizing Christian Maxwell's GPS fixed location during those hours, he did notice one irregularity. Maxwell had called in sick to work the day of the homicide, which by itself was nothing. But his phone's GPS triangle placed him in another location other than his condo across town. And for several hours it pinged off one lone tower, as if the phone and therefore its owner were stationary during the time of the homicide. Again, by itself that meant next to nothing, since many people call in sick from work, and then run errands, go shopping or play like adults will do. There was no crime in that. Richard had done it himself many times. But it piqued his interest, nonetheless, and stirred him to look closer.

Most investigators already knew that triangulation of GPS signals had multiple factors. And Jenkins was equally aware that included geography, interference from structures and landscapes, a network's size or aerial capacity, as well as signal strength, to name a few. And pinging for a phone's Long/Lat GPS was a tool easily utilized as we built stronger networks and added new towers. Most cities had cell towers every six to twelve miles apart, and the federal mandate of the E911 program made that even more defined. Set up so that 911 operators could typically locate at least the general vicinity of emergency callers in distress. We were getting to a point where a caller's position could be defined within a few feet.

In his perseverance, Jenkins located the only possible location available to Maxwell's phone and determined it had to be a motel. With very few businesses surrounding the Lat/Lon address, it wasn't difficult piecing that much together. Jenkins then pulled up Google Maps and took a quick online street view tour of the area in question. It appeared to be an industrialized section of the city with very few restaurants and businesses to choose from. Other than the motel, none seemed likely, given the hours Maxwell's phone remained static. But the motel was a shit hole, and even Jenkins could see that on his monitor. His virtual tour revealed photographs of a rundown motel with its faded, red paint-chipped doors and gutters hanging dangerously close to collapse. It appeared an ideal place for addicts and hookers but certainly a dubious spot for a marketing executive to choose. That was unless he was out to procure any of the aforementioned products of ass or drugs. And, from his brief interview with Mr. Maxwell, that didn't seem the case.

What could a man like him be doing holed up for hours in a dive like that on an unscheduled day off? Certainly his place was a helluva lot nicer than that shit hole. Was he afraid of bringing a hookup to his place?

A curious step forward for the agent, it led him directly to the motel in person. Once his gold badge was flashed, alongside his confident smile, he'd been granted access to the guest registry and all the names of those who checked in and out during the highpoint of the homicide. He knew when the shifty clerk handed him the records he'd see many names, most of which he expected to be aliases. He doubted this was the kind of reservation most in good conscience would've wanted their real names associated with, but, whether or not the names were real, the vehicle descriptions and tags still could be authentic.

Those kinds of simple advancements, made by a seasoned professional tracking a killer, got authorities closer to Church than ever before. In a career of killing that spanned over a decade, no one had come as close as they were in that precise moment. And all because of a victim's personal occupation more than any other reason.

WITHOUT RECOGNIZING HIS skillset, Gabriel had become an artist in his talent of murder. Occasionally disposing of white-lighter corpses effectively had added to the randomness of the killings and equally given him an edge over the police. But that edge had become a line, and that line then became a challenge after he foolishly chose to murder a detective and his wife...and all to protect his lover from further involvement.

Church had always kept enough sanity to produce few significant errors in his killings. He believed in his heart that he could count them all on a single hand. The first came when he agreed to meet with a potential biographer to tell his tale to the world. His own personal folly to prove he hadn't been all that crazy from the beginning, and his only hope of finding some buried truth amidst all the bad he'd done over time.

The second mistake came from his growing affection for the man who agreed to write his story and teach the world his tale. While the third and harshest for him as a person fell into place when he murdered a young woman to silence her and protect Chris from further entanglement from his criminal past. But his final mistake had to come after he killed a detective, who'd stumbled onto Chris's name, and his innocent wife, who was nothing but collateral damage in his sordid and complicated existence.

It might've been comical even to Church had he listed each mistake he'd made along the way, and in the order he'd made them. But in the end he was oblivious to the series of events proving fateful to his freedom, as well as any chance he might have had in escaping all this with Chris by his side. But they were separated from every mistake he'd committed; all because of listening to a god speak directly to him about a mission to cleanse and his own promised guarantee of divinity.

What might've proved the most absurd in the face of each and every murder was that Gabriel wasn't nearly as certain about his original conviction as he'd been before meeting Christian at that coffee house in Seattle. And now, for the first time in his life, he was beginning to question his guardian deity, to wonder if he existed at all outside his barren reality. Had he known any of this with any clarity, he might have thought every tragic step he'd taken along his journey was now suddenly meaningless. The kind of meaninglessness that puts the barrel of a Glock 9mm into an open mouth after one quick silent prayer, just before the precipitous explosion.

Recently he'd gotten closer to that sensation of him nearing his resting spot. That place where he'd eventually liked to have called his home. But after he'd met that odd little writer and gazed into those inquisitive and desperately hungry eyes of his, he was making his own connections without knowing the full extent, but time wasn't a good companion in those days after Keen's murder. He was nearing something final, that much was certain. But with every good or possibly tragic future occluded from him, he'd simply have to wait for whatever dark figure fast approached him along the way. Hopefully they had some answers to many of the questions forming in his brain of late. Questions like whether he had a future bound to Chris or whether he could somehow initiate a forced amnesia of his past life once they did make it out alive, free, and whole.

JENKINS DEPARTED THE motel with a copy of each guest's registry cards during a three-day period, beginning right before the murder and for the three days after the fact. Along with that, the front clerk had offered him an empty shoebox that he crammed full with copies of each credit card receipt, DL license copies, as well as the motel's guest book signature page during that three-day span. Not surprisingly, the shoebox consisted mostly of handwritten receipts for cash in forms of carbon copy. And considering the location of the motel, its disheveled exterior, and the age of vehicles currently sitting in the parking lot, Jenkins knew most patrons there were more amenable to offering cash without a lot of questions.

Back at the precinct it took a mere two hours of vital records search to eliminate many names off the registry, and he was able to purge nearly all, save for a select few. He had developed instinct over the years, but it didn't take a super sleuth to question the reasoning behind someone like Christian Maxwell, a respected businessman and local native, checking into a rundown dive motel a mere fifteen minutes from his luxurious high-rise condo downtown. It proved to him that something was afoot. After meeting the man at his home, he could tell he wasn't a killer. In his perception, Maxwell didn't have the backbone to commit such a horrific crime, but he had a secret that he'd been trying to hide, and Jenkins knew he'd uncover that secret somehow.

The registry cards that guests were required to sign had a place for a name, a vehicle description, their tag numbers, as well as general information such as email addresses and length of stay. Naturally Maxwell's name was absent from the cards as well as the registry. But running a list of vehicle tags against owners wasn't a difficult challenge utilizing their database, and what remained became a list of five or six names that didn't match to DMV records. This became the list he decided that needed a closer examination.

Agent Jenkins realized the importance of discretion when it came to checking into dump dives like that one, usually for sexual trysts, drug vacations, or simply to remain anonymous like when celebrities attempted to maintain anonymity. He remembered reading in school how even Oscar Wilde used an alias when he checked into the Paris Hotel d'Alsace, and recalled that pseudonym had been *Sebastian Melmoth* he'd registered under. And on a whim, Christian mockingly registered under that same name. Wilde remained at the hotel during the final five days of his life, where even the hotel management, upon finding his body, attempted to arrange funeral services under his false moniker.

Therefore, the agent never expected to see Christian Maxwell's name written down, but Oscar Wilde didn't have to register a vehicle, which Jenkins knew would surely be sitting within eyeshot of the front desk clerk. And beside one of those names that he hadn't eliminated yet was a hastily scrawled description of a car matching one registered to a Christian Maxwell. It appeared he'd registered under the name of Carlos Danger. The agent smiled when reading that. Knowing he was aware of a fact he doubted the front desk clerk had been even cognizant of; that Carlos Danger was the pseudonym mayoral candidate Anthony Weiner had used during many of the sexting messages with a twenty-two-year-old, then unnamed, woman. Someone who had been a lot of things to Mr. Weiner, but one thing for certain was that she hadn't been his wife. That scandal may have effectively destroyed his career, and, at the very least, forced his resignation from Congress in 2011. It seemed that Maxwell had a similar sense of humor as his own, he thought as a faint grin emerged.

Procedure suggested that he re-interview the marketing director to gain his own answers of why he'd registered in that shithole motel on his day off, and so close to his own residence. And particularly in Jenkins's mind why it had occurred on the exact day of Detective Keen's murder. But the agent wanted to exhume every available clue prior to forcing his hand or allowing a suspect to learn any more of the case he was currently building. Though he didn't believe Christian Maxwell was capable of the detective's murder, he did think he had to be more involved than what he admitted to. And every fiber of his investigative impulse told him there was more to uncover in Maxwell's odd behavior. So he decided then he was on the right path and had to see it through wherever that led him.

With a copy of *Carlos Danger*'s receipt card and his signature on the registry page in hand, Jenkins decided to revisit the motel to grill the front desk clerk a little more. He hoped he could mine sufficient recollections, but he knew how much time was becoming his enemy. It was going on two weeks since the murder. With every passing day, he suspected the clerk's memory would fade more and more, being pushed aside by countless nights of excessive partying and every stranger's face that arrived some time close to dusk, with their twitchy pupils and shaking hands, ready to pay cash for a single night stay.

The agent didn't know the reasons why Maxwell had chosen that location, but he couldn't have chosen a better spot if he'd tried. That section of the city was turning fast into a mecca for the drug jungle. If someone needed to score a fix, they headed there; if they wanted not to be seen with a twenty-dollar hooker that was the place to go. Secrets were monetary exchanges there, and no one would've openly approached a police officer to inform them of something they'd seen or a thing out of the ordinary, as if such a thing existed down around those desolate streets.

Loath as he was to admit it, Jenkins had always found those places a little intriguing. While other agents hated crawling around the filth and human refuse trying to solidify a lead, he felt strangely different. He was drawn to the dank, dark corners and hidden settings where junkies, criminals, and reprobates hung out. Those dangerous whereabouts they liked to call their safe harbors. How could anyone, he wondered, hate the places that offered up the best leads or gave surefire insights to the targets he hunted. He had to admit that it gave his heart a jumpstart every time on the rare occasions he found a need to traipse through crack dens and burnt out foreclosures to locate a criminal informant or a suspect in a robbery homicide.

He knew where Maxwell had stayed during the hours of the Keen homicides. He even considered that the man had specifically chosen that as his out-of-the-way location where he might clean up after committing the crime. Somewhere DNA wouldn't be splattered around his condo in his haste to rid himself of the evidence before it laid a breadcrumb trail back toward the murders. But that wasn't likely.

The odds were more likely that he'd used the motel as a meeting hub with his coconspirator. Someone Jenkins suspected had a better grip on the art of murder than the erudite man whom he'd met earlier. But there was certainly the question of motive. Because when he ran Maxwell's background to that of the victim in Keen's notes, the unfortunate Shea Baltimore, Jenkins had come up empty. Maxwell and Baltimore's paths shouldn't have crossed, and, without motive, the agent had little to go on. So, with every article from the investigation in hand, he headed back to the motel, hell-bent on getting answers to the questions rattling his brain.

The clerk was as nervous as he'd been the first time. The agent could tell the kid rarely came in contact with police, and he stammered and spit out his rapid answers too quickly. His wide eyes seemed to practically scream, "Hey, I don't get paid near nuff for this bullshit. What the fuck's the owner gonna say when he finds out?"

He only rented rooms and handed out keys, Jenkins suspected. Simply an hourly wage employee whose job it was to ask few questions, collect cash, and lock-up after his shift was over. Twice in one week he'd had a visit by the police. Or what he would've assumed were police, since the agent doubted he'd ever heard of the CID. He figured the young man had chosen this as his profession because it sounded easy; he didn't appear the type with the inclination for manual labor. If he lived in the neighborhood, there'd be few choices for jobs, even low paying ones. Manning the front desk at a dive motel might sound perfect to a slacker, and he had that shirker scent all around him. Certainly he wasn't equipped to handle being grilled by a detective with questions about recent lodgers.

"What can you tell me about this guest?" Jenkins asked as he slid the registry and receipt across the counter.

The young man's pitted face appeared dumbfounded by the agent's abrupt question. He began to stammer, and his eyes darted over the guestbook the agent had slid in front of him.

"I don't remember everyone who stays here, ya know," he said in a voice that creaked like air escaping a rusty pipe.

"Well, if you remember anything, it'd help me out. And you do wanna help me out, dontcha?" Leaning over the counter, Jenkins invaded the man's personal space. He was using tactics he might use when interrogating a suspect rather than a witness, but he didn't care. The kid rubbed him the wrong way, and his hostility seemed appropriate to his cause. The younger man was clearly nervous. His pupils appeared to be scanning the room for exits and reminding Jenkins of a coon snared in a hunter's trap right as the figure was approaching with a rifle slung in his arms.

Why was he so jumpy?

The kid was probably using the motel for his own small drug trade, though nothing that would equate him to the FBI's top ten most wanted.

AFTER GETTING THE job at the front desk of the motel, little Howard Abrams, known to his friends as Howie, began renting rooms that came with more than just the tiny complementary bottles of soap or shampoo. It was hardly organized crime, but Howie learned fast how he might supplement his meager income by renting rooms that came with street drugs for an extra fee. Most of his regular clientele came in the form of other kids his age. Those who wanted to party in privacy, usually with a girl, a bag of crystal or speed, or a select group of junkie associates desiring nothing more than to get lost from their empty hours and do so under a certain guise of security.

A word-of-mouth business, barely profitable for the amount of risk, Howie thought himself quite the middleman. Someone with talent, and one who could recognize how to connect all the dots between illegal product, and the accessibility and space of a cheap room to the regular patronage, he was growing into his own small-time cartel.

But because of his own criminality, Howie became the perfect eyewitness. His gaze was forever trained to the parking lot and to every guest arriving and leaving the motel. He knew more about those who checked in than any other clerk who worked there because his survival to stay outside of prison relied upon it. He remembered with great detail every resident. Specifically those who didn't have that road-weary, blank expression on their faces or the frustrations derived from screaming children in the backseat and wives with little patience.

He remembered Carlos Danger checking in. The name itself had piqued his interest because it hadn't matched the face of the man who signed the registry that night. The guest didn't look as if he had enough Hispanic in his bloodline to be a Carlos. And who had the last name of Danger anyway...except for maybe a wannabe spy? To Howie, he appeared more like a businessman who'd chosen the wrong motor lodge from the freeway, and chosen poorly, but must've been too tired to traipse back to his car and then onto the expressway just to find someplace more suitable.

"I remember that dude; he checked in on my shift, and he only stayed a single night," he said enthusiastically. Howie began to piece the puzzle together. The agent wasn't here for him but looking for someone else. And the sudden realization of his safety changed his mood considerably.

"He wasn't all that memorable; paid in cash. I think he was here for the usual; ya know what I mean?"

The agent looked at Howie. "What do you mean by the usual?"

"I think the dude was here for a hookup," he said.

"Why would you say he was hooking up?"

"Well, he may have rented the room alone, but he was waiting on someone else. I could tell."

Then he leaned over and whispered to the agent, "And I think he was a fag since it was a dude that showed up. I was on duty when the truck pulled up, and I saw a big dude knock, then walk into 212. And I didn't see him leave, not till the next morning. It was all hush-hush like."

HIDING HIS EXCITEMENT, Jenkins tried to display his professional calm face, but he wanted more. "Did you see what the man was driving?"

"Yep...an older two-tone Dodge pickup. Beige or faded yellow over white if I recall correctly." But before the agent could absorb all he'd heard, the eager and more relaxed clerk interjected. "I even got the tag number, well part of it anyway, the second time I saw it leave the parking lot."

In the following half hour, Howie explained why he remembered the incident in such detail. He lied enough through his reasoning, but Jenkins could see that he was covering up for something. Regardless of why, it had become ingrained into his memory. And he offered the agent something fresh and new that he hadn't known before the interview. Howie began an energetic conversation and offered an ample description of the Dodge's gruff-looking driver, as well as the first few numbers of the tag that he'd glimpsed as the Dodge peeled from the parking lot in a cloud of smoke and rubber. After the truck departed, only a few minutes later, his guest, Carlos Danger, came into the office to drop off his key. He looked upset, he told Jenkins. Like a man who'd recently left the gravesite after burying his father or something. It sparked an imprint and then stamped it into his memory because he hadn't seen another man with that teary-eyed expression of sadness in a long while.

Chapter Eighteen

GABE SAW HIS future as something covered in a death shroud. He couldn't see past those petty labors of his own simple survival, and anything else he viewed he did so through an existential lens. He hadn't been given the same opportunities of a high-cost education that Christian had. And because of that, he'd never read Sartre or Kierkegaard. But if he had, he surely would've understood those concepts better than most because he saw life as an absurdity with very little meaning in the grand unraveling scheme of it all. But somehow all that changed slightly after he ran across a person eager to listen to his interpretations and learn how he'd developed his outlook.

Christian Maxwell was a soul unlike any other. He'd been the only one anxious to delve into Church's past and study his childhood. He was like a scientist, plumbing the depths of Gabriel's history because he didn't fit the mold and appeared like an unfamiliar mechanism Chris wouldn't quite discriminate to a single category. He was an enigma he needed to study further, maybe in part due to how much he admired or loved him, or maybe it was how Chris's mind worked. Church gave him that much of an advantage, thinking the writer was in his own way smarter than he was. But whatever the reason, he was someone who'd become important to him. And for the first time in his miserable life, he was beginning to see a future with possibilities, which was a feat within itself.

He reminded himself he'd be seeing Chris in a couple of days, and that knowledge comforted him in ways that he knew he couldn't fully explain to anyone else. He'd determined it was finally time to have that long-awaited discussion with Christian. The one he hoped may change his life for the better. He finally felt he was near ready to broach the subject of him and his lover getting off the road for good, of him ending the mission that had consumed every measure of his life thus far—one where he might be able to stop the killings once and for all.

Although he had his reservations that he'd be able to completely ignore the white-light radiance that had bathed each and every victim. He did think he'd be able to at least ignore the booming voice in his head, the one that had always directed him to murder. For as long as he could remember, the voice had been his only companion, and the simple act of disregarding it was more than a little disconcerting. After all, what if that was the wrong choice to make—something he'd never be able to entirely extricate from his brain? What if he couldn't ignore the voice and the killings started again when he had Chris in tow? That would place him in the same danger Church had willingly accepted as his own personal fate.

As much as seeing Christian was a comfort to him, it was also a little disquieting. He didn't know how the conversation would go and couldn't see beyond the point where his friend might see his compromise to a difficult situation, or his willingness to change. Or even whether Christian would simply walk away once their last night together was over for good.

AGENT JENKINS ISSUED a BOLO (be on the lookout) notice for the two-toned Dodge truck and its mysterious driver. And his notice went nationwide. He'd arranged for his witness, Howard Abrams, to meet with a sketch artist to further follow-up on the new lead. His confidence grew when he began to think he had enough to procure a search warrant of Maxwell's bank and residence. His working theory was that Keen had inadvertently stumbled onto Shea Baltimore's killer, and, for reasons unclear to him at that moment, Maxwell had hired someone to eliminate the detective. Possibly to hinder the investigation further, he suspected, or because he'd learned something else during the inquiry that the killer had found somewhat troublesome. But his focus was not the homicide of Shea Baltimore but that of a law enforcement officer on the job. And he wondered what ramifications would twist out for his career should he successfully close the cold case murder of the Baltimore girl while simultaneously bringing the detective's murderer to justice.

The vehicle's approximate make and model, alongside a generalized suspect description, were little to go on. Still, if the driver of the truck was somehow connected, he needed every possible officer to be on the lookout for it before it traveled too far, hence the issued BOLO. While patrol units kept a vigil for the Dodge, he'd approach a retired magistrate and hopefully obtain his warrants. If Maxwell had paid someone to murder the detective, he'd surely have paid a hefty sum, which would be revealed by his bank statements. Regardless of how Agent Jenkins may have framed his investigation when he spoke to whatever judge or magistrate available to him, he actually had very real and perceptible doubts on Maxwell's guilt. He wasn't ready to fully commit to the belief his suspect had nothing more than a passing connection to the detective's murder, or that of his wife. But because he excelled in his line of work, he learned how to master the art of keeping his cards close to the vest. He knew that every investigation, as with any police procedure, began by tossing everything you had early on against the wall, then studying whatever remained after the other debris had fallen. So he'd explain it as the way his mentors had taught him: his *Best Reasonable Standard* led to his personal belief in his suspect's involvement, and he could offer Keen's own notes should that become necessary. He hoped he could do that in a verbal request rather than a signed affidavit request. Those were the kind of details that had the potential to turn ugly when questioned by defense attorneys in a crowded courtroom.

IT TOOK VERY little time for the BOLO Jenkins had issued to go nationwide. And when a Deputy Sheriff in Sonora, California began researching the man he knew as Bobby Johnson, the pieces began falling into place in a dangerous puzzle. The artist sketch and partial plate were enough to prove there were legitimate questions about the man's identity, and it sent an icy chill shivering down Corso's spine as he read the notice. As protocol, the partial plate had been entered into ALPR, the Automated License Plate Readers system. The Department of Homeland Security had been working for years to get the database set up nationwide, but with much furor from citizens who felt the plan was overreaching and a clear invasion of their right to privacy.

Still, mobile ALPR use was widespread through most US law enforcement agencies, at county, state, and federal levels. The deputy knew a partial plate on any all-points bulletin was only as effective as the officers who utilized them. An individual notice would become a single drop of water in a sea of alerts and informational posts crashing against the rocks. If Bobby's Dodge, or whoever he might actually be, was stopped in a typical traffic situation, it only improved the chances he'd be detained or that the BOLO issuer would be contacted.

Deputy Corso had seen his share of BOLOs before, but this one had very little information posted to explain its purpose. It gave only a partial plate, the Dodge's description, and generalized suspect description, with a pencil-drawn sketch below that. Staring at the picture, Bleu thought it could've been just about anyone. It favored Bobby in size and weight. But the police artist had included a three-day growth of unkempt facial hair for his suspect. And that did bear a striking similarity to Bobby. But with all its vagueness, he suspected the BOLO would go predominately unnoticed by most officers, though it had been of great interest to him.

He felt a wall of guilt and embarrassment toppling down to bury him. As he reviewed the notice, he stared into the image and recalled how he had done the unthinkable when he allowed the man to climb on top and fuck him shamelessly in the confines of that modest motel suite. If this was the person named in this BOLO, then his first inclination was the more obvious. That fact would come to light, and his secret life would be exposed whenever he pursued it.

The background voices of officers passing through the precinct startled him back to reality. His palms were fast becoming clammy and cold, and Bleu nervously scanned the room as if he'd suddenly found himself caught by a revealed lie. The notice had the typical contact information for the issuer, and he saw it originated from the Seattle CID, with the name and telephone number for a Special Agent Jenkins posted in the alert. He sat befuddled for a minute, wavering on whether he should call the number and begin his long-winded fabrication of how he'd run across the Dodge and its driver. But then he decided that it was better to wait. Using the same desk PC all the officers shared collectively in the bullpen, he began researching the CID, the agent himself, and attempted to learn any information possible as to why the CID was looking for Bobby. Most BOLOs offered a scenario as to why the bulletin had been issued and explained the criminal offense, often elaborating as to the danger of the suspect in question, whether or not the suspect was armed and considered dangerous, and why they were wanted or implicated in any crime, but this had nothing of the sort.

Maybe Bobby was simply a witness to a crime. Maybe he was the key to a larger offense but not actually guilty of anything. Bleu knew how ridiculous the idea was. Still, it crawled like hope across his gray matter as proof that he hadn't recently slept with a killer himself. He had to be wanted for something important because, after all, he suspected Bobby Johnson wasn't his real name, and good people didn't pretend to be someone they weren't. Not unless they were already as guilty as shit.

Bleu whisked up the bulletins he'd pulled from the communal fax, hiding the BOLO of the Dodge inside the stacks of other alerts, and then headed to his cruiser. He'd have to think long and hard about what he was going to do with his new information. Maybe occupying his brain with his typical patrol could help him forget about it for a bit, but he somehow doubted it. He needed to consider this heady thing, and he wanted sufficient time to digest it before making any rash moves that could end his career or even worse.

"WHAT ARE YOU doing now?" Gabriel asked over the phone.

"Would you believe drinking a screwdriver and lounging around in my robe?"

He could hear the smile creeping across Chris's face, even across all the miles separating them.

"I took the rest of the week off because I guess I'm getting excited about finally being able to spend some quality time with you."

A brief lull in the conversation seemed confirmation of his happiness. Both men it seemed were allowing the call to wash over them like a satisfying summer rain. Most of their recent conversations had gotten too heavy, and it was nice to have one decent talk that didn't include all the strain they'd created in their lives.

"Yeah, it's gonna be sweet," Gabe whispered into the phone.

They rarely talked during the daytime. Most calls happened in the wee hours of the evening. But the night before, Chris had begged Gabe to call him the next morning. He hadn't offered an explanation as to the change in protocol, but his eagerness was coming through in waves. Gabe didn't mind, though; it was pleasing to hear his lover's voice. It felt as if it were a mooring rope tethering him to a safer shore. They didn't discuss police or murder investigations or anything as dark as that. They talked about the minutia of everyday life. And Christian offered the news of what he'd found, in the way of a bed-and-breakfast near the midway point and all the plans they'd have to cram into their brief time together. What didn't need discussing was sex. Their first day was already allocated for lying in bed and screwing like high school kids whose parents were out for the evening. And they discussed doing other, more traditional, things as well: movies and dinners and even a long country drive through the unfamiliar countryside.

"WELL, WHAT ELSE do you have in mind?" Chris asked.

"I thought I'd turn you inside out, like my pockets at closing when the bar's thinning out." Gabe offered mischievously.

With the conversation having taken a decidedly sexy spin, Christian felt his cock growing stiff under his robe knowing Gabe was in the same boat with little else to do but jack for relief. "You're making me hard with the prospect, mister," Chris replied cheekily. "But hang on to it. Or rather, don't hang on to it. Not until we get together."

"Per usual, you ask a great deal of me," Gabe said with a throaty chuckle.

With his illicit afternoon vodka and juice beginning to loosen his once taut wiring, Chris began spitting out reminders of their earlier times together. It was like reliving old pleasant memories; ones that were, in fact, not that long ago. They could've discussed any number of ancient histories. Chris might've discussed college parties or Gabe talked about those he'd met through decades of drifting. But it was almost like they were trapped in that one point where they'd first met; always yanked back to the single joyous time where anything more was a stretch to their faculties, as if it were a sweet nostalgia recently pulled back into the light.

"Yeah, that really was a fun and weird weekend," Gabe said in closing to one of Chris's stories. Then with a haunting silence on the other end of the line, Chris jumped to the conclusion it had brought something back with it. A monster recently reawakened from its slumber.

"Hey, buddy. I hope I didn't bring back any bad memories," he whispered coyly.

"Bad memories are pretty much all I have," his lover said assuredly. "Well, besides the ones we had that weekend."

With his tone lilting up in the end, it seemed Gabe's way of reminding Chris he had experienced some good times, despite the shit storm that had become his life this year.

After a long awkward pause, Chris finally said, "Well, babe, just hold to the safety bar till the weekend. Don't forget we'll be together soon, and I can't fuckin' wait."

"Right, buddy," he said as if he'd just remembered something that had escaped his brain.

"And keep your paws off your dick, boy—I want you primed and ready for me alone."

Chapter Nineteen

AFTER DISCONNECTING FROM the call Chris walked around his apartment feeling either a little lost or a little drunk; he wasn't sure which. He didn't know what to do with himself after his conversation with Gabe. He was running on enthusiasm and raw tingly nerves, and it felt like it had been years since he' had anything like spare time to kill. This could all be the plot for some great novel he'd one day write. Even though he knew how insane that image was. First of all, he didn't have sufficient talent to describe his attraction to a killer like Church. Not to mention it would require an admission of his guilt, a practical 200-page confession inside a slick paper jacket with his face on the back cover. He pictured himself signing copies of his book in a trendy, well-lit shop. He'd be seated at a table in the unfamiliar surroundings of a strange metropolitan city. He then pictured his own smile fading as two men in dark nondescript suits pushed their way past the line of eager patrons awaiting his signature. Clearly intent on arresting him right there in the book store while all his fans watched in horror.

A bizarre chain of events led him to this point; an unexpected series of challenges where he met a killer and then found that he'd fallen deep into the rabbit's hole of that murderer's abnormal life and circumstances. He wasn't able to write that kind of tale. He knew no reader would ever find it believable. That was what Gabe represented to him, the danger of the unknown and the constant struggle of understanding what had created him and what propelled him forward.

And then there was the sex. And that single prospect alone kept him tangled with excitement. He had gone through those intimate moments over and over. Usually at night, when he lay under the covers feeling more alone than he had before meeting Gabe, who'd certainly transformed his life into something completely alien. And that didn't look as if it were going to change anytime soon.

IF SOMEONE WERE to inject Gabe's veins with sodium pentothal and then ask him to speak every secret he had buried in his heart, they would hear Christian's name slurred through the furor of his hallucination. Mixed somewhere between the tales of murder and the white-light incoherent ramblings, a picture might surface of his true and unadulterated feelings for another person. Surprisingly for some, it wouldn't be a family member or a longtime female companion or a beloved pet. It would be another male.

Most of our sexuality can be divided into subset categories, and, where Christian was concerned, it began with his hero-worship and adoration. He saw a distinct image of a confident and powerful man. One he couldn't deny possessed every physical and personal trait that he felt he lacked most. It began that simple, though it changed quickly.

For Church, it was slightly different. He saw someone who cared enough to learn more about him, someone who appeared genuinely concerned about his well-being. That had been a first for a man years on the run, where all his time was spent alone and his life was all but untethered.

He couldn't deny Christian had a calming effect on him. Lying next to him in bed as he slept safely burrowed in the crook of his arm gave him an unexpectedly peaceful feeling. For the second time in his life, he was discovering how much he wanted to protect someone other than himself. He wanted to become that white knight guardian he'd pictured himself to be. Not since he'd driven out of his parent's driveway back in Tennessee, leaving his little sis and mother alone, had he felt that sensation of being a defender of the meek or dutiful. And despite that, he wasn't a man prone to guilt; even he recognized how difficult that particular decision had been. He was leaving frail figures behind, those ghosts of his past who were either too young or lacking in sufficient backbone and grit to stand against the likes of one such as his father, Bennett Church.

Gabe had wondered many times since meeting Chris if this hadn't been his salvation, his one chance to abandon all those specters from the past. A humble do-over for those innocent faces he saw standing in the rearview as clouds of dust and smoke as his Chevelle tires squealed their getaway. He had a chance to finally make it right. A chance to save one life in the least, when he hadn't had the courage to save those who should've mattered.

Sprawled across his bed, still gripping the burner phone, he stared at the ceiling and contemplated his life completely. It was usually the man on his deathbed who counted all his regrets, as if they were treasured coins stacked in columns on his nightstand. But he wondered how much of an albatross he'd become for those around him. He'd killed many people during his lifetime, and a few he knew had been innocent. Like Shea Baltimore, who only died because he'd made a single mistake when he decided to fuck her without considering the outcome. And then there was that detective and his innocent, attractive wife. She'd been a nice enough woman, someone who stirred some confusion in his head when he thought about how good she might be in the sack. And there was Christian Maxwell. The one person worth anything to him because he'd stuck with him despite knowing every awful thing he'd ever done.

A trail of bodies discarded in his wake, like so much litter and refuse scattered along the interstate. Not to mention every white-lighter whose life he'd snuffed out. At the direction of a God he knew he was finally losing contact with. His instinct and confidence to know he was doing something righteous and good was fading into the background. And he suspected Christian was the cause of all that.

Shaking off the bad vibes, he stood and headed toward the shower. He hoped standing under a hot spray would rinse away the perceptions he'd allowed himself to wallow in. Like so much dirt or highway dusts circling the drain. As he stripped out of his clothes and stepped onto the grimy lime-encrusted tile, he wondered if he was going to tell Chris about his tryst with the deputy. He'd already told himself he never suspected Maxwell was remaining faithful to his memory, though in his heart he knew that was nothing but a full-blown lie. Although he considered sex a natural inclination that all men needed on a regular basis, he actually doubted his lover had attempted it with anyone else yet. He wasn't the type to require a little passing-night strange with some anonymous trick just for relief from a full set of balls. He was far too much in love at the moment. But as the water and suds mixed and collected at his feet, Gabe knew if he were to think about it for very long, any prospect of his lover's infidelity would've made him feel slightly disappointed...and maybe even a little angry.

CRUISING THE STREETS of Sonora in his patrol car was a challenge the next afternoon. Bleu couldn't keep his mind focused on the mundane tasks of his job. Before his shift began, he'd stopped in at the diner for breakfast, as had become his custom. With every friendly face of each denizen in his hometown whenever they passed him at the counter with a gentle slap of appreciation on his back, he felt a cold shiver racing beneath his skin. He wondered if this was going to be the beginning of the end, one where he'd no longer be able to wear the uniform and bask in the community's respect as he had before.

He'd learned to cope with secrets he'd been carrying before then, but this was entirely different. If the gossip mill ran amok with stories of him being gay, that might be one thing. But if news broke that he was removed from the force or fired for having sex with someone who could be a wanted killer, then he knew the stories would never fully dry up. They'd crisscross Tuolumne County like a fire left unchecked, and he felt perpetual worry with what that might mean for his father and the staunch reputation the man had so sorely prized.

You probably should've thought about that already, he chastised himself.

The voices bouncing in the hollows still echoed with his father's timbre, and every word he heard was laced with disappointment and sullen surprise. He'd wanted to be a cop for as long as he could remember, and now his dick was going to upend that life and change his fate forever. He worried that he'd have to move away. And while leaving Sonora might have been a hopeful prospect, as much as it would've been sad to leave his hometown, he naturally assumed when it did it would come after a job offer at another precinct and something in law enforcement, since he'd made that his chosen field. Not this kind of embarrassment or this type of forfeiture for every plan he'd once made for his life. And that was a little discomforting.

But he knew one thing for certain. He wanted to question Bobby before making the call to the Washington CID offices. He wanted to know if he was even correct about his assumptions before alerting authorities. Hiding under all his shame was still a small distillation of hope buried in the sand.

After a few hours of that single thought occupying his mind, and just when he figured he couldn't take it anymore, he decided to drive over to the Queen of the Mines Lodge after work and confront the man. He didn't know Bobby well, or whoever he actually was. But he had spent time with him in public and even more wrapped in a sweaty embrace. Still he couldn't gauge how the big man would react after hearing Bleu grill him on who he was, or why he might be wanted by the authorities.

He couldn't call ahead since they hadn't exchanged telephone numbers. And as he weaved through those same city roads he'd driven throughout his adult life, he found himself unconsciously taking back roads and boulevards he rarely found himself driving. He wasn't doing it intentionally, so, when he noticed his surroundings, he immediately guessed it must be like sneaking back to the scene of a crime. But this wasn't any typical call that he might've monitored on the police band, it was his offense. And with every block his cruiser passed, and every corner he took at higher speeds than normal, he felt as if he were closing the gap from everything he'd created in his life to whatever end sat perched under the shade of those tall pines on the outskirts of downtown.

"So, deputy, you feeling a tad bit horny? Thought you might stop by for round two?"

He could almost hear Bobby saying the words. And with that, a pit inside his stomach began to expand with every mile he passed, taking him closer to his destination. Just after six in the evening, the sun was drooping lazily over the horizon as he pulled into the parking lot and noticed the two-tone truck that had started it all. It was still parked just where it'd been left, and the sight of it suddenly turned that pit into an uncomfortably sized boulder in his gut. He got out slowly, instinctively reaching his hand to finger the holster on his right hip—a reflex—a gesture he performed every time his dispatcher directed him to a scene of potential violence or where dangerous elements could alter an outcome.

He'd almost hoped that Bobby's Dodge wouldn't be parked in the lot, but there it sat. He was able to walk up beside the dusty beast—that had clearly seen its share of mileage—as he sauntered bravely up to the motel door. He inhaled deeply and forced a congenial smile to his face. He gently knocked once, in a sound that felt familiar and affable. Then he simply waited.

Chapter Twenty

BOBBY PRACTICALLY ENGULFED the whole frame of the door as it swung open. He stood there, obviously fresh from a recent shower, with his dark, tousled hair still dripping with water like the last remnants of a summer rain. Across his broad, naked chest, damp spots were still visible buried among the fur of his chest hair. With a wet towel in one hand, it was clear to Bleu that he'd been planning on heading out soon. He was wearing nothing but his tattered Levi's, and standing there barefoot and shirtless, he appeared the epitome of masculine sexiness carved in stone. He didn't say a word, simply leaned against the doorframe and smiled back in a lascivious broad grin with a twinkle forming in both pupils—evidence to Bleu that his earlier assumption had been a correct prediction of the man's mood.

Corso's eyes were drawn to the open top button of the denim, as if the man had forgotten it in his haste to reach the door. Or had it been more purpose than accident, he wondered? The open fly barely covered the crest of pubic hair and enhanced the trail of fur that crept farther into his jeans like a sensual invitation and a begging of future exploration.

"Well, hey there," Bobby said as the grin stretched wider. "I didn't expect to see you tonight." Though a statement, it was also more. Peering first right and then left suspiciously, he quickly stepped aside to allow the deputy to enter.

"Sorry I didn't call first," Corso stammered, "but I didn't get digits the other morning, 'cause you were still sleeping. And I didn't want to call the front desk to have them ring you."

"Not a problem," Bobby said emphatically. "I'm glad to see you now."

Entering the motel when sober was a strange sensation for Bleu. He was nervous and began to instantly regret his reasoning for the visit. He thought he was coming off like some love-struck stalker, and that made his stomach queasy. They'd met, they'd fucked once, and now he was standing there unannounced, and he could once again hear the words rattling around in his head: *"Thought you might stop by for round two?"*

"Are you headed out?" Bleu stuttered, eyes flashing toward the closed door.

"Eventually, maybe grabbing supper or a drink," Bobby said in a fashion that seemed to leak sexual innuendo in the smallest of ways. "Take a seat, buddy. You just coming off a shift?" he asked waving to the open salon chair?

"Hate to pop up uninvited, but I was hoping we could talk." Bleu gingerly took his seat. He watched the man he knew as Bobby move across the room like a shadow and felt the atmosphere in the small room dip to match his mood. Even in the dimly lit motel with the curtains drawn, he could still make out the small gestures of a man who appeared cornered and uncertain.

"Sure, deputy, what's on your mind?" Bobby said as he moved cautiously to an available chair, feet from where the officer sat. Grabbing an open-back rail chair the motel graciously provided its guests to fill up the empty space comprising the kitchenette, he hoisted it across the bare rug and assumed a straddled position. His legs splayed apart as he towered over the chair back, which appeared to Bleu to be his rather obvious attempt to tease and tantalize his visitor with his shit-eating grin and casual posture.

"So, what are ya waiting for?" Bobby said after too long a pause invaded the room and the silence seemed deafening.

The deputy hesitated before muttering, "Well, I wish."

But, before he could continue, his face went cold and he felt distant, as if any hold he once had of wherever he was headed suddenly released its grip. Whatever he'd intended to say was now lost to the ether, like some smoke signal caught on a breeze.

"Well, you know what they say. If wishes were horses, even beggars would ride," Bobby said with an impatient grin. Bleu thought he looked as uncomfortable as he was, but maybe for different reasons.

"Umm...what?" Bleu asked, confused. He'd carefully planned what he was going to say before he arrived, but now he couldn't quite grasp how he needed to broach the subject. And the man wasn't making it easier, sitting there in that seductive stance and eyeing him hard with his annoyed furrowed brow.

"It's just a saying I heard as a kid," Bobby said flatly. "Something my mama used to say." Then to the officer's relief, he rose from his chair and grabbed a half-full bottle of bourbon from a counter in the kitchenette. "I don't know about you, but I think a drink's in order. Can I splash some in a glass for you?"

WITHOUT WAITING FOR a response, Church dragged out two cups and poured two full glasses for him and his guest. "I don't have any soda handy, so it'll be straight...then again, you like 'em straight, right?"

Like the beggar's quote, Church had heard another phrase he suddenly recalled: "cutting the tension with a knife." That was the stifling feeling he was getting in that dark motel room in that second. He knew the deputy had something he desperately wanted to say, and at first he assumed it was gonna be his declaration of his undying affection. He had a way about him. He'd always been fairly confident that he excelled in the sack, and the proof came through in the faces of every man or woman he satisfied. Many times they'd crawl back for more and offer themselves up like sacrificial lambs of sorts. He'd thought this was what this was at first. But now he could see it was something deeper, more important, the blank concerned stare on the lawman's face said it all.

"Spit it out, deputy. What's got you racking your brain so?"

"Back at the station I noticed an all-points bulletin. It seems someone's interested in your old truck, maybe even chatting with ya up close and personal."

THERE. I'VE LAID it out for Bobby to address, and he thought he'd done it with enough casual ease that he hadn't startled him. But without knowing otherwise, he would've been incorrect.

"All points, huh?" Bobby said without expression in his voice, and Corso's spine muscles tightened as the man moved closer to hand him the plastic cup full of bourbon. Almost as if he hadn't a care in the world.

"You know, dude, I really doubted your name was Bobby," the deputy offered bravely. "You didn't strike me as a Bobby then, or now."

"To be truthful, it isn't," Church said, retaking his chair and swilling his booze in a big gulp. "Actually my name's Gabe."

"Good to know," the officer said as he forced a smile and tried to remain calm. "I always like to know the name of those I fuck."

"Or get fucked by," Gabe said, correcting him.

Then, there it was again. That crooked self-serving grin of his; that suggestive, nearly evil smile, which had been so alluring from the first moment in that fateful traffic stop. He certainly was full of himself.

"So it is your Dodge that Washington wants to find? You're admitting that much?"

GABE BRIEFLY CONTEMPLATED what to say and then decided, rather rashly, to be more honest with him than he ever had—with the single exception being Christian, naturally.

"Yes, they might be looking for my truck. And certainly they wish to get me in an interrogation room for a chat."

"You wanna say why?" Corso asked, as he sipped slowly from the cup, never taking his eyes off him.

Church tried to appear relaxed, though in truth he was performing rudimentary tasks he'd grown accustomed to, such as figuring the distance to the door and what it'd take to overpower the deputy. He became frustrated when he remembered his trusty Glock was presently stowed in its usual hiding place, and that was in the Dodge outside and too far away in that split second to do him any good. He was pissed at himself for being foolish and unprepared, which wasn't like him. He hadn't stayed as many steps ahead of the police by being as sloppy as he felt then. He needed his firearm, and mentally he was kicking himself for not having it close at hand—somewhere that he could get to it quickly. Yet to an outside observer, one would never have seen how busy he was, running scenarios and calculations in his head because his confident expression never faltered. He became a thing of cold stone, barely readable to anyone, even to the deputy who was mere feet from his chair.

"The BOLO I saw was pretty short on details," Corso prompted quietly. "It didn't say what they wanted you for. And I'm still hoping you'll tell me; maybe give me a reason not to have to take you down."

"Bold and fearless, like I figured you'd be," Church said without completing the thoughts running through his brain. When the officer finally looked down at his cup, Church could see a wave of shame creeping over the man.

"Before we discuss me, deputy, I have a question for you."

The sound of an engine pulling up in the lot outside momentarily broke the tension hanging in the air. Church considered for an instant that it might be Corso's backup police arriving. But when he didn't see blue-and-red lights streaming through the closed curtains or hear the rush of voices of excited cops about to burst through his door, he turned back to Bleu and said, "You obviously have your own issues, buddy. I presume you're somewhat closeted at work, and Sonora isn't that big of a city. Surely you've risked some sexual encounters other than me."

"What does that have to do with the price of tea in China?" Corso was surprised and slightly angry.

"Well, I was thinking that everyone has secrets, right?"

The sound of a car door slamming and then the muffled words of a male guest arriving back at the motel could be heard over the dead quiet in Church's room. The man was arguing with a woman, presumably his wife. Then heavy footsteps trailed off as the newcomers entered a neighboring suite and another door slammed, suggesting they'd taken their heated discussion inside.

After a brief pause, Church continued, "I was just mentioning how we all have something to hide, and before I told you mine, I wanted to ask you yours."

LIKE GUNSLINGERS IN the Old West, both men were at a standoff, and the deputy was considering the weight of the gun holstered on his right hip. He didn't want to have to draw, and part of him hoped he wouldn't have to. He still thought an explanation was a possible way out of the nervous energy building in his chest.

He was confused about what Gabe wanted, but glared back when he finally realized his former trick wanted to hear his confessions first. He figured if he wanted to hear any of "Gabe's" truths, he'd have to respond in kind.

"Yeah, no one at the station knows I've sucked a few dicks in my life—so what?"

"That's not what I wanted to know, officer. I wanted to know if you ever loved anyone, and, in particular, if that person might've been male."

"The punch line here being you have?" Bleu asked

Gabe's demeanor changed from the deputy's question as if he had to suddenly confront that lone fact for the first time. "I suppose I have," he said finally. "I ask you the same thing because I know what it means to be in love. It is, after all, the single reason I'm here in Sonora."

The minutes in the motel felt all but incomplete to Deputy Corso. Each second seemed to linger in the air as if it were awaiting its own form of acknowledgment. He'd seen it before. It was the same reason suspects never spoke freely during an interrogation. They were waiting for the time to be over, their chance to have others show their own hands before the waterworks began. It felt like that. And, in the labor of those seconds, neither man said much at all.

"When you find that one person who eventually connects you to the real world, it makes you better...don't you agree?"

If Gabe had expected an answer, he didn't wait to hear one. Instead, in the failing light of the motel room as dusk turned into evening, the officer could see the man tearing up and pupils that took on a distant, longing gaze. He could tell that whatever memory the man was navigating, he was doing it solo, and his presence as an added passenger in that journey was not only unnecessary but unwarranted.

"But what do you do if the struggle to keep that person safe becomes an overwhelming challenge, like God or destiny is working too fuckin' hard against you. Like someone wanting you to fail?" Gabe's voice trailed off as if those last six words were intended for his ears alone.

The deputy had the sudden impression he'd walked into the middle of someone else's play, and he didn't know the whole cast or know the setup. It was that kind of sensation that demanded one wait patiently. As if he could simply ask someone during intermission to explain the parts he'd missed. But it wasn't going to be that easy.

"So, you are wanted for a murder?" Corso asked, downing the last gulp of alcohol courage.

"Probably many," Gabe replied, staring off at some invisible horizon line in that dark, confining room. He was already gone. In the middle of some dying declaration of sin that made him realize the obvious. The cop in him knew he was suddenly confronting a caged animal, and that made him even twitchier.

But Gabe didn't look caged, nor did the expression on his face change. He still looked relaxed, despite his confession. In Bleu's perception, he was an engine running on idle, a man who didn't appear all that desperate or all that dangerous. Not that the deputy would've allowed himself to grow slack like his adversary. His open palm edged minutely closer to his holster, but with a glance to imply the bigger man had already suspected that outcome, Gabe stood slowly, so as not to startle his guest into any impulsive action.

And he said rather quietly, "You need a refill, handsome. And now, I do as well."

MOVING GINGERLY TO the officer's chair, Gabe extended his hand to grab Bleu's empty cup. He clearly saw how brave the deputy was when Corso offered his cup to Gabe without any indication of pretense or noticeable alarm in his eyes. He knew this had to be an odd predicament for the lawman, who was sitting all tranquil and pretty in that motel room with a confessed killer. A man he'd recently wrestled naked with on that same queen-sized bed mere feet from where he sat presently.

"Wish I had some ice to offer, but I didn't know you were coming by," Gabe said with a smile tossed over his shoulder. He filled both glasses with bourbon, but then, with a reflective look, he decided to splash some cold tap water in their drinks in lieu of ice.

"Less than straight, but we like that too," he said, returning Corso's glass to him.

He was sporting that suggestive, somewhat sinful, grin of his. The smile the deputy was learning now could be both endearing and deceitful at the same time. "We certainly don't need you to get foggy from the booze, deputy," the man said, retaking his own chair across the room.

"I have to assume you came here without backup?" Gabe asked with cold measured words. "Maybe you just wanted to see if I was really wanted by another agency somewhere...before you had to admit to your superiors how you came to know me in the first place?"

Corso smiled over the rim of his glass. The man was certainly clever. Or at least he could read the situation well. But knowing that became a tad unsettling. This man was a criminal, after all. But to his credit he had guessed correctly. The deputy hadn't arranged for backup, and now all he felt was green and unsophisticated, since he hadn't actually told another soul that he was going to the motel. No one knew he was even there.

He knew there'd be no cavalry topping the hillside behind him. He was alone and with someone that'd casually professed to be a killer. Corso had to fight against the instinct of reaching for his service weapon, which was the only consideration racing through his brain in that moment. He suspected he could reach his gun, but the man sat closer than he'd have preferred, and he didn't like his chances it wouldn't go quickly south.

Yet he had to acknowledge that inside all he really felt besides the twinge of raw nerves was something he could best describe as *curiosity*. The man had mentioned about being in love with someone and some rambling statement about it being why he was in Sonora in the first place. Could he have an accomplice Bleu hadn't met? Was a stranger about to come barreling out of the bathroom with a gun in hand?

AS IF BY telepathy, Gabe saw concern flashing in the younger man's pupils. "You don't have to worry; we're all alone here," he said, scratching the three-day growth of irritation building on his chin. "In fact, the man I was speaking about isn't anywhere near California." Then thinking further down the path, he added, "He also doesn't know I've murdered anyone. That's a secret only you and I share."

His lie was intricately crafted on the spur of the moment. He knew his best chance of making it out unscathed was ricocheting somewhere between slim and none. But he couldn't fathom the addition of one more brick into the mortar of that prison wall that he believed was quickly circling Christian. It had been his fault from the beginning. That much he knew. And the lunacy of piling body over body to protect someone he once considered innocent had placed Chris down deep in the same scurry hole where Gabe now hid. He had red neon flashing in his brain now, thinking of how idiotic this whole thing had become and how quickly it had managed to swell out of control. He'd never meant for any of that to happen, and he felt the shame of his own ego, like when he first agreed to let his writer ever tell his tale.

The air had become thin where he was. Cold arctic winds blew on his face as he stood on the edge of that unfamiliar precipice. His awful realizations were suddenly made whole. He was finally beginning to understand things that had escaped him: that everything he had wrought upon the world now had no ambiguity. He understood with instant clarity that this was his first big-picture viewing of that exact spot where his destruction would come to fruition. In his mind, he could see a litter of sprawled, awkwardly bent figures on the ground below. And for every face he could barely make out, he noticed it was the face of someone he recognized most.

He saw Christian Maxwell's face on one, Sissy Bennett's on another. Even Shea and the detective were there, lying broken on the earth beside the detective's once-pretty wife. Every rumpled form became a cadaver then, and each face was puckered skyward, wearing a lifeless, glassy gaze. Even the color of their pupils had drained away, and every expression he could read seemed burned to an alabaster white.

Chapter Twenty-One

GABE WONDERED WHAT Chris might be doing in that same moment, the instant that would change everything for him.

"Let me ask you," he said, turning toward the deputy sitting in that corner chair obscured by shadows. "Is your mother still living?"

Corso's face seemed shocked by the randomness of his question, and he stammered back, "No, she died when I was hitting my teens. Why do you wanna know?"

"Mine, too, at least I suspect she is, might not be, but let's say for argument's sake she is. What would you say was your mother's best quality?"

"I dunno. Haven't thought about that," the lawman stuttered, clearly astonished at how suddenly the conversation had turned.

"My mother was a weak-willed woman, but she loved animals," Gabe said in his most reflective tone. "She would've been surrounded by animals if her husband had allowed it." Then moving slowly to refill his glass, he said, "But he was an asshole who wouldn't have anything of the sort. In his eyes, a house pet either earned their keep or they became worthless."

CORSO WATCHED AS the unlikely transition washed over his one-time lover. This was completely out of Gabe's character. But he sat rapt with attention, and, for the first time since arriving, he wasn't thinking about his service weapon.

"My mother—Sissy was her name, by the way—used to find all kinds of strays when we lived back in the boonies. Dogs, cats, orphaned fawns. Just about every species ended up hobbling up to our farm. And she'd name every single one that popped up. The names didn't stick for long 'cause eventually her husband would traipse off to the woods, pulling the stray dog in question by a leash or the freshly born kittens screeching in an old tow sack."

The deputy was transfixed. And, though he'd been listening to the story, he replied with, "So you were raised on a farm?"

IGNORING HIS QUESTION, Gabriel was already lost. He was remembering the fields of his Tennessee youth and his long walks over swaying bluegrass with its vast stretches of empty space, speckled slightly by the occasional sagebrush or pin oak sapling.

"The bags of kittens eventually found their way to the shallow waters of the creek out back. The pups were never heard barking though. Just a single shot explosion of my father's handed-down Remington bolt action."

After a substantial pause, the deputy asked, "Why are you telling me this?"

"Because, officer, that was something I remembered about my mother that was good, and I figured you had some good memories, as well. Are there any you want to share?"

"I think I'd rather know what you're wanted for by the Washington police." Bleu said with effort to keep his words level and predictably calm.

With a resolute *humph*, Gabe retook his chair and, after a silence which seemed to last an eternity, he finally said, "Okay, then let's get to it. But remember, deputy, my story may have a bearing at some later point."

Church began to speak about the last few years of his life, but consciously kept Chris's name out of every fabrication he weaved for the lawman. He noticed how blindly captivated Corso seemed to be as he skirted closer to the edge of his chair. He also noticed how his fingers were no longer twitching nervously. Like when his guest had been heavily contemplating pulling his firearm and attempting to take him by force of the gun alone. But if he'd done that, Church mused; he wouldn't hear the whole story. And even through the darkness of his confession, he smiled at that notion.

The story he spun borrowed parts of his own reality. Some parts he simply made up or recounted from newspaper articles he'd read once or television shows he'd seen in countless motels. He wanted it to sound believable, and even sufficiently gory, but he needed to leave some things out. Like the part where he met Christian Maxwell and any involvement he may've had in his murders of Shea and the detective. It wasn't all fiction...but it was close. Close enough for government work, he thought, remembering what the ole rube had said to him once.

He told the officer how he liked the idea of being hunted. Distracting him and making him nervous whenever he mentioned how it made his dick hard even thinking about it. Gabe shifted his weight and readjusted how he sat in his chair. He wanted to observe the wet embarrassment as it turned the deputy's face red. He used plenty of vague terms when it came to cities and victim's identities. He wanted the officer to be inquisitive, even ask for more. He was good at reading others and knew Corso wasn't just intrigued with his narrative—he was lapping it up like milk from a cat's bowl.

"You have questions, I'm sure," Gabriel Church said rather flatly.

"Why?" In his confusion, Corso couldn't even finish the question, though it wouldn't have been necessary; that he knew. Church didn't want to sound insane, even if he truly was. This had been the driving force of wanting his story told in the first place. It had been the catalyst that had altered his future from that first second, that moment when he foolishly believed he could tell his story and not sound like he'd simply fallen off his beam.

He didn't want the deputy to look at him with those same eyes that Chris had. His early staged expression of shock and fear that he'd somehow managed to power through over those early days. He had, at least, learned that much from their time together. So, he tried to play down the whole white-lighter mission thing, shrugging his shoulders and feigning confusion to stall for time. It was better that they think him crazy for one sin, in lieu of another.

One thing was certain to Church: his Glock 9mm couldn't help him here. He hoped he could divert the lawman with his wild stories, and he hoped he could move fast enough across the room that he might force the young man from his chair to wrestle him to the ground and wrench the gun from either his hand or holster. He knew that was his only chance for making it out of the city alive and free. Even with this flooding realization filling up his brain, he was regretting it. He didn't like the idea of one more corpse lying in his wake, particularly someone as sexy and smart as the deputy. Before he could fully react, the lawman broke his concentration.

"You've killed many people then?" he asked.

"Enough to matter," Gabe said coolly. "More like an outbreak of mortality in whatever city I found myself."

"Without any reasoning...just random slaughters?" the deputy asked.

BLEU WASN'T EVEN trying to hide his disgust. He was more alarmed as to the *why,* more than the deed itself.

How could he have not seen that during their conversations?

He'd trusted the man. Enough to follow him back to his motel. He'd gotten naked and even fucked him, and suddenly it was incalculable then that he hadn't seen it more clearly. What kind of officer was he, not to see that glaring fact staring him down, he wondered? That single shock outweighing everything else in that one particular moment.

AND THE SURPRISE Gabe saw on his face gave him the green light to act.

It's now or never, he thought, as he flung his body forward and pounced like a juggernaut against the chair where his lawman sat. Corso's training must not have prepared him as much as it should have because in that split second the bigger man towered over the deputy. With his free hand, he grabbed for the deputy's right arm and twisted. Clearly Bleu thought he was trying to stopgap him from reaching his service weapon, and it was surprisingly effective as a technique.

It was difficult to fend off an attacker from a seated position, and Gabe utilized that. He forced Corso backward by propelling his body onto his, and, with a jerk of his knee, he went straight for the deputy's crotch. He then heard his own words echoing in his skull as he thought, *Now that's a policeman's ball I can really get behind!*

THE PAIN WAS excruciating. Corso heard the muffle of all his oxygen being expelled from his body while simultaneously trying to wrestle the killer off his chest. He felt a small explosion in his gut as his testicles were crushed in the force of Gabe's attack. He knew it was a death struggle, but all he could remember was how this was a first for him. Throughout his career on the force, he'd never actually had reason to fend off an assailant or been as close to dying or killing to survive. Hell, he'd never even had reason to fire his weapon in the line of duty.

Strange, all the odd things that race through one's mind whenever it should be occupied by other, more important things.

Both men were struggling for the gun, but Corso was handicapped by the killer's size and position. Not to mention the intense pain from a spiral fracture at his elbow received when Gabe scuffled to prevent him from drawing his Glock from its holster. As they fought for control of the weapon, Bleu heard the sounds of heavy breathing in his ear. It sounded wet and anxious, much as it had two nights before, on a bed that sat mere feet from where they were brawling.

The killer was stronger than he was, and carried his mass as his advantage. But eventually they made it to the floor, where they tussled and rocked back and forth while the deputy was pinned underneath. To any outsider it would've looked like a scrap between pubescent boys in the throes of an argument. But this wasn't male posturing for the attentions of some high school cheerleader, this was life or death, and the lawman did his best against greater odds.

With his gun free of the holster, Bleu stretched his arm wide, trying hard to prevent the killer from liberating it from his clenched fist. Straddling Bleu's body like some perverse sex act, Gabe grappled for the .22 as he tried to confine the deputy's gun arm against his broad chest. With forearms crossed like a man in a coffin, the killer was yanking with all his might to keep the gun from leveling at his core. His breathing was like a freight train barreling through a tunnel, and, even in the waning light, Bleu could see that his attacker was grinning.

Flashes came in a myriad of images as Bleu recalled his youth. He'd known boys his age once who seemed to relish the torturing of insects and small foraging animals they'd run across. His brain locked onto a memory. A time when a boyhood friend named Thad and he were hiking through the woods and they'd run across a possum lying dead in the creek bed. It had looked dead, but there wasn't any decay—simply a lifeless carcass for scavengers to feast upon. But Bleu was young and didn't know the stories of possums. And when Thad found an old empty Coke bottle, he forced it up the animal's asshole then roared with sadistic laughter. Later, Bleu remembered how possums liked to feign death, and he wondered if the animal had been alive after all. He wondered if it'd remained motionless throughout the assault just to survive. Either way, he reasoned later, the small animal would've died anyway, having been unable to extricate the bottle from his mutilated innards. Thad was one of those boys: the kind who hurts the innocent just to see the outcome. He'd decided not to remain friends with Thad after that, and they never played again. He didn't want to associate with anyone that he thought could be that cruel. And now, as he looked at the killer huddled over him and saw him smiling, he thought this man was exactly like Thad.

With Gabe yanking his arm painfully backward, the deputy was still able to twist his wrist and his finger somehow found the trigger. He heard the abrupt bang of discharge, and, being closer to the gun than ever before, he saw for the first time the gases as they propelled through the air. He knew gunpowder didn't have cordite. It hadn't been used since the last war, but to the best of his recollection he did detect an odor of charcoal and sweet banana, and that was a thing he hadn't expected.

Corso hadn't seen where the barrel was trained, but, by the sound his assailant made and the expression on his face, he suspected he'd caught him somewhere. But, even after the blast, Gabe never stopped fighting. Even with a wounded look and that grin finally faded, he appeared angrier, and his steel-gray eyes filled with water as he fought through the pain.

BOTH THE KILLER'S hands were gripping the deputy's wrist as he pushed him hard to the ground. Then with every bit of effort he could muster, Gabe swung his elbow wide and smashed it into the lawman's chin. The force of the unexpected blow had everything built inside it. Every bit of frustration and anger he had with himself for not choosing to leave Sonora sooner, as well as not being able to help Chris more. The deputy was hit with every bit of Gabe's exasperation. Dazed and unsteady, Bleu shook his head unconsciously, like some idiotic character in a cartoon from his youth, a man stunned while stars danced above his head. The damage had been done, and that second changed Corso's fate forever by giving his attacker a better chance to react.

With a closed hand, Gabe brought his arm back in a high arc overhead then drove his fist hard into the younger man's jaw with all his strength, thus completing what his elbow had only hinted at. The officer was all but unconscious, though he still rocked back and forth as if he might recover. But it was enough that Gabe could wrestle the gun from his hand and then stand quickly as he towered ominously over Bleu's crumpled frame on the carpet.

Though it would have been impossible to see, Church was trapped in a moment that seemed frozen in time. What appeared less than milliseconds was for him an hour of deep reflection. Standing over the deputy as blood soaked his side and drained onto his Levi's, he stared at the man who he'd once fucked and had even found some idle pleasure with. He had the lawman's gun, and he had the same mission he'd had since arriving in

Seattle. But it was another difficult challenge he regretted more than he'd been able to explain.

Whatever presumptions he once had were suddenly falling away like scales from his eyes. His whole life had been a mission from God, and he'd been ordained to become that angel of death and retribution. He'd been sent to earth for the sole purpose of maintaining balance to the world and keeping the *judged ones* in check. The white light had directed him, and he'd felt the warmth of that radiance whenever he bathed under its glow. Those echoes rattling constantly around his brain reminded him that he had been more than just a poor kid from the wrong side of the tracks, with simply bad parents and no future. That he was destined to become someone special, something more than the sum of what his life had been before. Everything he'd ever known was focused on that one idea. That was the only security Church had ever known; that sense that he was important to someone, somewhere, and that, even if there hadn't been anyone else, then at least he'd been important to God. But as he stood there with the muffled sounds of the deputy regaining consciousness there at his feet, he was beginning to understand the exact extent of how wrong he'd been.

Maybe I'm simply evil. A dark cloud that drifted through the cities he traveled through, a shadow damaging every person he ever met and came in contact with. And that included Christian Maxwell.

A sparking in his brain brought images of Chris back to his mind. He felt a serenity wash over and envelop him. He saw his lover's crooked smile and his perfectly white enameled grin, and in that memory he felt pleasure. He was filled to capacity with that feeling of love, and his need to protect the only thing of value he'd ever experienced in his life.

That drive of protection coursing through him had cursed him once before, and it would curse him yet again. It was the reason he brought the gun up, then took level aim at his former tryst lying so helpless on the ground...and the only reason why he fired.

"You see, deputy, we all end up like cats in a bag and then tossed in a river to drown," he whispered to himself.

Chapter Twenty-Two

THINKING ONLY ABOUT his excitement, Chris tossed his suitcase on the bed then yanked bureau drawers open before pulling out a stack of rolled socks and underwear and carefully stowing them in the bag. He thought, with a smile, that he didn't need much because he intended to remain naked as much as possible. He caught himself humming a song, though even he hadn't fully recognized the tune. It was just his mood coming through, the wellspring of lighter days where he might be able to leave some behind in Seattle, at least for the time being. He had his rental car waiting downstairs and his reservation confirmations tucked in an inside pocket of his luggage. He was ready for a change and could barely contain his joy.

The midday sun exploded through the high-rise windows and danced effervescently on the floor of his bedroom. He knew within hours he'd be pulling into Central Point, Oregon and then he was to wait in the parking lot of a diner they'd chosen as their meeting spot. He knew he'd hear the Dodge before seeing it, the creak of axels and struts needing oiling as it lumbered up next to the rental. He knew he'd be ecstatic upon first sight of him pulling up with his windows down and sporting that shit-eating grin he'd missed so much.

Then after one helluva long embrace, he knew he would be relegated to the passenger seat. He knew his lover well enough that he'd demand to drive. He'd want to be in control of their rented Audi for the whole of their brief weekend together, all the way during their drive to the B&B, but he didn't mind. He liked watching Gabriel behind the wheel. He knew it gave him a chance to relax and finally shed some of the weight from all that abstinence and awful isolation he'd felt of late. But before he could pack any toiletries he heard a ring coming from his nightstand drawer and a chill raced through his blood. Was Gabe calling to make sure he'd made it to the highway already?

He knew the only person with the number to that phone was Gabriel. But because the way the light splashed at his feet and the tune he'd been humming was still fresh in his mind, he never thought to assume the phone call could be anything but good news.

"No, sir, I haven't made it to the expressway yet," he said breathlessly as he answered the phone. "Just give me some time. Or are you that eager to see me?" he asked with a lilt in his voice and a smile that even Church should feel over all the miles.

"Yeah, that eager, boy," Gabe said slowly, although his voice sounded off.

Of all the conversations the two had shared over many months—their late-night calls and their long-winded discussions that never seemed to end—they had very few secrets left between them. Christian knew Gabe, better at times than he knew himself, and he heard a tincture of something in those few spoken words, something he didn't recognize. And an icy grip seized his lungs and held tight.

"Is everything all right?"

CHURCH SENSED THE distress in Chris's question, then felt the alarm in his voice as it rose exponentially.

"Just fine," he lied. "I wanted to catch you before you left's all."

"Why?" Chris asked him. "You want me to bring something?"

Human nature as a whole is flawed. Church knew it long before then, and he'd mentioned that fact many times during their early interviews. "Everything crumbles," he'd said late one evening while they drank from a bottle and their speech became slurred. It had become a wedge between them, one that Chris constantly struggled to overcome. Was he worried more than he should be? Church simply looked for the worst in people; saw only the dark around every corner and every bend. That's how he'd stayed alive through all his offenses. How he'd remained free when most would've been apprehended and confined in a brightly lit hospital unit for the criminally insane.

But in that instant, all he wanted was to calm the disembodied voice on the other end of the signal. He didn't want an outpouring of hysteria or any tears and crying. He knew he'd already lost too much blood, and he didn't think he could stand the added strain.

"Just don't make the trip," he said in a quiet grimace he hoped was undetectable. "There's been a slight change of plans, and I think our vacation might be postponed."

Chris repeated what he'd asked earlier, "Is everything all right?"

But avoiding the question, as he wanted to offer comfort to Chris, Gabe whispered softly, "If I sound strange, it's because I'm behind the wheel. I had to leave quite unexpectedly from the spot where I'd landed."

Then, almost like a treasured afterthought, he said, "Ya know, it was Sonora. I'd forgotten I hadn't mentioned that to you before."

CHURCH'S VOICE WAS labored and trailed a bit near the end of his words. Christian felt panic rising in his chest. "You told me I shouldn't know where you were at, not exactly. You said it was safer that I didn't know."

"Well I'm telling you now," Gabe said with a lilt in his voice. "It's friggin' gorgeous here too. A place I think you'd have liked to have seen. It's buried near the base of the Sierra Nevada foothills. It's all gold country around here, with trees and mountains that seem to extend far beyond the horizon."

This rambling discourse wasn't like Gabe at all. Panic was escalating into a burning heat, and it was quickly circling his heart. And suddenly every worst fear he could imagine was coming into focus.

"Well, don't worry. We're gonna get to see it together, buddy," Chris stammered his words nervously, burying all the horrible pictures he was visualizing in that moment, that thing that was happening on the other side so far from him. "Tell me, Gabriel, what's happened? 'Cause you don't sound the same, and you're starting to scare me."

"I had to shoot a friend," Gabe said. The words sounded drunk and slurred, like when together they'd tipped a bottle of bourbon back at the Mayflower Park Hotel, sitting naked and cross-legged on the floor while sharing stories of their childhoods.

"He's not dead, though. At the last minute I figured I couldn't do it. He was just doing his job and a really nice guy. He has a bright future. Besides I merely grazed him, so he'll survive." A humble lie of omission, he wasn't as certain of the deputy's fate as he made it sound. There'd been too much going on then, and one split second or one millimeter no wider than a few strands can make all the difference between bright future and a dark grave. But Christian didn't need that worry, so he carried it alone, as he should. The bullet came from his gun; all of this was his responsibility.

Questions should've fallen from Chris's lips like waves crashing over the Niagara. Questions like Gabe's use of the word "friend." Or how he knew this person was a nice guy with a bright future, or even how any of this could happen without him knowing a single detail.

It rushed up from nowhere and slapped him hard across his face, and the only thing he could think of was how unpredictable Gabe's words had sounded. But even before he could say a thing, before the words could form across his tongue, he heard a guttural noise and recognized how much pain Church had to be in right then. And for reasons still unclear to him, he knew that meant peril for one or both of them. And in that second his questions refused to come.

"You know, Chris," Gabriel began, "I've never known anyone quite like you. You kinda made me feel like home. Like I had a place to go outside the world, one where I could feel safe, secure, and peaceful...even though I didn't deserve it."

With tears filling his eyes, Chris instinctively covered his mouth with an open palm. It was his vain attempt to stifle any sounds he knew would surely come in an uncontained eruption, and he didn't wish to do that to his lover. He wanted to scream as loud as he could because whatever this meant, he knew it had to be extremely bad. Gabe would never talk this way. Something was terribly wrong.

This meant he had to be running, possibly with sirens from police cars speeding at his heels. He could be wounded, maybe even mortally—and that image alone opened any floodgates Christian had hoped he might suppress. Wetness came in streams along his cheekbones, but they gratifyingly came silently. He hadn't wanted Gabriel to hear him blubbering on the other end. Not when he needed him most. He felt as if he was covered beneath a heavy winter blanket comprised of apprehension, and he didn't know quite how to wriggle free.

"You put me back together, son, and I'm grateful for that," Gabe whispered over the sound of rubber pounding blacktop.

"Can you make it somewhere safe?" Chris asked him. He gurgled through his words actually. They sounded fraught and anxious, a belly of some volcanic explosion about to occur and not at all like the calming question he'd intended it to be.

"I have the small problem of a gut shot I really need to deal with, and I've been driving all night." Church said. Chris could imagine him glancing down at the Dodge's bench seat stained red. "But I wanted to talk to you; lots to say; I figure."

The way his lover was measuring his words, along with the notion that he might never see Gabriel alive again, was too much. It took hold and refused to let go. Chris gasped hard trying to hold back the inevitable wall before it might crash down and bury him.

"You don't need to fret, my love. I've made it out with greater scars than this."

He was lying; both men knew that. "I want you to know how sorry I am for dragging you into my shit. I never intended for any of that you know."

"Sshhh, don't talk. Pull over somewhere and try to get some help." Then with his wall shattering out of his control, he screamed, *"For God's sake, stay alive...for me."*

The last words were a whisper, a trail of hope and promise that he'd guessed would come too late.

"Live or not, buddy; this is the last time we're ever gonna talk."

With his stomach aching like he'd suddenly reached the bottom of his fifth, Chris collapsed beside his bed still gripping the phone in white, hard knuckles. "Why?" he stuttered. "Fuckin' why?"

"Because, baby. I can't keep making the same mistakes over and over, and I can't keep doing to others what I've done all my life."

"There's a place," Chris cried into the phone. "A place we could go, get away...stay together, forever."

After a pause Church whispered back, "There's no such place, not for us and not now. But you have to know I loved you; that you fixed my ills, nonetheless. When you finally find that one person who somehow connects you back to the world, it's supposed to make it better, isn't it?"

"It isn't over for us, baby." Chris said, but even he had heard the wincing pain beneath the promise. It was as empty as his future plans now.

"I didn't think it possible before, but I'd figured aways back that you must've been born with my initials stamped onto your ass cheeks," Gabe managed with an audible grin. "You were my salvation when I wasn't that for you."

Over the background noise of wind whistling through Gabe's open window and the din of traffic sounds off in the distance, Chris had heard the weight in every single spoken word. He knew the big man was crying, the same as he was. And he pictured those tears intermingling with Gabriel's furry bearded chin, and the way his eyes crinkled at the creases whenever the sun blasted him directly in his face.

He knew he was instantly broken now, possibly forever. He doubted that he'd be put back together, just as much as he doubted Gabe would somehow survive his wounds. Some fables don't end with Humpty's shell getting reassembled; that much Gabriel had taught him. And the only thing he was aware of, and could be so certain about, was how peaceful and loving

Gabriel sounded during the call. He'd accomplished something for him anyway, Chris thought. Maybe it had been too little, too late to do them any good, but it was something, nonetheless.

They talked for a while longer that afternoon. Gabriel's voice was laced with saccharine Chris had never heard him utter. It had simply been too hard to hang up for either of them. They knew that once this conversation ended, everything else would follow suit, and nobody could've wished for a more bittersweet ending. After some time, when the tears were drying up and Chris could tell that Gabe was in too much pain to continue driving, he allowed him to say goodnight.

Not goodbye because that would've been a word neither could have offered with conviction. There was more crying and despair to get through, and behind all the cold reasoning of everything that had happened to transform their lives, Chris still had some semblance of hope beating in his chest. Hope that Gabe did, in fact, pull the Dodge over to the side of the road and did, in fact, find a way to heal. To survive whatever wounds he had. That he'd somehow made it safely back onto the highway and was going to continue driving nonstop until he found that restful spot he'd always talked about, a place that Chris knew had to rest just beyond that next rise somewhere across the blacktop.

Chapter Twenty-Three

ALL HE COULD remember was searing pain.

The white-hot feel of a poker shoved mercilessly into his side to remind him he was about to die. There was delirium as well, accompanied by the muffled sounds of activity swirling around from disembodied voices. Where blue-and-red flashes of light danced across black asphalt and streaked in pools of gas and oil from the wreckage. Then sudden blinding realization hit him like a wave. His name was Gabriel and there had been an accident. There were police and an ambulance nearby, and he was a fugitive. A killer who had lived his life on the run from the law, and he was about to get caught.

It was true. People do have flashbacks of their life in those moments before death. His childhood flickered by like old film footage sputtering on an ancient projector. Images and senses as disembodied as the voices of the emergency responders he could hear circling his truck.

As blood seeped through his shirt, making him feel like he was swaddled in a wet rag, he recalled the moments that had brought him to that point. The gunshot wound from the deputy that he knew was the precipice about to surely end his life. He saw the blacktop right before he spun recklessly out of control. He recalled the smell of burning rubber from tires on his once beloved Dodge pickup that had taken him so far across states. He couldn't remember the actual crash. Instead of hearing the noise of violently crumpled metal or sounds of squealing tires, all he could sense was being suspended in a vacuum as if he were encased in cotton, where all sight and sound became frozen in time.

His arm was wrenched uncomfortably under the shell of the dashboard, which was nothing but twisted carnage by then. Gabriel could hear sirens screeching in the distance and knew, anxiously, that more police were heading to the scene. Another troublesome thought to consider. Shaking off his confusion, he began to assess the immediate situation. He had lost consciousness, the blood loss too severe to keep control of his vehicle. The Dodge had careened off the roadway, and by some fortune he knew he didn't deserve, hit a tree and a guardrail but thankfully no other cars. Covered in blood and still pinned in the wreckage, he hoped no one had spotted his wound as a bullet hole and not simply a result of the crash.

The pain was unbearable as he shifted his weight, trying to free his body from the crushed dashboard of the broken Dodge. He couldn't determine which hurt worse, the mortal gunshot wound at his side or the consequential pain caused by the accident. All he could wrap his head around was his need for flight more than rescue. He suddenly felt very foolish. He'd allowed himself to get trapped by his own stupidity, and it had occurred with something as mundane as a traffic mishap. How could he be the type of man who'd escaped so many close calls in his life only to get entombed in his own truck while police stumbled onto the scene and found a wanted killer?

Trails of wispy smoke from the engine block rose to greet his nostrils. The oily, corrosive smell of spilled fuel seemed to be the only thing tethering him to reality. He had to escape the debris as well as the police because there'd be questions that he couldn't answer. And there was a handsome deputy lying somewhere in his wake.

"How you doing there, buddy?" he asked. "You hanging' tough for me?"

Gabe looked up and saw a paramedic poking through the open window. His heart skipped a beat at first because he thought it was a cop, and, even through the intense pain, he still noticed his skin crawl with that awful prospect.

Nodding, he forced a bent smile to his lips. All to show he was conscious and aware of his predicament and somehow bearing through the pain quite well.

Then the two began a most unusual dance. That point where trained professional meets innocent victim, where all those minute seconds of life and death become so vitally important in the grander scheme of everything. The paramedic was male, younger than Gabriel, and seemingly at ease, despite the cacophony of sights and sounds swirling around him. He was good at his job.

"These firemen are gonna get you free in a sec," he said with a carefree sort of grin to relax his charge. "Then we're gonna get you all the help you need. But first, can you tell me where it hurts the most?"

"My pride," Gabe said with a snort.

"I see," the younger man chuckled back. "I'm gonna check you out for a moment."

He began carefully patting Gabriel down as he inspected for any extended flesh.

"Whatcha doing there, buddy?" Gabriel whispered with a salacious smile and suggestion of impropriety.

"Just getting to know you better," the man chortled back. "I got a lovely wife at home, so I don't need to get my jollies feeling up a big guy such as yourself. Can you tell me your name, dude?

"Gabriel...Gabriel Church" he said. He was immediately surprised that he'd blurted out his real name, which wasn't like him at all. It must've been due to the pain, he figured, or possibly how nice the paramedic seemed.

"Well, Gabriel, I'm checking for bloating that might suggest internal bleeding. I'm also checking for anything metal sticking out of you."

"I think I'd know if I had something like that going on," he said expelling air in a humph of exasperation.

"You'd be surprised, fella. Sometimes people don't even realize when they have fragments sticking outta their bodies. Not until we get them extricated anyway."

Grinning through his discomfort, Gabe shifted farther away with an audible grimace. He was trying to prevent the paramedic from running a hand over his bullet-holed gut, and even through his smiles, he was working feverishly on his next move and possible escape.

THE MAN LYING on the ground was strangely fascinated by the carpet. An atrocious color, balancing somewhere between a beige and the pigment of rotted hay, it somehow reminded him of his childhood. How odd to be considering the choice of rugs as his own blood was forever staining that fucked-up carpet in a motel room at the Queen of the Mines Lodge. He had been shot in the shoulder by the bullet of a Glock 9mm. It was only a grazing wound, but it had happened nonetheless, and now he knew everything was about to change, and not for the better.

His name was Bleu Corso. He was a deputy chief in the Sonora Police Department in Northern California, and he was bleeding from a gunshot wound. Despite the pain, all he could concentrate on was how he'd done the unthinkable—he'd discharged his weapon at a suspect for the very first time, at least one that wasn't a simple paper cutout hanging at the range. And that by itself should've been enough. Though he had to admit there was another glaring detail he needed to add to an already cloudy mix. That being said, he had recently slept with that same suspect in that very motel room hours earlier, before any of this had escalated into what it'd tragically become.

"This is gonna make for one fucked-up report," he whispered aloud.

Grabbing his shoulder above the pierced flesh, he tried to stumble to his feet and regain his failing composure. He'd already heard the sounds of doors being thrown open after the exploding gunfire and knew by the rustling footsteps outside that some keenly observant bystander had already phoned 911. He reasoned his uniformed colleagues were already en route, and where that should've made him feel better it actually worked just the opposite. There'd be questions. Ones he wasn't fully prepared to answer, secrets hanging on an edge of being exposed. Things he hadn't admitted to anyone and was barely beginning to understand. And there'd be other questions, such as "Who's the mysterious shooter?" and "What are the circumstances surrounding this tragic crime?"

The physical pain burning his shoulder subsided long enough for Corso to feel his heart sinking into his gut when he heard the faint siren wail of approaching patrol cars as they turned off Euclid several miles away. It wouldn't be long now. His mind raced to all the possible scenarios he might tell, but, with each calculation, he seemed to be coming up empty. There were no lies he could tell to explain this shit, he thought as he rubbed his forehead in worry. There wasn't any fabrication he could muster that even sounded plausible to his own ears, much less his captain or associates in blue. He pictured himself being carted off in his own cuffs. Even though he knew he'd done nothing illegal per say, but he had danced precariously over the line of decency. And even if he weren't arrested for some unknown crime, he was certainly going to lose his job, his standing, and his reputation.

He pictured his father then, and that image brought a soaring shame flooding over him like a cloud. Bleu knew that he'd be disappointing someone whose respect he'd worked very hard to acquire. Hell, all of Tuolumne County would be rocked by the news he muttered in his own head. There wouldn't be anyone talking about his bravery after his sordid and unnatural affair came to light.

"Yes, he may be a queer, but have you ever noticed how handsome he was in dress blues?"

No matter how hard he rubbed his brow, he couldn't seem to displace the humiliation he knew was coming. And as if to remind him, the sirens got louder and closer. He lied when he told himself it had begun simply enough. He'd noticed a man at a gas pump standing next to a Dodge two-tone pickup. Tourist trade, he'd figured a hunter possibly, someone driving up the coast to land a ten-point buck and enjoy the scenic vistas offered by the Sierra Nevada Mountains. He'd considered then that stopping the vehicle came only as a seasoned lawman scratching an uneasy itch. But even now, as the blood was still oozing from his red-stained shoulder, he had to confess that it had been something more than protocol, more than any desire of protecting his hometown from any new and potential threats.

He'd stopped his quarry, not to assuage some police instinct, but because the man was simply drop-dead sexy. Even from a distance and across a busy roadway and a parking lot filled with cars, he'd seen that clearly. He'd been stopped breathless in his tracks by the sight of such a brawny man as he leaned against the open door of his cab and gassed up that dilapidated old Dodge, wiping his forehead of sweat and scanning the street like some hungry bird of prey.

The big man refueling his vehicle, wearing an open plaid shirt over a skintight tee of dingy white, made a rustic picture. Maybe it had been his blue jeans or the calfskin boots. Maybe it had been the package he displayed like a trophy, or the way the light played across those iridescent pupils of his—eyes that, from that expanse, the deputy couldn't begin to tell were blue or gray or some other shade lingering in-between. The man stirred his loins as much as piqued his interest, and that was the reason for the traffic stop that began the whole torrid tale.

But now, as he lay on a stained rug in room 212 of the Queen of the Mines Lodge, all Bleu could do was consider what a wrong turn he'd taken. Even now he knew he couldn't have guessed how badly things were going to sour. How the man he first knew as Bobby Johnson, and then Gabe, would become a friend, then a lover, and finally a most unusual suspect. The man who'd shot him in an awfully ragged gun battle, reminding Corso of a shootout at the OK Corral. He'd escaped, but the deputy had clipped him—that much he knew. As Bleu stumbled to his feet, he felt his shoulder scorching red-hot and the numbness creeping frighteningly down his side. It felt as if his dead arm had suddenly become firewood, immobile but still burning, dissolving into ash before his very eyes.

Scrambling for support, the deputy grabbed the arm of a nearby chair, then forced his body upright. Unsteady, he felt winded as he strained to fill his lungs with oxygen. He couldn't decide if it was the result of the struggle or the bullet resting too dangerously close to his spine. If he hadn't turned quickly enough, he suspected the shot might have shredded his carotid artery. And instead of being simple unsteady on his feet, he would've been *straightforward dead*. What he didn't know then was how accurate a shot Gabriel was or how he'd trained his self in the use of firearms over the years.

THE VERY FEW accomplishments Gabe's father, Bennett, could ever own were the times when he took his only son to a neighbor's wooded field to shoot game or merely take turns with target practice. Bennett would grab his old Smith and Wesson that hung on the rack in the living room, then pull a couple of cold Budweiser's from the fridge. Then, with his rifle slung over his shoulders and two beers swinging like corpses from the plastic, Bennett would bellow out for his boy, and he and Gabe would head out to the woods together—another Americana fiction pulled from a Norman Rockwell lie. But it was one of the few good memories Gabe ever had of Bennett, and the only time he'd ever recalled them bonding as father and son.

After he left home, he found himself drifting aimlessly across the states for years. Poor and directionless, he knew that the only thing he actually possessed in abundance was time. In a constant struggle of boredom, Gabriel found one thing he enjoyed more than most was scanning for the red clay stretches of long residential country road and searching out the vacant fields that he knew were so plentiful across this nation. He'd become quite adept with finding those remote spots, even when they were so well hidden off any beaten track. They were perfect spots to fire his stolen Glock 9-millimeter and test his skill and marksmanship. Once he spotted an ideal location, he'd park his truck, and, as he slowly stepped out into the cool morning air, he was already taking aim at whatever small game might've caught his eye. They could've been ducks swimming lazily across the water or birds idly circling the pastures above his head, but, once he spotted them, he was firing almost immediately—to test his accuracy. Occasionally he'd spot some blackened fence posts off in the distance, and in his mind he pictured they were a line of advancing rebel soldiers. And with every shot fired, he was ending a life and felling a soldier. He was breaking apart the threats of that encroaching line of single-file dangers.

As a result, and out of that lonely isolation and single-mindedness of his character, he'd actually become quite good. Enough so that when he took aim at the deputy, he'd hit his intended mark, as he'd expected. He'd told himself, in the unpredictability of that moment that he only wanted to wing him. To stop him in his tracks, like those advancing lines of soldiers in his past. He'd wanted to reach the door and, hopefully, his eventual freedom, and he knew any escape rested in the proximity of his Dodge and that blacktop minefield of a parking lot that separated them. After all, he'd seen the deputy naked. They'd shared laughs and beers together. And he intuitively knew he didn't really wish to kill the man. After all, he liked Deputy Corso. Still, in his head, Gabriel knew he was indeed quite capable of such an awful act.

Yes, he was capable, if he felt he had to and if his back was truly and fully against the wall.

His freedom meant more to him than any of those combined hours spent joking as friends or drinking cold beers on tap, and even those tentative moments in the sack when sweat ran like tears along his spine and the younger man had stared seductively back into his own eyes, piercing him like a laser and telling him to go deeper and harder.

In a parallel moment, shortly after Deputy Corso had rummaged the empty motel room for any loose fabric to clot his bleeding shoulder, Gabriel Church was staring out the cracked windshield of his beloved Dodge as lights flickered above his head, reminding him of a nighttime carnival. It became the usual pandemonium of every sight and sound that accompanies such an accident that occurs on a fairly untraveled road after dusk.

The attractive EMT was back then, leaning in with his handsome face and glassy eyes. He was attempting to remain calm for the driver at the scene, but Gabriel could see past his cool demeanor. He must be relatively new at this, Gabe thought.

"Don't worry there, buddy, we'll have you out in a minute" he said in quite even tones.

Somebody put a cock in his mouth and shut this guy up, he thought, rather bemused.

Yes, he was in pain, but triggered more from the bullet wound in his gut than being trapped inside the twisted metal of his pickup. Seeing the steam wisp and curl from the bent hood of the Dodge meant the radiator was damaged. And, even through the pain at his side and the discomfort from being confined beneath the steering wheel and the misshapen, crumpled floorboard, all he could think of was the loss of his vehicle. That same vehicle he'd owned and maintained for so very long—the same one in which he'd zigzagged across numerous states over a period of many years. That same place he'd often slept when money was tight or motels weren't an option to consider. It'd become the single creature comfort of normalcy for Gabriel Church, and the last thing of any real value he still possessed. Having to consider abandoning it was a finality he couldn't rationalize, and it was as immediately unbearable as the portent of blood seeping through his shirt and collecting near the waistband of his jeans.

He figured that his reality was likely dealing with a mortal wound. He'd fallen into the exact predicament he'd feared throughout this whole adult life the most. He was surrounded by police cruisers and bleeding out faster than expected, and the best of his many unpleasant options was that he was about to be arrested for shooting a deputy in a motel room in Sonora. It was the finality of a bug hitting the windshield, the impossibility of escape, and even in the light-headed fog of too much blood loss, he thought about Christian Maxwell.

As blue lights flickered in the night sky around him and the air and background noises became an irrevocable conclusion, he considered what Chris might be doing in that precise moment. How excited he must've been at the prospect of meeting him in that bed-and-breakfast they'd planned days earlier. Then his entire outlook turned because he knew there wasn't going to be a few days of idle relaxation to hope for. A shade of despair crept in suddenly as he realized his meeting with Christian was now never going to take place. The loss of that hope and the fear he'd seen Chris for the last time became a loss that he felt was too excruciating to bear. But whether it was instinct or something far more disturbing, Gabe had the foresight to locate and stow the Glock 9mm that had protected him so many times before. Slipping the gun into the small of his back, hidden by his jeans, he hoped no one would catch sight of it until he had an occasion to use it for his escape. He also grabbed the disposable cell Chris had given him. That was a little more difficult, as it'd been thrown onto the floorboard, and he was forced to twist painfully to scoop it into his fingers.

In those moments, all he could believe was that his whole existence had been like making love in a burning building, an indiscernible tenuousness with each and every act, where all his emotions hung on single fragile thread, and always with a threat of breaking in two. And all because of choices he'd made in his life, particularly those where he'd killed in the name of a God he'd never really known anyway.

Chapter Twenty-Four

BY THE TIME he found the strength to make it outside, Bleu could hear the distant call of sirens as his buddies were surely speeding toward the scene of the disturbance. He hoped no one had spotted his cruiser parked in the lot because, if anyone had, it meant an officer could be wounded, and that would mean a shitload of police were headed his way. For his precinct, the scanner code was 11-99, an indicator that another officer was down or injured. Even the code sounded ominous to him. An 11-99 was the type of code that nestled in the back of every officer's brain. Though he'd never responded to one himself, it was the type of radio call that very few units ever joked about.

His thoughts were racing at full speed. And, as the wailing sirens grew louder and closer, he was struggling to come up with a plausible story he might craft from nothing that could still salvage his job and reputation. Firstly, he was in his cruiser after hours, a small infraction, but one that could spell trouble further down the line. Secondly, he was visiting a man in a motel room without backup. And finally, there was the indisputable fact that he'd been acquainted with a man he now suspected was a serial killer, as evidenced by his presence at the man's motel and the shooting that had now made him a victim. And none of this could be adequately explained without outing himself in the process.

A trained officer rarely freezes in the headlamps. He, or she, faces danger enough to learn better how to react. Even in a humble town the size of Sonora, there were risks to wearing the badge. And with all his skills intact, Bleu Corso still couldn't come up with anything in those tenuous moments that might save him. And it wasn't just embarrassment, or the loss of his career. It was facing his father after the news broke and trying to explain his sexuality to someone else. Particularly someone like his father—a man he admired and respected—when he hadn't fully faced that realization himself.

Minutes later, as the first of several black-and-whites pulled into the parking lot at the Queen of the Mines Motor Lodge, all Bleu could muster was a quiet "Sonuvabitch." It was like standing on scorched earth with only a faithless prayer for rain. Then flashes in his head reminded him how nothing ever grows strong on burned soil, and when he recognized Officer Donovan leaping from her cruiser as she raced up to greet him, he thought of dying crops and barren harvest as it weighed heavily in his mind.

"Deputy Corso, are you all right?" She called out, oblivious to her training. Her first duty was to secure the scene, and the younger rookie hadn't yet pulled her service weapon.

"I'm fine," he hollered back, still clutching his bloody shoulder in stoic fashion. "Just grazed here, but the suspect got away from me. I'm sure he's headed out toward the highway. Get an APB out for me, will ya?"

Before she'd even reached him, she'd already turned back toward her cruiser to call an all-points bulletin. Bleu smiled as he noticed she'd yet to un-holster her sidearm and didn't even know the make and model of the vehicle she was supposed to radio in.

"Rookies," he muttered as he shook his head in embarrassment. By then another deputy was out of his vehicle, and, with more years on the force than Donovan, he'd at least pulled his firearm and was scanning the parking lot for any suspects. Corso couldn't really blame the other officers, though, since there was so little crime in Sonora. And a shooting that didn't involve a drunken redneck was a rarity indeed, much less one that involved another cop.

By then the asphalt lot was filling up with guests who'd come out of their rooms like curious cats. Some were furtively peeking through curtains or steaming up windows in glassy-eyed wonderment. Corso figured some had to be locals, and staying at a motel during the week meant that whatever they'd been doing inside wasn't anything they wanted others to know about. He'd seen at least one face peering out that looked scared. He assumed it wasn't fear of being at the scene of a shooting as much as fear a reporter might film their vehicles in some background shot when they were never supposed to be there in the first place. It always seemed to Bleu that the smaller the town the bigger the secrets. And he had to admit that he was no exception to that rule.

"I called for a bus," Donovan said as she slipped up beside the deputy unnoticed. "I need the vehicle and suspect info to call in an APB, though. That is, if you're feeling up to it."

"It's a two-tone Dodge pickup, least five years old with gold over white, though heavily faded and beat-up," Corso replied, trying to remain professional.

He knew that he already obtained the trucks tag numbers from that earlier radio check. But he didn't want to give that out unless he had to. In truth, he wanted Gabe to get as far away as possible. If he was questioned about it later or someone noticed that he'd failed to give such significant information at the scene, he could write it off as something he forgot to mention due to his immediate blood loss and trauma. Yet it was a calculation that only worked because he was two-stepping the dance rather quickly, and all to music in his head that no one else could hear, and all within a moment's notice.

"Was it a traffic stop gone bad, or did you stumble onto something?" asked Simmons, the more seasoned officer, who'd arrived after Donovan. And though he had a few years over the rookie, he was still unfortunately an underling who Corso liked but now was forced to lie to.

"Yeah, I spotted the vehicle pulling into the motel lot and decided to make a routine stop. Not sure why now, but I suppose it was a good call. Before I could run the tags, though, the suspect fired without cause and sped away."

There, the lie that would either work or end him in one fell swoop. He knew he had to say something, but even as the words slipped out, he was already scrutinizing his statement for possible flaws. Maybe a guest had seen him entering the motel, instead of the shooting outside in the lot that he was describing now. Or maybe someone had heard the scuffle inside the room. Yes, there were numerous fuckups that might be brought up, questions he wasn't sure he could answer effectively. But he had to offer something, and, being the senior officer at the scene, he hoped it probable that he could control the investigation, or at least turn it to his advantage in some way.

"I called it in to Captain Kowalski," Donovan said abruptly. The words sent shivers down Corso's spine as he smiled over his shoulder curtly. In his head he was contemplating all the ways he could kill the bitch in that moment, but even he had to admit she was merely doing her job and following protocol. Any officer-involved-shooting required the presence of a supervisor at the scene. It didn't matter that, as a supervisor himself, it was usually him they would've called. He was both a victim and the officer whose weapon had been discharged. That alone meant Kowalski had to be summoned. And that brought new tensions clawing up his back like tiny spiders.

GABE FELT JEALOUS as he watched the speeding lights from every passing vehicle, all the while knowing those lights were traveling closer to the only man he had any real feelings for, while unfortunately he was headed in an opposite direction. But God has a knack for keeping us all perpetually occluded. He keeps us from seeing, with any clarity, the end of our journey, just as he does in the beginning, after we've all taken in our first breaths of life, after we've opened our eyes in amazement and stared out into an unfamiliar world, without any knowledge of where that road might lead us.

Gabriel put the pain of his gunshot onto some unattainable hidden shelf in the back of his mind and attempted to wriggle free from the metal carnage. He knew the sequence of events that'd surely follow; they'd free him from the truck then place him onto a gurney to load him into that waiting ambulance. At some point, they'd see his wound wasn't a result of the crash but instead a bullet hole. And somewhere between the highway and a hospital, the police would then be notified. He suspected they'd be parked beside the ambulance bay as it pulled up.

I have to free myself quickly or risk incarceration and questions I can't answer.

He knew the one thing that most emergency responders didn't expect to see at a scene of an automobile accident was a victim disappearing before receiving medical treatment. Had this been a police chase where the suspect crashed the car that might have been a predictable outcome. But by all appearances this was the simple tragedy of a driver falling asleep at the wheel and inadvertently going headlong into stone and guardrail. For Gabe, this was what he was hoping they'd believe was the case.

After the handsome paramedic checked for any spinal injuries, then cuffed Gabriel's neck with a protective collar, it took two men to wrestle him out of his truck onto a gurney. Covering his seeping wound with his flaying arms and the flannel overshirt he'd been wearing, he was able to keep them focused on maneuvering his sizable girth onto the waiting stretcher, not noticing the gaping hole at his side.

"Hey, fella, before we go to the hospital, can you grab my glasses outta my truck? I can't see a thing without 'em, and I think they fell to the floorboard," Gabriel said, trying to smile through the wincing pain. He'd timed it perfectly because they had yet to load his gurney into the ambulance, and he'd successfully shown how little pain and danger he was in. But this killer didn't wear glasses and his lies were compounded by his feigning lack of discomfort.

After a reflective pause, the attractive paramedic decided to be that nice guy he claimed he was. Nodding through a comforting smile, he quickly turned and headed over to the crumpled pickup to search for imaginary glasses that had never existed in the first place. While the other male paramedic was busy prepping his unit for the trip to the nearest hospital, Gabriel seized a free moment. Quickly lunging to his side, he slipped off the stretcher and ducked unnoticed to the side of the ambulance. Even with his stature and impressive physique, Church always maintained a certain amount of fortune when he slipped into so many places unseen. He had a knack for dropping out of sight or unexpectedly fading into nearby shadows at his whim. You couldn't be a successful serial killer without a certain amount of either luck or skill whenever it came to subterfuge or being invisible when you needed to be.

Clutching his side, Gabriel skimmed the line of trees at his right as sweat began to bead his brow. He noticed the same woody barricade he'd have driven headfirst into, had it not been for the guardrail that prevented it. It had been merely his bad luck when his engine block clipped a large stack of boulders. Monolithic stones that may've broken apart countless years earlier before tumbling down the mountainside, dangerously close to the road, stopped only by that same railing that'd miraculously protected his death.

His head was swimming, though he couldn't tell whether it was the result of the intense pain and burning, gaping void at his side, or simply the accident playing havoc with his brain. He lumbered to the protection of the trees and scurried into the cover of darkness that it provided. Grabbing a tiny oak sapling for support, he turned just before he disappeared from view entirely. He saw the kind medic still rummaging the floorboard of the Dodge for those invented glasses that he'd begged for. He couldn't see the other man but assumed he was obscured by the ambulance. Fortunately, the police cruisers had parked a distance away. They were blocking traffic and setting a perimeter for the medical first responders to work their magic. Therefore, no one ever saw the sole victim of a hapless automobile accident slipping up the hillside away from medical assistance or the officers called there to render aid.

Chapter Twenty-Five

IT'S ALL ABOUT perspective. Memories whittling away inside a brain; carving out and extricating all those small burrows they encounter in their search for new homes. Memories like Gabe's whiskery jawline, and those wet whiskey-scented breaths of air whenever he was pulled in for an embrace or a passionate kiss. These were going to be the things he'd remember for a lifetime, he suspected. And even as his tears fell and his chest was racked by unrelenting sobs that he couldn't quite completely expel, he was capable of holding onto that one memory at least. In that second, it became his single greatest lifeline and the one thing holding his head above all those overlapping waves.

He had his doubts. He had very real fears that Gabe wouldn't survive the gunshot much longer. But Chris knew he couldn't be certain. Because even he couldn't see the whole path ahead of him and didn't wish to, not while there was still a tiny sliver of hope that he could cling to. Maybe Gabriel could make it to a hospital. Maybe he'd scramble from beneath whatever hell he'd found himself in because, after all, he'd done it before.

Later, the phone could still ring and he'd hear his lover on the other end. Gabriel would begin another unusually twisted tale of how he'd somehow made it to safety. Or how he was recovering fast and would be back on his feet soon. And in all the time he'd known Gabe, Chris had seen many times how much the man relied heavily on his own good fortunes. Chris could almost see that bent smile on Gabe's lips whenever one of his escapes went off according to plan. And indeed, to any outsider it did appear as if he had some heavenly protection surrounding him, as he himself had often described while they lay in each other's arms at night. He'd whisper to Chris about how he'd always had angels watching and protecting him, especially during his getaways. And all things being equal, he, too, had to admit how many times Gabe could've been stopped, how many kills might've been avoided with minimal effort from someone else's part. Yet somehow he always managed to slither out from under any possible threat unscathed. His escapes happened like clockwork, and usually without anyone even knowing Gabe had been there.

Hankering for self-medication, Chris wiped his eyes, then headed to the dry bar in his front room. He poured vodka into a tall glass, splashing the softest whisper from the lemon-lime sodas he kept stocked in a tiny fridge for guests. If Gabe were here, they'd both be drinking bourbon. He did so love his whiskey, and, considering his childhood in Tennessee and Kentucky, it was probably expected. He didn't know where Gabe was when he'd called. All he knew was they were supposed to meet at the B&B for a much-needed reconnect. But that was before his terrible call with a breathy Gabe whispering his sad goodbyes over the line.

He'd crossed the Rubicon; that much was now a certainty. His life, absent of Gabriel's influence, could've easily slipped back into old habits. But as he considered their last time together, he didn't even realize that he'd placed his drink on the table and then walked back into his bedroom. He awoke to find himself mindlessly stuffing clothes into the same bag that waited patiently atop his bed. That same luggage he'd been filling for a vacation with his lover away from the big city lights of Seattle. He was performing the mundane task of packing without any conscious awareness—jarred back into the moment as if he'd risen from his body and was watching himself from some metaphysical plane outside his perception. He witnessed himself cramming shirts and socks into the bag while wiping remnants of tears from his red, aching eyes. And as he observed it all, he suddenly felt slightly better.

He had already rented a car. It had been Gabe's suggestion, and a wise one. He already had a room reserved, had taken the time off work, and cleared his calendar. There wasn't a good reason not to go, he figured, but if he stayed he knew he'd drive himself crazy waiting for a call that may or may never come. He told himself that he'd be closer to Gabe, at least. And besides, he needed to do something, even if it didn't make any sense. He'd drive the distance alone, and, if he had to, he'd search every hospital and jailhouse within two hundred miles of the B&B. He had a plan—that was something, and the only thing he could currently wrap his head around.

HE FELT SENSORY overload, a jagged, bony finger poking him in his bloodied side while terror screamed alarms inside his head. Flickering blue lights danced across the asphalt below him as he clambered up the hillside.

Pushing past the latticework of low-hanging branches, Gabriel stumbled forward through the lack of any trodden path, the steep incline making it increasingly difficult in the dark. The sounds of voices and slamming car doors grew softer from the distance, overshadowed by the chirping of a hundred hidden locusts making a cacophony of music in his ears. And as tiny stones crunched under his feet and began sliding back down the ravine, his own breathing came out in ragged, intense bursts, far too loud for his liking. As the killer scrambled up the rise, he feared the sounds of brambles and rocks being displaced might alert those below to his direction, but he knew he had little choice in the matter if he intended on making it to freedom. As he ascended the slope, Gabriel darted between saplings and old growth pines, trying to steer into the shadows and away from the cast of moonlight shining overhead.

The wreck had been caused by him blacking out, and, as he trudged into the safety of the tree line, he suspected he might lose consciousness again. The thought of him dying beside an interstate at the base of the Sierra's wasn't necessarily a bad way to go. Better than what he figured was planned as his destiny. But if one thing had protected him throughout it all, it was his firm belief in his instinct and the particular drive that compelled him forward and away from danger. Somehow he knew he'd get out of this sticky predicament, like he always had before. And at least he still had his trusty Glock in hand, if it came to that.

Gabriel had killed many people, but none he considered collateral damage or innocent—save for the exceptions of Shea Baltimore, Detective Keen, and his sexy soccer mom of a wife. As he brushed past branches and searched the ground for secure footing, he suddenly realized how many innocents he'd actually killed in the grand scheme of things. It was hard not to visualize the faces of those he'd killed that were never intended to be white-lighters or those whom God had commanded him to eradicate.

With more to consider than his guilt, Gabe made it far enough uphill to not be seen by anyone on the road below. The pain was intense, and he was out of breath from the climb. He stopped long enough to lean against a large California black oak and ran his palm across the wound. He was exploring it for the first time since he'd been shot, and, in the darkness, he felt a wet stickiness on his lower back, the same as in front. He figured this was good news because it meant it was a through and through. And without a bullet still lodged in his gut, his biggest fear was losing too much blood.

The deputy carried a .45, which could cause an obscenely large bullet hole when fired. But in his head, Gabriel suspected if he could simply stop the bleeding, he might stand a chance. But it wouldn't happen unless he got a safe distance away.

When he felt he was far enough away from the scene, Gabe found a boulder to rest against for a minute or two. Pulling out the cheap disposable, Gabe stared down at the buttons for what felt like an eternity. The steam from his hard breathing was making tiny clouds in the cool night air, and though he knew he could always call Chris for assistance, he remembered how every action he'd taken in those last few weeks had been the result of trying to protect him from even more involvement. Besides, calling seemed unmanly—as pathetic a concept as he could imagine. An alien notion, since he'd spent his whole life alone. He'd never needed to ask another person for help before, and even asking Chris felt a pitiable thing to his character. But looking down at the ever-growing stain on his blood-saturated shirt seemed to become the quantifier that finally made that decision.

It took a few rings for an answer, but he was secretly elated when Chris said, "Oh thank God, there you are."

Gabe heard the panic in his voice, but it felt strangely soothing knowing that someone else out there still cared or worried about his well-being. "Well you know me, babe. No one can pin me down for long."

"I'm heading in your direction in the rental now. I couldn't wait around for you to call me back."

Gabe felt a half smile emerge. This was a connection that neither man could've ever described. But, in some moments, they felt as strong and undeniable as any love affair in straight society.

"I don't know where you are, not exactly, but I know I can be there in a few hours. It's Sonora, right?"

Without answering the question, Gabe said, "That'd be good, 'cause I'm still in a bit of a pickle here, and, frankly, I could use the ride."

The silence over the line told Gabe that Chris was suddenly putting a heavier foot on the gas pedal, as if it were even possible to race to his side faster.

"Can you fill me in while I drive?" Christian asked quietly?

"Not now...still feeling the heat on my backside, lover, but later for sure. There's a bar slash diner in Sonora. It's called Dotty's and it's off I-120. Find it as soon as you get into town. That's where I'm headed now."

"Even driving all night, I won't be there till tomorrow. You gonna be all right till then?" Chris wouldn't have forgotten the last call from Gabe and knew there was a bullet they had to contend with.

"Can you stay on the line with me, for a while?" Chris asked hopefully.

"Sorry," Gabe whispered back.

Chapter Twenty-Six

BLEU'S MEETING WITH the captain went better than expected. Maybe it was his ability to bullshit his way out of trouble, or maybe it was respect for years of service. But either way, Kowalski seemed to accept his story with a grunt and an acknowledging nod. Even to the deputy, it seemed far too lax a response considering an officer had discharged a weapon and an "unknown" suspect was loose within the general public and a real threat if cornered, as he secretly could attest.

Hiding in the commotion of the moment, Bleu allowed paramedics to address his wound while he spoke to Captain Kowalski and others at the scene. After the location was successfully locked down, he was boarded into an ambulance and sent to Sierra Emergency Medical for a proper follow-up. There would be more questions to answer, and he had to remember to keep each one straight in his mind. But even he sensed he couldn't quite prevent what was coming; inevitability was staring back at him. And the outcome didn't look promising.

"It looks worse than it is," the deputy managed to say with a smile. The paramedic, a younger black woman with kind eyes, didn't look as if she much believed him.

"Oh, I hadn't realized you graduated," she said with a smile. "I graduated from Oregon State before I decided to get my EMT cert. So where did you get yours?"

Chuckling through a knowing grin, Bleu decided it was best to allow the professionals to work. He'd been bandaged back at the motel, but while en route to the hospital she was checking vitals and busy with a clipboard for an endless array of questions. "Are you allergic to any medications; do you have any conditions that prevent surgery...*blah, blah, and blah.*" He was a seasoned officer and knew the questions were more for appearance than anything else, a distraction from the pain and a mundane litany of useless information, since he knew they'd be asking those questions again during intake.

"I've never had an officer in my bus," she said patting his shoulder in a comforting manner. "I've had gunshot victims here, but no policemen. I guess it was bound to happen sooner or later."

"Then I guess it's a privilege to be your first. I promise to be gentle."

Why is it, Bleu wondered, *that people always have to somehow make it about themselves, even with his blood-stained shirt as proof to the contrary?*

"Sugar, you're in good hands," she said softly, hovering over the uncomfortable gurney he was confined to. "Besides it looks like a grazing wound. You'll be back on the job in a day or so. And now you can say you've been shot in the line of duty, huh? Maybe even take some time off on the city's dime if you want?"

He could smell the faint odor of perfume when she leaned over his body to adjust the wrappings on his shoulder. He wondered if it was normal for a paramedic to wear cologne and perfume on the job. It seemed strange to him and somehow unprofessional. When she reached over his chest, Corso noted that she had a nicotine patch on her left arm.

"Trying to quit cigs?" he asked, breaking the silence.

"Trying is right, deputy, but it's a hassle."

"How'd you know I was a deputy?"

"Honey, anyone I see in a uniform with a badge gets called deputy. It's who I am."

"I gotta admit I feel kinda naked here," he said.

When she furrowed her brow in confusion, Bleu responded by saying, "No gun. They took my service pistol at the scene. It's protocol whenever an officer discharges their weapon," he muttered back.

"Well, no worries darlin'; you won't need it where you're headed. And besides, they surely wouldn't let you keep it anyway, no matter how important you think you are."

With that, she rested her hand on his undamaged side and quickly began extricating him from the equipment meant to monitor his vitals. Their pleasant conversation worked better than the clipboard. Because he'd forgotten all about the sirens wailing in his ears, and before long they were pulling into an emergency bay at Sierra Medical. He was hopeful they'd release him in just a few hours and he could get home. It'd been one helluva day, and he was exhausted. Home was looking pretty darn good about then.

As the deputy was being unloaded, nearly thirty miles away, Gabriel Church was crisscrossing a wooded hillside in the dark, still clutching his gut as if holding back his insides. He heard the sound of voices from the road below just as they found the empty gurney in unexpected fashion.

"What the hell? Hey there, Josh, you missing anything special? Like Mr. Roadkill possibly?"

Gabe could hear alarmed male voices rising and falling over the still mountain sounds of the forest. Then scampering feet as someone raced over to the cruiser to alert the officer parked up a stretch and trying to prevent late-night travelers from inadvertently stumbling into an accident already in progress. The sounds grew more distant as he traveled up the hill. He began to arc his direction in an effort of reaching the road further away the carnage of his beloved Dodge, as well as any black-and-whites he suspected were en route if not already there.

If he could make it even a mile up the road, he figured he might be able to procure a ride and escape the inevitable. He'd use his Glock if needed. He'd wave down a passerby and then forcibly acquire a vehicle at gunpoint. He'd avoid the main streets and then race back to Dotty's Place where he'd meet up with Chris the following morning.

Then, he hoped, all would be right with the world.

But even he knew he couldn't prevent what was coming, not fully anyway. Pushing through bramble and dead foliage, he wanted nothing more than to be back where it began...back at the Mayflower Park in that rain-soaked city of Seattle. He pictured himself sitting in one of their baby-soft leather chairs, sipping his first glass of champagne while watching Christian towel off from a shower that followed sex. They hadn't ever drunk any champagne, he reminded himself. But it was a hazy, what-if memory. Or it might've been one of those things that hadn't happened yet.

In that exact moment, he sensed he was closer to getting caught than he'd ever been before. It felt unnerving, like waking up next to some tragic fuck he'd procured at a bar, stuck together in a culmination of sticky drying amore that some called love. Different from any white-lighter murder turned sour, it was real danger, and actually, for the first time it did feel real—something he was sorely unaccustomed to. His prior kills had gone off without any hiccups. He slipped in unnoticed, took control of his environment, and seized every moment like a maestro. He snuffed out life as quickly and mercifully as any state-sanctioned execution. He always prided himself in the careful way he dispatched those whom he'd been called for. He always performed the tasks meticulously, and always with his usual measure of compassion.

There were mistakes, sure. But for the most part it generally played like a movie in the back of his brain. Those rising crescendo swells to underscore a tension building and every heartbeat bringing the audience to the edges of their seats. Then a visible white flash of a knife blade arcing in the overhead light or even a stealthily dropped rope or garrote over the unsuspecting neck of a targeted white-lighter. They were all quick and relatively painless kills in the grander scheme of things. They were intangible enough to feel like make-believe for someone like Church. But now, racing breathless through an unfamiliar terrain, the blood seeping out his side like a constant reminder, he was certain he was suddenly facing his reality head-on.

"You don't tug on Superman's cape. You don't spit into the wind."

Even a line from an old Jim Croce song offered valuable insights.

He heard the sound of approaching sirens echoing over the mountainside. And even through the noise of such a big man lumbering through the growth and brush, his heavy breath coming out in steamy billows like a freight train, he knew they were getting closer every second. He was dizzy, confused, and cold, despite the sweat that was speckled across his brow. In his efforts to escape, he'd all but forgotten his wound and seemed oblivious to the blood loss that was taking a dangerous toll. Stumbling toward a fallen log, he stopped briefly to catch his breath, and, looking up, he was surprised to see Chris standing in a clearing break, not five yards away.

"What the fuck?" he muttered as he wiped the perspiration before it could drip in his eyes. *Chris is here. Thank God. Well, he made it here awfully fast.* He was standing with arms outstretched like a savior on the cross. But he wasn't making any effort to run to Gabe, and even through the moonlight, he could see that Chris was smiling and that made him feel safe, better in a way.

"How'd you do it? How'd you find me?" he asked raggedly. The words came out jumbled and barely audible, more incomprehensible than not. As he reached out to the fallen log to support his weight, he felt coarse bark in the palm of his hand, so he knew this had to be real. Then he raked an arm across his face and shook his head to clear the haze, and, when he looked up, Chris wasn't there anymore. He scanned the trees for any comforting sign, but even as the miasma faded, he realized he was only half-expecting to see anyone. He was alone, after all, and standing on a not so gently sloping hillside somewhere in the deepest part of the thicket. And he was bleeding to death.

But for every man there is a moment of unpredicted fortitude. That point where you are called to push harder than you'd ever pushed before. And for Gabriel, it must've been then, in those dark woods with deliverance five yards ahead and just beyond his reach. So he moved forward, disregarded the pain and the blood that was running down his leg as if he'd pissed his own jeans. He pushed branches and vines aside and stumbled headlong over the rise. And although it felt like hours, the reality was that in twenty minutes Gabe had made it to a soft spot and walked out of the woods, like a stage actor pushing past the curtains on opening night. Across the way he could see asphalt as it bowed across a highway bend, and he realized he'd made it to the road. With his trusty Glock in hand, he thrust his body forward and headed down the hill to greet the first strangers that passed him—anyone not driving a police cruiser anyway.

Chapter Twenty-Seven

DISOBEYING EVERY ORDER given back at Sierra Medical, Deputy Corso decided to stop in for a drink before heading home. He'd been properly bandaged and seen by the best emergency doctors in the county. One of the few perks of a being a policeman shot in the line of duty, he supposed. Everyone treated him generously, almost like a hero—if they'd merely known the truth. If anyone had actually known he hadn't exactly stumbled onto a gun-wielding madman but, in fact, had gone willingly to the motel. And not in a simple traffic stop gone awry but to interrogate his lover and make sense of the mystery that surrounded him.

Stopping in a bar he'd never frequented, he was suddenly glad that nurses had provided him with an undamaged shirt to walk out of the hospital with. Although he still had his uniform pants on, he at least didn't look like an off-duty cop. He actually looked like every other resident in Sonora, a man stopping in for a quick drink at a dive bar where he hoped no one would know him by name. The bandaging wasn't visible under the bare white T-shirt he'd been given by the staff, so there shouldn't be any questions to answer. The bartender, an overweight but lovely woman in her fifties, met him at the bar still clinging to the dishrag she'd been wiping the counters with.

"What can I get ya, handsome?" she asked with a smile.

"One fifty Bacardi rum, straight up," he said with a nod.

"Damn, son, you have a rough day? Usually I'd suggest rubbing alcohol since it may have some flavor in the glass, though it may be harder to keep down...but what the hell."

Another world-weary soul, Bleu thought. After all, that was the kind of response expected from bartenders in these kinds of establishments.

"You could say it's been rough," he mused.

"You wanna tell me about it?" She slid the drink over and leaned across the mahogany as her ample bosom came close to spilling the glass before he could yank it up.

"Naaa," he said, nodding politely. "You probably hear your share of stupid stories behind that counter I'd guess."

"They don't pay me just to look beautiful here," she said with a wide grin.

"Oh, then it's not your bar?"

"No, but there's some pride in simply being the cog and not the gears," she whispered back. "So, what's got ya appearing so down, good-looking? You don't strike me as a fella who has a lot of bad days in a row."

He smiled back and thought how strange it was that this affable server could draw a bead on him based on such a brief initial impression. Even judging him better than he might've had tables been turned? And he was a cop. She'd assessed him immediately and even engaged him with a smile. She had allowed him to unload his burden whatever that might've been. Almost as if in another life she would've made a right and proper therapist. No doubt she'd grown quite effective in keeping customers sitting on their barstools for hours. It was financially beneficial to keep her regulars engaged and talking freely. At least, that was until their wallets and purses went dry. Bleu was amazed at how much better she was in judging a simple stranger. Better than he was. And after all, a tragic miscalculation from a friendly face is what started him down this fucked-up trajectory in the first place.

But his troubles were too unbelievable to dissect with any outsider. So he shook his head with a knowing expression that implied, "You wouldn't believe me if I told you—so let's not even go there."

"Well, Sadie's here if you need, doll." And with that she went back to her duties, rushing off to another seemingly lost soul at the end of the bar, maybe in hopes of better conversation.

Sipping slowly from his rum, Bleu stared down at his glass, lost in thought. He'd misjudged Gabe, and it held hard ramifications he knew he'd have to face later. Flashing back to their first meeting on the side of the road seemed a bit pivotal in retrospect. A handsome face staring out from that old and weathered Dodge and a sardonic, sexy grin beaming up as blinding afternoon light played games with the deputy's head. Yes, he recalled, the man had looked as if he'd been bathed in a halo of radiant light. But Corso knew it was nothing. Just a simple fact of where the sun sat in relation to the time of day. And merely circumstantial based on the spot where he pulled the truck over.

And Gabe was no angel; that much was certain.

He knew he'd be required to fill out a lengthy report, one that described every single event leading up to the shooting. And he knew there'd be long discussions with the captain. He could already picture that conversation: Kowalski's brow furrowing as he stared back in disbelief of all the lies Corso intended to drop in that office. But there was something else troubling him more then—the notion that someone could meet a stranger quite innocently. Then foolishly imagine they knew who or what they were and what they were capable of. Then find they'd woken up to something quite the contrary, something dark and unexpected. He'd fucked a killer. How was that not going to stick with him forever? Would he judge every other stranger he met based on his inaccuracy of that one man? Was this how the wives of killers on death row felt?

"He was a nice and quiet fellow," they'd say. *"No one ever suspected he was as evil as all that!"*

His head hurt with everything racing through it like NASCAR. And since they'd given him some over-the-counter pain meds at the hospital, he figured he'd best not test his luck driving all loopy. He turned up his glass and swallowed the last of his rum with one gulp. Tossing a twenty down, he called over his shoulder, "Thanks, Sadie, but I gotta hit the trails."

"You certainly come back and visit me soon, my lovely," she hollered loudly. Corso detected the lascivious fantasies creeping into the older woman's head before he closed the door behind him, every syllable of her goodbye positively dripping in innuendo.

WIND WHISTLED THROUGH the cracked window of Chris's rental in long beseeching whines as headlights flashed past him in the far lane. His foot already ached from the heavy pounding of the accelerator because he couldn't get there soon enough. Chris tried to put that last phone call from Gabe out of his head because it was a distraction he didn't need. It wouldn't give wings to this red Chevy Malibu from Avis, he figured, so better not replay the conversation over and over. It made him more anxious and encouraged even more dangerous speeds.

The Malibu he'd chosen hadn't been his first choice over the Audi; the gas tank was smaller than he'd preferred for such a long drive. But it was conveniently already in the lot when he arrived. Even when he was signing the papers, he kept thinking how many stops for fuel he'd have to make. And every stop meant a delay in his trip he didn't need.

Tossing his hastily packed bag into the backseat, he'd jumped on the highway as fast as he could and raced into the night with more on his mind than in all his recent days combined. He thought about Agent Jenkins, worrying if he was actually closer to apprehending Gabe than he'd let on in that difficult meeting. Glancing into the rearview, he wondered if he could even spot a tail if someone was following him. Naturally, Gabriel could. He had skills of self-preservation that Chris had never even considered. Then again, he'd come from good family stock, and with money to spare during his formative years. Gabe had none of that, he reminded himself. He'd been tossed into the world penniless and without any direction. Forced into a cold world with nothing but his wits to rely on, and he'd done the unimaginable—because he survived. And at times he even flourished, but not presently.

He knew his upbringing had been the polar opposite of Gabriel's, which would've been the epitome of the wrong side of the tracks, as his mother had reason to proclaim. And what he knew of Gabriel's childhood had formed him from the ground up, somehow twisting it from the root, growing it into something ugly and beautiful at the same time. Certainly, it was the cause of his twisted pseudo-religious fantasies he spoke of. Those same stories Gabe would tell in their quieter moments, the ones that frightened Chris the most whenever Gabe's silver-blue eyes flashed to the hurtful memories of his past.

Whereas his mother, an ideal image of white Anglo-Saxon-Protestant blood, would never deign to acknowledge anything she considered foul or unrespectable. Gabriel's mother must have been the incongruous backward twin to her. He'd heard enough to know Gabe idolized his mother, Sissy, as someone weak and indecisive—and certainly not strong enough to stand against the tormentor Bennett Church. Still, his mother wasn't a strong symbol of womanhood either. She was just as weak, but she had options that Sissy sorely lacked. No, his mother wouldn't have stayed in a marriage when her husband beat or berated her, Chris surmised. But it was apples and oranges because if the Church's had money and reputation might've Gabe turned out differently than he had?

With a single hand on the wheel, Chris rubbed his eyes hard, partly to shake off the nonsensical bullshit running through his brain and partly because his eyes ached. He hadn't even been on the road long enough to be so fucking drained. There were still a few too many hours of driving left to go, and he had to wonder what might happen when he got there. Would Gabriel be all right? Would he be pulled into a police chase with a bloodied passenger beside him, whispering him on like some Bonnie and Clyde sort of ending to his life?

It flashed suddenly in his head—the call police would make to the Maxwell family. The late at night ringing of a telephone, that coughing unsettled answer from his father as he scrambled to pick up the landline. He smiled at the image he'd fabricated. How wonderfully upset his mother would sound in the background, worried more about what others might think once they read the papers than how her only son was found inside a wrecked car, bullet-holes sprayed across the side panels, and a dead serial killer holding his hand in a sordid unrealistic death pose. *Jesus, how gruesome are my ramblings becoming? It must be a symptom from my time with Church.*

As he drove, Chris scanned the businesses right off the freeway. When he saw a familiar sign for a drugstore chain, he exited quickly, then circled back. Once inside, he practically ran the length of the aisles until he found a teenager in a ridiculously oversized shirt stocking shelves.

"First aid kits, you have them?' he asked, out of breath.

A wispy bearded juvenile pointed over his shoulder without ever looking up. "Aisle four," he muttered.

Christian chose the most expensive kit available and ran to the front to pay. He didn't know if he'd need it, and rather hoped that by the time he got there, he wouldn't. But for Gabe's sake, it was better to be safe than sorry, as that old adage goes.

Back on the interstate, he picked up his pace since he'd lost valuable time at the drugstore. Thankfully, it was that golden hour where traffic was sparse and cops expected speeders. He hadn't had a chance to hook up his phone to the Chevy's Bluetooth so he was forced to use his cell's GPS app. After a few hours he was on the I-5 southbound, keeping his eyes peeled for the 518 exit toward Fresno. It wouldn't be long now. The closer he got to Sonora the louder his heart pounded. And even though he'd given up smoking years earlier, all he could think of was taking a long luxurious drag of a cigarette as something to occupy his hands.

Strange anxiety squeezed his chest tighter every mile-marker he passed. It felt like standing in a party and watching an ex-lover, who he'd never truly gotten over, chatting up an attractive stranger. It was buoyancy of the heart. An overwhelming sense that he'd just remembered he'd misplaced his lottery ticket only moments after the winning numbers were announced. He didn't know what to expect in Sonora, but the occasional bumping irregularity of rubber against uneven blacktop was that inkling, he feared, of unsteady things to come.

"I'LL NEED TO take your car," he said with a furrowed brow and menacing stare.

Church successfully pulled over the first car he saw circling the bend. He'd been walking on the driver's side of the highway, hunched over and clutching his side like some wounded motorist in dire need of a ride.

"You get to where you're going by relying on the goodness of strangers, while still always expecting the worse," he once told Chris. And remembering the clever killdeer bird of his Kentucky and Tennessee youth, he decided to appear like someone hurt and needing assistance. He was, after all, just such a soul. As he stumbled along, clutching his bloody side, the headlights lit a flare behind his back and shone a path before his feet. Naturally he would've normally faked distress, but he didn't need to. He was already stranded, hurt, and in powerful need of a fast getaway.

The middle-aged man behind the wheel went ghostly pale as Church shoved the barrel of the Glock through his open window. This poor dude was never gonna stop to offer help to a stranger again. But it couldn't be helped. Leaving him standing by the side of the road, Gabriel gingerly climbed in behind the wheel and drove away, tires spinning as the dumbfounded motorist-turned-pedestrian began reaching into a pocket for his phone.

Remembering there weren't possible exits before he'd smash headlong into his own accident, he spun the steering wheel wide, sending gravel and dust flying as rubber scrambled to find traction. Pressing the pedal to the floorboard he powered past the man who'd so graciously offered up his vehicle. He was still standing there, his cell phone plastered to his ear, a dumbstruck expression still visible when the headlamps brought him into frame.

Church was bleeding heavier now from his trek over rocky terrain, not to mention assembling the required nerve it took to perform a fast theft of a car at standing gunpoint. It had been one of those things he'd never done before. And even through the prodigious pains he felt in doing it, he now knew there was one less thing he had on his bucket list to scratch off. Heading into town, his stolen Acura blew past several police cruisers heading in the opposite direction. He knew they had to be racing to the accident, hoping to make an arrest for a wanted criminal. But all he could wonder in that moment was how many cops did a little city like Sonora actually maintain? Maybe, they'd called in the state police already. If so, that meant getting out of town was going to be an even bigger challenge.

Chapter Twenty-Eight

STARING AT HIS bedroom ceiling, Bleu couldn't sleep, despite how tired he felt. The drugs the hospital had given him were beginning to take effect. He was at that balance on the width of a blade—on one side he was too exhausted to sleep, and on the other, he was in enough discomfort to feel somewhat alive. He was picturing three critical days in his life that were unlike any others he'd ever experienced. Three consecutive days from a simple traffic stop to this hellish moment in time.

He was remembering the man who shot him, and that overshadowing manifestation of pure sexuality. When he'd given Gabe's description to the other detectives at the scene, he'd left out some of the details. Particulars like how incredibly deep and blue his eyes were. Or how strong and intensely powerful his presence appeared. He wasn't a man; he was an all-consuming force of nature. His honeyed voice twanged with a slow Southern drawl, those piercing glances that shot through him like finely tuned lasers, sent there to extricate all his secrets. Or even the way the sweat poured off his body during the hottest throes of their lovemaking. Yes, he had held back a bit.

Just the memory of that night sent lifeblood coursing through his cock. It bobbed into life and tickled the glory trail of hair below his navel. It felt good against the coolness of the sheets he lay under, and even now it made his heart race with anticipation. If Gabe were captured alive, he'd tell his story to everyone. The night he slept with a closeted cop of Tuolumne County; that same officer who later shot him in the very same motel where they fucked a night earlier. His lies to officials, particularly those to his captain, would be irrevocably exposed. Bleu Rould certainly lose his job and maybe even be charged by the District Attorney; something like accessory after the fact, or obstruction...maybe even something more creative.

His father would hear the news. He worried that he'd be rattled by the gossip running rampant in a little town. It would be necessary to have conversations with his dad that he'd hoped he'd never have to make. Dad wasn't in greatest of health, Bleu remembered. He was old and somewhat feeble. Maybe in the back of his brain he'd always assumed that he could hide that side of his life until his father died. If only to spare him the pain and embarrassment it could cause.

No one can ever really plan for these kinds of things, he mused. Those conversations that we all know are inevitable: the bedside confessions of the dying, or the emotional surrenders of overstating love to a family member, and doing so honestly and openly, with every fiber of one's being...one more time to be safe before they slip from your grasp.

No, we don't ever plan for those kinds of talks. We just hope that we are ready by the time they are forced into our hand.

Hearing the sound from a distant police siren echoing on the air, Bleu stirred in his bed. It was late in the night by then, but that particular noise could awaken every nerve in a policeman's body. Even off-duty one wondered which officer was answering the radio call. Or what they would find when they got there. Would they find a college kid's party going too loudly, a domestic disturbance, or something even worse? Would they stumble into a gas station robbery already in progress? How many outcomes could transpire when one was not there to offer assistance? Bleu understood it was one of the many character flaws that made for a good cop. But it could play hell on someone's mind if they didn't learn to compartmentalize job versus sanity.

Kowalski had instructed the deputy to take the following day off to recuperate. But he still encouraged him, with a serious tone in his voice, suggesting it may be beneficial for Corso to show at the station at some point in the day so that they might get a more formal debriefing from him on the shooting. The implication being that it might still get somewhat sticky wasn't hidden well under his flowery façade of concern. Kowalski's primary interest was clear in Bleu's mind, and it had little to do with the officer's health or well-being after a shooting. He did intend to stop by the precinct later in the afternoon, but not before he took a long investigative trip through his hometown. He knew Gabe was no doubt long gone by then and that there were blockades being set up on all the major thoroughfares out of town. But something didn't feel right in his gut, and if it helped to drive around town looking for a beat-up, two-tone Dodge, then so be it. He felt a nagging sense of uncertainty, but one he intended on investigating while he still had the time.

HIS MOUTH WENT dry, as if he were already a corpse. He needed water, yet he wanted whiskey. The drive through town had been thankfully uneventful, though every car he passed and every noise outside the stolen Acura sounded like a cacophony of terror-inducing cymbals crashing in his eardrums. The blood he'd lost while running from the accident had finally trailed along his leg and reached the top of one of his socks. And even sitting behind the wheel, he could feel its sticky wetness. Strange how he could even notice that, given the substantial discomfort he felt from the burning bullet hole.

He'd been lucky throughout his entire killing career. He'd never received major injuries, nor had the authorities gotten as close to his backside as they were in these moments. Certainly, he'd never experienced a wound as great or as possibly life-ending as this one. It hung overhead like a dark cloud, causing him no small amount of consternation and grief. There were many scenarios in which Gabe had foreseen his own death. Many involved gunfire and police chases, while another, less ignoble, end came from that pesky atrial hole in his heart, finally causing him to *stroke out*. Hopefully during a furiously involved sexual act—if he had any say on the matter. But none of his scenarios consisted of him wrecking his truck into a crumpled heap on the side of the road. Or hoping a man like Chris Maxwell might be able to race to his defense and be the one to free him from his messes like the little girl he felt he was since he'd been forced to ask for help.

Out of all the defects to his personality, there was also that goddamned genetic abnormality he'd been born with. Congenital, they'd told him, even before he knew the meaning of that strange sounding word. Maybe it was inherent, or maybe hereditary, but whatever it was, ASD (or atrial septal defect) was one more chip he was born to overcome. It hadn't given him any trouble so far, but others, like Chris, had heard it beating a single vibration off the norm. Generally it happened after sex, or usually when he was drifting off to sleep. That misshapen sound of a valve in his chest struggling to stay closed.

Thump-thump-thump. It beat loud and often like a metronome working overtime. It created one additional pounding sound, which most people would never have even noticed. But Chris had.

As he lay his head down atop Gabe's hairy chest one night, Chris had heard the irregularity—the slight and subtle change in rhythm—and he was inclined to ask Gabe about it. Chris had broached the subject far earlier than it normally would have come up in conversation. And that was assuming it ever would, since most people who slipped in and out of Gabe's life were mere distractions in a long journey to nowhere.

He rummaged through the man's glove box and found napkins and a dirty old rag he could use to slow the bleeding. Once he found a busy fast food joint, he pulled into the parking lot, then drove to the back, away from other cars and out of reach of the streetlamps overhead. Then he began the best job of bandaging his wounds that he knew to do. He'd have to lose the car soon—that much was obvious—because by now, it surely had been reported as stolen. He had less than an hour until the search was on for the Acura and the armed suspect driving her. But in the meantime, he could stop for a minute, rest back in the seat, and finally relax. Even quietly listen to the radio until he was forced to make his next move. He decided to abandon the car somewhere near Dotty's Place and try walking there. He'd hide in the back or near the trash bins until Chris arrived. It was sloppy, but it was a plan.

As he sat in the dark, music playing from the car stereo, he thought about Father Kait for a minute. He was instantly thankful he wasn't here to witness this. To see how Gabe's life was uncoiling in such a disastrously awful fashion. Fortunately, he was unaware that the old priest had succumbed to the same type of stroke Gabe had once figured would be his own. If he had known this, that his friend the cleric was dead, he may have actually felt worse. But only because he may have thought the priest could actually see his fucked-up situation from his heavenly perch on high. Yes, he would've hated that—so in this one particular circumstance, his blind occlusion of the fact became his single best salvation.

In every war there are those who fight, those who bend at the knee and supplicant, and those fools who try to play both sides, thinking it safe to work one flank against another. But those people always seem to fail, spectacularly so. And then there are those who simply die, willingly and without the soft patter of the drum lines and 21-gun salutes. They are as important as any facet to the war, and, in many ways, more important than all the others combined. Church would've been one of those.

He would've been one of those who died fighting on a hillside, as his wave of clawing fellow soldiers whipped a path behind his back. He was never supposed to be the hero, though he'd never been afraid of death. He wasn't a conspirator either, though he was craftier than some. He wasn't anything, he figured. Just a wall of flesh and muscle sent as cannon fodder toward an advancing line. And as he sat there bleeding in a stolen car at a Jack-in-the-Box parking lot, the ramifications of every action he'd ever undertaken seemed suddenly lit by unusual clarity.

All of his life had been spent in a mission for God, he'd thought. And if the last few months had taught him nothing, he was certainly learning that divinity couldn't possibly work this poorly.

"I used to believe in God," he said quietly over the music from the radio. "Now all I do is spend time praying he doesn't exist. Isn't that a kicker?"

There was no one in the car to hear him. He was speaking mostly to himself and to a man he was beginning to think wouldn't make it there in time. He hoped the soft words he'd whispered could somehow hit the airwaves and reach Chris's ears, who Gabe knew was surely racing like a bat outta hell to find him. With that, he turned on the ignition and pulled into the street cautiously. He began heading toward Dotty's Place, and all he could think was how normally when you found yourself in a hole such as this one the best advice was to stop digging. But that didn't appear to be Gabe's inclination. Instead, he pushed the accelerator down and hit the onramp toward the southbound highway.

BY THE TIME his rental pulled into Sonora, Chris was road weary and his butt sore. The one thing keeping him going was a pit in his stomach that grew exponentially with every mile marker passed. His throwaway phone sat in his lap, and his eyes darted from his normal cell and back to the disposable. He wanted to pull over to check the GPS for that Dotty's restaurant Gabe told him about, but the traffic coming into town was unrelenting.

When his lover mentioned he would've liked it here, he wasn't joking. It was beautifully green and the mountains picturesque. He could see himself living here. And when a native of Seattle tells someone they have a lovely town that was surely saying something. Finding a break in the parade of cars, Chris took the next exit available. It was that period of predusk, where the sun was dipping below the mountaintops along the horizon. A perfect time of year for vacationing. Late enough in the year to be cool without the cold, and days long enough to enjoy the scenery in hikes and on horseback. No wonder there were so many cars traveling through.

As he was scanning for an empty lot to park and manage the GPS, the other cell in his lap began to ring and vibrate. It startled him enough that he nearly weaved into oncoming traffic, but he shakily regained control and fumbled for the phone.

"I'm here." His breathing was anxious. "Where are you?"

They often spoke in broken interrogatives. A subtle common tongue shared in a private self-induced connection, which neither man really understood. For two such very different people from very different backgrounds, they had a certain interdependency that linked them solid. Chris assumed it came from their bond of sex, whereas Gabriel assumed something else entirely.

"I'm at the diner. It's called Dotty's Place; off I-120. Remember?"

"I'm on my way," Chris said flatly. "But now that I'm here, tell me just how bad it is?"

"It's fine." He knew Gabe was lying.

"Get here soon, 'cause we're getting outta here for good."

Gabriel gave fast directions to the restaurant, telling his friend all the best routes available, as if he'd been Sonora born and raised. Even now, with the turmoil bubbling around them, Chris thought, he still had to maintain his confidence and superiority over other men. In a way that made Chris feel better because Gabe didn't sound as weak as he had during that last desperate phone call.

The white clapboards and ancient faded signage announcing "Dotty's Place" to the world caught him by surprise. It wasn't at all what he expected it to be. But he also didn't know the history made for Gabriel in those last few days at that restaurant-slash-bar known for their steaks. His nerves were electric as he pulled the Malibu into the lot. The ten to fifteen cars there couldn't begin to fill the immense space. It was clearly a spot favored by those folks who'd stumbled out of the bars and needed something with carbohydrates to soak up all the alcohol.

He didn't see Gabe anywhere after he pulled into an empty space to park. He craned his neck wildly, searching every car or any place that he might be hiding. After a minute of his heart pounding, he grabbed for the disposable to call, but before he could complete the call, his passenger door opened and Gabriel slipped inside. Chris was tempted to throw his arms over his lover's neck and kiss him passionately, but he was met with an open palm.

"It's neither the time nor place, babe," Gabe said gruffly. "But later...I promise."

"God, how I've missed you," Chris muttered.

Then immediately he began taking stock of the situation. Glancing down at the blood on Gabe's shirt, he made a nearly inaudible gasp. Fear widened his eyes as he reached to inspect the wound.

"It's fine really," Gabriel said. "We just need to get out of here. The police are looking for me. They'll have every highway outta town barricaded by now. Let's find a safe hole and hide. We can worry about this hole then," he said, indicating the gaping bullet hole in his shirt.

"I have a med kit in the back seat," Chris announced. "But you know this town better than I do. Where do you want me to head?"

As he placed the Chevy in reverse, he looked at Gabriel again for the first time he'd seen him in weeks. He was thinner than he remembered, the beard on his chin more unkempt than before. The miles apart hadn't done him any good. He was ragged and beaten down in a way he'd never seen him. But even as rough as he looked then, it still felt whole and warm simply being in his presence.

Gabe thought for a minute, a confused look on his face, before he blurted out the words, "There was a motel I was staying in. It's where the shooting occurred, but surely by now it's been cleared as a crime scene."

"You wanna go back to the same place you were shot?" Chris shouted more loudly and effeminately than he would've liked.

"Why not?" Gabe murmured as a sadistic grin began to emerge. "No one will be looking for me there, for heaven's sake. You can rent the room while I stay in the car hunkered down. It's not like they're gonna give you my old room," he chuckled.

"There are other motels we can choose from," Christian offered bluntly.

"Yes, but they'll be looking for me everywhere, but least of all in the exact spot of the crime. After all, it's the hole I was nearly ended in."

"I think you're losing your mind."

"I can see how that might look or seem possible," Gabe muttered as he stared out the window and scanned the streets.

"I know it sounds haphazard, but, if you think about it, it makes perfect sense." Gabriel turned to stare into Christian's hazel eyes. "As long as that prick of a manager doesn't see me, then it's an ideal location."

"What happened to your truck?" he asked, realizing he hadn't even asked yet.

"Well, bit of a tragedy there," Gabe began slowly. "Yep, I banged up the Dodge pretty badly, I'm afraid."

Chris surveyed the big man once more. He knew how much he'd loved his beat-up old pickup. He'd traveled the length of the states, literally from coastline to coastline, in that trusted heap. And he'd done that feat more than once. It must have been held together by duct tape and prayer, but somehow he'd managed to keep it alive and running. Now that it was gone, Chris knew it represented more than a mere loss. It had been Gabe's sole and prized possession. Having to abandon it must have hurt him more even more than that thumb-sized hole in his gut.

"You've got loads to fill me in on, buddy," he said smiling over at Gabriel to show him he wasn't really concerned.

No sir, I'm not worried at all, not even in the slightest.

Chapter Twenty-Nine

"I REALLY NEED to look at that wound," Chris finally said. But by then Gabe was lost in thought. His eyes darted back and forth across every street and alley they passed. Eventually he mumbled some inaudible acknowledging grunt but seemed trapped by whatever he expected to see outside his windows, like a wagon train of cars barreling out to ensnare the Malibu.

"I'm not much of a doctor, but I can try," Chris said in a last ditch effort to break the silence.

"You'll do fine. I have faith," Gabe said distractedly. Foregoing those possible threats outside the car, Gabe twisted around to look at Chris again. It was clearly painful for him, but the half grin he forced on his face made all the difference to his lover. "As soon as we get a room, I can strip for you," he said, flashing his pearly whites and showing that characteristically tiny chipped tooth in the bargain. It was always about the sex with him.

"I remember having to strip when I was a boy, for my mother." But when Chris looked back confused, Gabe blurted out, "No...I mean when I would go off playing in the tall weeds and hanging around the woods for hours, to get away from Bennett, my mom would make me strip to my undies when I came home. She was looking for ticks; you see. But it was a strange ritual, me standing there in my tiny white underwear as she examined me head-to-toe. And she'd always find a couple. Then she'd yank 'em off 'fore they could bleed me."

Not wanting to take him away from that one good childhood memory, Chris still felt the need to say, "Ya know, that's actually the first time I remember hearing you ever call her 'Mom' and not 'Sissy.'"

Gabe didn't respond, instead turning to look out the passenger window again in silence. After fifteen minutes, he began giving more detailed directions to the Queen of the Mines Lodge. Telling Chris to turn here or follow that street all the way down. Like Dotty's Place, it wasn't anything Christian would've expected. It was sad and rustic at the same time. White connecting cottages, with a few unconnected ones, perched atop a hill that backed up to heavier, undeveloped forest at its rear.

"What the hell would make you choose this place?" Chris stammered, confused as he turned into the parking lot.

"Remember, park at the end there," Gabe said quickly. "There, beneath those low-hanging limbs."

Gravel dust filled the so-called courtyard as the Chevy wheeled around to a space away from everything. "Sonora's an old mining town," he said rather proudly as Chris turned the ignition. "Everything round here has something to do with mines or gold."

"It looks like you like this sort of shit." Chris grinned. And it did appear Gabe was pleased. Even through his obvious pain, he seemed almost boastful of the fact he'd stumbled onto this old motor lodge on the back ass of nowhere.

"It isn't the Mayflower, you understand, but it'll do till we can get free of this town."

Church dropped his seat back with the lever on the side and then managed to lean to his right and close his eyes and cover his face. To anyone who saw, he was a road-weary tourist with too many hours behind the wheel.

When Chris got out, his legs shook with tremors. He'd actually been behind the wheel far too long, and it wasn't an act.

Fifteen minutes later, he was back at Gabe's window, tapping lightly. "All clear," he nodded. He was swinging a large key ring in his hand to illustrate that it wasn't a typical key card, but a single key and a ridiculously oversized key ring with the lodge's logo printed on it. This was unlike any motor lodge he'd ever stayed in. But then it occurred to him that this was the only motor lodge he'd ever stayed in.

Surreptitiously they slipped inside the room while Chris tossed his luggage and the med kit on the queen-sized bed, then locked the door, and set the latch.

"It's gonna feel nice to have a shower." Gabe breathed in short bursts as he gingerly sat on the edge of the mattress.

"First things first," Chris said. "Take your clothes off." With a dismayed expression, he added, "I can't believe this. I've been waiting weeks to say those words, but now, in this shit hole? Come on, hon." He opened his bag and pulled out his shaving kit. "I have some antiseptic pads I think—"

"If you had to stay in a lot of the places I'd stayed, boy, you might not have put off killing yourself another day."

"Good to know your sense of humor's intact."

Gabriel stood up and gently extricated himself from his bloody rag. Kicking off his boots with his toes, he slipped out of his jeans like a dancer. He wasn't wearing anything underneath. Chris had nearly forgotten that fact. He went commando most days, and he wondered how many boxers or briefs Gabriel even owned. A rank scent of manhood hit the air as Chris began examining the bullet hole closely. Amazed, he said, "This thing went clear through."

Gabe nodded, pleased. "Good, I thought so. That means if it didn't pierce the kidneys I might survive this."

There were countless cuts Chris noticed, tiny abrasions and scratches all over his massive frame. He didn't know they came from Gabe running through the woods at night, but, as he opened the medical kit and began sterilizing the main injury, he took care to find every other mark on his lover's body and clean it properly as well.

Once Gabe was patched and had taken a half-dozen baby aspirin from the med kit, he lay down exhausted, still naked and odorous. "I'm gonna tape some plastic over the bandages and run you a hot bath. You've lost a lot of blood and your best bet is to rest here for quite a while till you get your strength back."

"Sounds like a plan," Gabe muttered, but before Chris could do anything he heard the slow steadied breathing of a man in sudden slumber. He'd fallen asleep almost immediately, so Christian resigned himself to sliding close and lying next to him. He watched Gabe's burly chest rise and fall, and then listened for the sounds of irregular beating in the hollow of that ribcage.

Most every resident in Sonora knew Deputy Corso on sight. He'd become a fixture and a symbol of rural Americana, from his faded boots to the embroidered star emblem on his chest designating him as a city law officer. Most residents had grown up knowing his family and many of them remembered seeing a tow-headed kid running the streets before the streetlamps ignited after dusk. He'd grown up in this little California town, becoming that square-jawed picture of a respectable man that people knew to count on. After all, this was his hometown. As he drove his cruiser in and around the tiny establishments, pausing to examine the back alleys and nondescript spots where a man might hide, he thought about all that would change once the armed suspect was arrested and everyone heard the stories he could spin.

He felt that if he could find Gabe before the others, then he might alter the outcome, though he wasn't exactly sure how he was supposed to do that. There'd been great danger in the big man's eyes. A certain disregard for any consequence, and that fact chilled the deputy to his core.

"You know I kinda like the idea of being hunted. It sort of makes my dick hard, as if you couldn't tell."

Gabe's words had been revealing, he remembered. They fairly screamed psychopathic delusion. But even during their brief exchange back at the motel, Bleu had seen other shades of the man poking out around the edges. He was smart in a level sort of way. He appeared to have compassion too. Had he not, he might've easily jumped the lawman before their conversation went any further. It wouldn't have taken a lot. A bounding leap across the room and he'd have been on top of him. He didn't need to give him a sterile explanation of what he was capable of. That spoke volumes, Bleu considered. If he could find him, talk to him, he thought he might be able to resolve the situation quickly and quietly without anyone else getting hurt.

Maybe a good officer's instinct, or maybe it was out of some sick need to see that spot where they'd made love that first night, but either way, the deputy was heading to the Queen of the Mines Lodge before he was even aware he'd been navigating there. Up the hill he drove, until he rounded the bend and saw the motel nestled in the encroaching tree line. He could see the room where the shooting occurred. Still marked by police tape, that may be the only indication anything untoward had occurred there. The sad little division known as the Criminal Investigative Unit of Tuolumne County was already long gone, and cars still sat in front of their rented cabins. What would prompt a person to remain in a rundown motel after a shooting? It wasn't like Sonora didn't have a wealth of shady no-tell motels.

Since he was still in uniform, it wouldn't look suspicious to have him poking around. So, after parking, he slowly sauntered over and maneuvered past the tape and went inside. He saw the bloodstain on the threadbare carpet and an overturned chair, but, other than that, it was empty. Any possessions Gabe had left were by then bagged as evidence and currently stored at county lockup.

There was a musty odor hanging in the air, and with the blinds pulled, it became a dark and uninviting room. Staring at the unmade mattress with the blankets crumpled haphazardly on top, he remembered their sweaty, tangled bodies there. Apparitions of their torrid sexual encounter brought back to bear. This out-of-the-way motel surely had seen its share of nighttime visitors, but none that began with anxious fumbling fingers and still ended in gunfire.

He didn't know why he was there. It seemed instantly stupid to him then, standing alone in a crime scene. But it was a powerful feeling, a sense of overwhelming history with secrets that swung pendulum-like from wall to dirty wall. As if by reflex, his right hand went to his holster and gripped his gun like a child with a *blankie*: with that same feeling of steady comfort, whether a boy or an adult man.

He had no way of knowing that Gabe was at that moment three doors down. And in a way that was a good thing, for both of them. Even the blackest of hearts still beats strong, and, if there were ever any kind of connection existing between Bleu and Gabriel, it was in that moment razor-wire thin and unbreakable. One happenstance or miscalculation may have changed the aftermath completely had Chris decided then it was a good time to slip out quietly for a bucket of ice or a lone deputy to have noticed that single blood patch on the steps outside room 215, leading to the door. Well, things could've gone bad fast, certainly differently than they did.

"Can I help you, officer?" A voice caught the deputy unaware as he spun around quickly, his hand never lifting from his service weapon. It was the lodge manager. Bleu remembered him from the commotion after the shooting, a lanky fellow in a ratty flannel shirt and jeans.

"Nah," the deputy muttered after collecting himself. "I just decided to take a gander at the scene, make sure they didn't miss anything."

He turned away and examined the floor, partially because it appeared professional, and in part because he was riddled with shame. Had the man known he'd been there the night before the shooting? He wondered. Had he known what kind of things transpired in that room?

"Most excitement we've had here in years," the man said with a slow drawl.

"I take it this place isn't yours?"

"No, hell no, I just watch over it for the owner. He was sure surprised to hear what happened here last night, though. He's outta town now, but I think he's gonna fly in. Not sure why since it's all over and done with," he said with a chuckle.

"I know you gave your statement to the other detectives already, but if there's anything more to add while I'm here, now's the time."

"I take it you haven't caught the bastard then?" the man asked, evading his question.

"We will," Bleu said with a confident grin. They walked outside the cabin as the deputy ran through locations and spots he hadn't checked yet, places where a man could hole up and stay unseen. After thanking the motel manager, he headed back to the cruiser, his hopes slowly dashing against the rocks.

GABE'S LABORED BREATHING filled the small space of the motel room, yet Chris stirred when he heard the familiar sound of rubber and gravel as car tires spun in the parking lot outside. Jumping up, he pulled the curtains aside and peered out nervously. His heart nearly stopped completely when he saw it was a police car that had pulled up. He was about to wake his lover when he noticed a single uniformed officer getting out. He didn't look like someone making an arrest. He moved slowly and methodically toward the room where Gabe had stayed. He didn't know what the cop was doing there, but since the motel wasn't circling with black-and-whites and he couldn't hear the whine of a helicopter overhead, he allowed himself a second for his heart to restart.

He didn't know then how important the man was in their ongoing story. He didn't know the man was named Bleu Corso, or the one commonality between them was in their shared experience of Gabriel's massive member. All he knew was his current fear and apprehension. And against his better judgment, he decided it was best to wake up his killer, if only to see how he might handle the situation.

He had tossed a blanket over Gabriel as he slept, and now he sat gently on the edge of the bed and begrudgingly nudged him back to life.

"Babe," he whispered, "I hate to bother you, but we may have a problem."

YEARS OF RUNNING had tuned Gabe's instincts into something akin to a trusty weapon. Jumping up, instantly awake, his hand went quickly to the nightstand where he'd laid the Glock. Even before Chris could calm him, he was standing somewhat vertical; naked, armed, and ready for the door to come crashing in.

"What is it?" he stammered, his eyes wild and piercing.

"Relax," Chris said, reaching up then grabbing his forearm to lower the gun. "A cop is here, but I don't think it's anything big."

Lunging toward the window, Gabe used the gun barrel and opened the curtains ever so slightly. The first thing he noticed, besides a Crown Victoria Police Interceptor parked in the lot outside, was the serial numbers painted above its grill. He remembered those numbers, having committed them to memory after that first traffic stop in Sonora. It was Deputy Corso. Back for more, or possibly just to check the scene of his recent mistake. He should never have shown at the motel without backup. And he should have questioned his story from the beginning. But he wasn't aware the lawman had run a search against a name. He'd simply hoped his charms would've prevented him from looking any closer.

"Bring me my pants," Gabe ordered over his shoulder. And his dutiful lover scrambled to collect the clothes strewn about the floor. Once he'd slipped into something he could fight in, Gabe went back to the window, but didn't look worried.

"Is this that the friend of yours?" he asked out of the blue. "The friend you supposedly shot?"

Gabriel didn't know exactly how Chris had made that connection so fast, and when he turned back to face him, he had a strange look of admiration in his eyes. "I was going to tell you all about it," he said flatly. "Once we were safely out of town."

"For someone you shot, he appears to be doing fine," he said.

"I told you it wasn't life threatening. I was aiming to wound, not kill."

Chris shook his head and whispered, "Well, now what? What do you want us to do?"

Gabe walked over and raised his mitt-sized palm and brushed it over Chris's cheek. "You let me handle it like always. I'm not going to let anything happen to you, not while we're so close to making it outta here...alive and together."

There it is. That firm decision I've waited forever to hear. A statement carved in stone, a testament that this time Gabe wasn't going to slip away on his own. That this time, no matter what happened, they were going together. Even through the anxiety of getting caught, he felt suddenly freer than before. A complete wholeness was encasing him in soft down-filled wrappings. And he smiled when he looked up at those silver-blue eyes and knew in that one fucked-up moment in time—everything had a meaning.

"There'll be time for that later," Gabe mouthed quietly, as if he knew what was going through Chris's head then. That if he hadn't spoken, there might've been tears. And there wasn't any time for that. On that score he'd been right.

Then the unthinkable happened next. Gabriel shoved the Glock in the small of his back and walked to the door, leaving Chris sitting on the bed. Before the deputy could get inside his vehicle, the killer cracked the motel door enough to occupy the space, and then whistled like a farmhand calling cattle for a feeding.

"Hey there, deputy," he called out smiling. "You wanted to see me?"

BLEU WAS STUNNED to hear that familiar twang so close. Turning toward the voice, he was instantly transformed into an alabaster statue, staring at the bigger man's frame as he casually leaned against the doorjamb like a man without a care.

"Yeah," he said slowly, desperately trying not to appear caught so close to the edge. "I was kinda thinking it was a good time to chat."

He began walking over cautiously, his boots sliding over the gravel and his fingers never straying too far from his holster. "Do you think this time we could do this without any pistols going off?" he asked as if he'd been manufactured from steel and iron.

"We're both armed, deputy. I can assure you of that. But all I want to do is talk for a minute. I know you don't owe me anything. But I'd consider it a gift."

He was smiling broadly, with that half-bent twist of his lips. He was strangely confident, considering one quick reach could've turned that parking lot into the OK Corral. But it was his straightforward bravado that pulled the deputy in closer, telling him this meeting wasn't going to end like their last.

Slowly, Gabe stepped backward to allow the lawman to enter his room, his back against the door, trying to appear nonthreatening. Warily, Bleu stepped past him, and was surprised when he saw someone else sitting on a bed, his face nearly as white as his must've looked.

"Deputy Bleu Corso, please allow me to introduce you to Christian Maxwell...an unarmed and innocent friend." He'd forced the words innocent and unarmed out with careful timing, trying to say much by offering him very little.

Chapter Thirty

CHRIS WAS SUDDENLY even more confused. Was he supposed to stand up and shake the deputy's hand? What's the protocol when you meet one of your boyfriend's tricks? Someone he'd exchanged gunfire with and someone who currently wanted him jailed?

"Take a load off, Deputy Corso," Gabe said, indicating an open chair in the corner.

"Well, we've been there before, haven't we?" The deputy finally allowed his nervousness to peek out unashamedly.

"I'm going to reach for my gun...very gently," Gabe said. "But I don't plan on aiming it anywhere. I want to show you where it is so you can see that I'm not grabbing for it."

With his fingers extended like holding up a dirty dolly someone had found on the roadside, he cautiously pulled the nine-millimeter from his jeans and then laid it down on the bed beside Chris.

"First off, my buddy Chris here isn't guilty of any crime you'd be aware of. You have my word on that." As Gabe spoke, the deputy thought how incongruous that statement sounded, but somehow still believable. Despite all the lies he'd already told him about whom he was, somehow this felt like real truth falling from his lips.

Jutting his chin forward Gabe said, "I want to talk about you and that dude over there who looks as if he waiting for the other shoe to drop."

Confused, the deputy looked over and noticed something he'd never calculated about the man: a peculiar kindness he'd missed in his overall assessment, which now blasted past that impressive shade of whatever-color eyes he'd supposedly been born with.

He looked strangely sad and imploring. Serious now for the first time since he'd seen him standing in the parking lot.

"One way or another, deputy, I'm getting my friend, Chris, out of Sonora." The sentence was a warning, as much as it was a threat. The words were positively dripping with determination and cold, steady resolve. Suddenly, it was clear to the deputy who this man was, what he meant to the stranger who'd stumbled into town. Weak-kneed, the deputy decided to take the chair in the corner, as unreasonable as that might've been had this been anyone else. He wasn't afraid then, though he knew that single act may turn out to be his last bad decision ever made.

"What happened before here...what crimes that may been committed don't concern you, Bleu. Not really." Gabe leaned closer, speaking soft enough to show true emotional connection with the lawman he'd taken to bed not that many days before. It was no secret to either of them there had been something between them, something more than sex, more than that small degree of history occurring first on the side of the road, then in a bar, and finally in a darkened motel room. It felt pervasive and alive, and even with the man's lover sitting a couple of feet away, it was as undeniable as anyone could know.

"Something tells me you have a few secrets of your own, boy," Gabe said decisively. He didn't want to expose anything out in the open or hash out the deputy's closeted career for anyone to hear. And besides, each of them already knew that fact, so there wasn't even a need. "Maybe some things are better served if they stay secret," he muttered aloud. "We all got our secrets, Bleu, maybe some worse than others, for sure. But wouldn't life be a lot easier if we all worked to keep each other's secrets buried?"

"You'll never make it out of town before you're caught," Bleu said, hanging his head.

"I've made it past a few barricades in my days, Deputy Sheriff Corso," Gabe said, grinning happily. "Question is, what about you, how you gonna fare through all this?"

"A hell of a lot better once you're out of town," he said more to himself than anyone else. "So where will you two go?" he asked.

"Better if you didn't know where, buddy," Gabe offered. "It was a pleasure having you," he said with a smile as he rose to shake the deputy's hand. The sexual innuendo hadn't been lost on Bleu, nor had it on the other man who was fighting to hold in his words. As Bleu rose and extended his arm to Gabe, he smiled wearily. He felt like he'd been beaten down or dragged for miles across the hot blacktop. It was a funny situation, one that would take years to unravel in his mind.

"Dispatch reported heavier coverage of officers along 108 and that corridor right beyond I-49. So try to stay clear of that for a while," Bleu said.

"Will do, deputy, thanks," Gabe blurted out awkwardly.

Before he left, Corso turned back to Chris, who was still sitting on the edge of the bed. He offered him a conciliatory, knowing nod, and, in kind, Chris returned the same gesture. It was a combination of thank you and good luck but hidden below the surface, in that spot that those two men might recognize, it was also envy: bitter and green. Where one man was expected to lose here, another was now suddenly destined to win.

By the time the cruiser pulled off the hill, Gabe was sitting beside his lover and seemingly just as confused.

"So now what?" Chris asked without expecting to hear the answer.

"Well…we wait here," Gabe began. "We clean up and grab some food, 'cause I'm starved. We'll hole up, maybe even fuck a bit, and eventually we'll hit the road once the barricades are down. Then it's open highway all the way."

Epilogue

THERE ARE NO tiny questions about love—either it's there or it isn't. When one person makes the ultimate sacrifice one would fully expect the rest of the story to fall into place easily. But it doesn't, life doesn't ever work that way. With the wind blowing in from the rental's windows being cracked, air flicked through Gabriel's hair as he slept against the glass. It was an achingly beautiful sight to Chris—his lover by his side. Though he was still recuperating, he was there, at least. Within physical reach of Chris's hand, and even with him behind the wheel of the Malibu, he wasn't exactly sure where he was supposed to be heading. Very soon, they'd have to drop off this rental and exchange it for another bought with cash. And there were problems with all his belongings still at the condo, which he'd probably have to give up. But for now there was open road and clear skies. Sonora was over a day in their rearview and everything somehow felt fresh and new.

They'd had a strange journey for both of them. Which already felt like eons had passed from that first afternoon at the Cherry Street Grinder when he looked up to see that frightening persona of a serial killer. Suddenly this felt like a child's delusion, so far from the actual truth. A silly effort on his part to write about, and therefore understand, someone so completely and vastly different than himself. He'd already decided to abandon his button-down conservative life in his wake, but only if Gabe could assure him the murders were done for good.

This occurred to him when it happened in the car a few hours past the Nevada border, with Gabe broaching the topic even before he could. He'd been staring at the mountains as they passed, stone-faced and overwhelmed.

"There is no God here," he uttered.

"Everything I thought was important is now gone...but there's still you and me. I have that—correction, we have that.

We'll have to run now, maybe change our names or hide ourselves away on some island somewhere." Gabe said with a grin. "We still have

Agent Jenkins on our tail. But I've made a career out of keeping off their radar, so maybe I could teach you a few things. But that island deal, now that one sounds pretty good indeed."

Without turning to face him, he reached out and grabbed Chris by the hand. He was gripping him tighter than he ever had before, almost as if his lifeline had somehow changed...that things he'd once found important had suddenly transformed into something new and possibly better.

Acknowledgements

Special thanks to Kathy Mac of MM Book Escape, because if it weren't for her, this series might've ended up very differently. I offer many thanks to my editor BJ and owners at NineStar Press, LLC who could've just as easily opened a vein rather than attempt another arduous book from me. And thanks to Todd Kirk and Richard DeVoe, as well as all the friends who showed me the way. Special thanks to the Gabriel Church fans who stuck beside me for the entire crazy ride. You are all flickering stars in my heavens.

A note to the Gabriel Church fans out there:

After my initial foray into the Gabriel Church Tales, I discovered how much being a writer had become my raison d'être, the justification for my very existence. The creation of strong characters, more than the process of writing is what sparked my interest and plagued my waking dreams. Gabriel Church was easily one of those distractions. He was (or is) a deeply flawed individual with profound aspirations and dark longings, and he fast became one of my favorite persons to while away the hours with. I didn't wish to leave him behind, but I chose not to sully his memory by dragging out his story to the point of exasperation to those who read and enjoyed his tale. He is an organic soul, even given his twisted nature and horrendous crimes. We are all sin in one form or another, but he was wise enough at least to recognize his defects, and like all of us with bent imperfections, he sought a way out and off the road he was traveling. I will continue thinking of him fondly as I hope others do as well. As I sit in my boxers typing at my computer well into the night, I have to believe he will be there looking over my shoulder inspiring me like he did for Christian Maxwell...to simply keep writing the story.

Many thanks, Rodd.

About the Author

Rodd lives in Dallas, TX, yet originated in the back hills and sticks of Oklahoma. To learn more one merely has to visit his online presence at RODDCLARK.COM. A fan of mystery and suspense, he is drawn to the journey as much as the tale itself. With deeply rich characters, all bent and misshapen by circumstances beyond their control, he enjoys taking his readers on often dark and disturbing flights of fantasy. He began his books with the Brantley Colton Mysteries and evolved into the critically acclaimed series The Gabriel Church Tales. He's enjoyed writing since long before he could legally drink and likes making new friends and fans along the way.

Email: roddtx@usa.net

Facebook: www.facebook.com/rodd.clark.96

Twitter: @RODDCLARK

Website: www.roddclark.com

Other books by this author

Rubble and the Wreckage, 2nd edition
Torn and Frayed, 2nd edition

Also Available from NineStar Press

Connect with NineStar Press

Website: NineStarPress.com

Facebook: NineStarPress

Facebook Reader Group: NineStarNiche

Twitter: @ninestarpress

Tumblr: NineStarPress